May you always win

David Ala...

ANGAKOK

DAVID ALAN MORRISON

Cover Design by Troy Johnson
Edited by Alyssa Graybeal

This is a work of fiction. Names, characters, places, brands, media, and incidents are either the product of the author's imagination or are used fictitiously. Any resemblance to similarly named places or to persons living or deceased is unintentional.

PRINT ISBN :978-1533568038
EPUB ISBN : 1533568030
Library of Congress Control Number:

ACKNOWLEDGMENTS

"To thine own self be true." Immortal words that are not only a phrase but a lifestyle. A sincere thank you is due to those who helped me bring Angakok to print: Holly, Mona and Darrin. Next time around, drinks are on me.

For Darrin Scott Murray, wherever you are. Thank you.

THURSDAY, JULY 7, 2005

2:16 AM

"LIFE'S LIKE A BUS," Rodney's grandmother liked to say, "if you don't make it, just wait—another one's on the way."

As a child, Rodney had no idea what the hell the old woman had meant. But as he stared down at the Harley Davidson roadster lying mangled at the end of Judah Street's cul-de-sac, he knew the old bat was wrong. The poor sod who'd been riding the motorcycle wasn't getting another life. He was history. The leather-clad corpse lay tangled in a heap at the base of the sandy hill that separated the N-Judah streetcar line from the beach road; his arms were twisted around his body, a braid of torn flesh and broken bones. A few feet away, a woman's body lay motionless in a heap, her bright red cocktail dress shredded, her pale skin peeking through the fabric like a human barber pole. Perpendicular to both of the bodies sat a black Mercedes convertible in which a leggy blonde in a leather miniskirt swayed drunkenly. She had bright red nail polish and was sucking on a cigarette, cackling loudly.

Rodney forced himself to breathe slowly. Pull it together, man. Shit. You can do this.

For the past two years, Rodney had managed to avoid responding to motorcycle accidents—until tonight, when the blare of the station house ripped him out of his bunk and sent him stumbling half asleep through the frigid fog to the passenger's seat of the ambulance.

Rodney's shift-partner, Ed Wentworth, a tall, lanky man with thick black hair, tossed the empty cup of his fourth Slurpie of the day onto the ground and began pushing through the swelling throng of onlookers, shoving them harder than Rodney thought necessary. No wonder the station guys called Ed "The Slurpie Bitch" behind his back.

"Get the hell out of the way, people!" Slurpie shouted. Then under his breath muttered, "Jesus fucking Christ! How do you expect us to do our jobs?"

"You drink too much of those things," Rodney said, following Ed into the crowd. "They're nothing but sugar, you know. Empty calories."

Ed shot Rodney a venomous glare and lit a Marlboro Red. "Well," he said, exhaling a cloud of smoke into Rodney's face, "should be just enough energy, then, to kick the fucking shit out of you for not minding your own God-damn business."

Rodney pulled his gaze away from Ed and turned to the thin blonde standing next to the Mercedes. "I didn't do a fucking thing," she slurred. "They came out of nowhere!" She squealed with laughter, then sucked in a lungful of smoke and continued. "I don't know who the hell they are. Do you?" she asked the short brunette who hung over the back door of the car vomiting a chunky brown stream mixed with bile. "DOES ANYONE HERE KNOW THESE TWO LOSERS? WHO ARE THEY?"

"You take the fag," Slurpie said, tossing his crash kit onto the ground. "Try not to kill anyone again, okay?"

Rodney felt his blood run cold. Shit. Shit. Shit. He should have known the guys at the station would find out about what happened in Kansas sooner or later. Shit. Rodney knelt beside the mound of leather and wiped away the puddle of blood that had accumulated at the base of the biker's neck. He pushed into the flesh to feel for a pulse.

"WHO IS THAT BITCH?" The blonde screamed again. "DID ANYONE SEE HER RUN INTO ME?" The blonde stumbled and recovered. "It's not my fault."

Rodney felt something squeeze his ankle and jumped back when he heard a tiny crunch of bone under his boot. He looked down and saw he had just crushed the biker's pinkie finger. How did the hand get there? What was going on? The leather-clad body shuddered and the corpse's arm jerked. Rodney checked the neck again, this time finding a faint pulse. Shit. Shit. Shit. Not again, God, please not again.

He ripped open the biker's jacket and jerked the lid off his crash kit. "SLURPIE! ED!" He screamed. He yanked out a rescue breather with one hand and opened the biker's mouth with the other. Three breaths, thirty compressions.

"What the hell you doing?" Slurpie's voice sounded gruff. "They're gone, man, gone."

Rodney threw himself onto the biker's prone body. "Get the docs on the line, now!"

"They're gone."

"Fuck you, Slurpie! Nobody dies today."

"Look, asswipe—"

"This guy's not dying. Now get the docs online or the station's gonna find out you're smoking on scene." Fire burned through Rodney's body. Sweat broke out along his brow. "This guy's not gonna die. He's not!" Rodney pressed on his rib cage and started counting. This guy's not going to die, he repeated to himself. This guy's *gonna live. This is not going* to be Kansas all over again. If it's the last fucking thing I do, this biker guy's gonna live.

FRIDAY, JULY 7, 2006

2:16 AM

APRIL STOKES THREW OPEN the sliding glass doors of her penthouse, stepped onto the patio and spread her arms wide to let the bay breeze blow across her naked flesh, feeling a sense of renewal as the salt air caressed her lean stomach and teased her nipples. As the lights of the city blazed through the thin chiffon curtains, she breathed deeply, sucking into herself all of its seductive scents. She inhaled a faint whiff of marijuana from one of the apartments below and smiled. How often she had dreamed of returning to the City by the Bay! She returned to the apartment and wiggled her toes in the bearskin rug, feeling its coarse fur against her feet before lifting it off the floor and draping it over her shoulders. In the old days, she would have felt the material to be too heavy. But that was before the change.

God, how she loved furs! The very idea that blood once flowed through this beast and now its carcass lay decaying in some forsaken landfill while she, April Stokes, had its hide. It implied that things were just as they should be.

She gazed at the city from the shadows of refurbished buildings that had sprung from the rubble of the 1989 earthquake. The apartment stood a mere three stories tall, but because of its location in North Beach, she could still see all the way to Chinatown on a clear night. San Francisco's traditionally chilly summer had retreated into hiatus, leaving a cloudless, warm July night in its wake. She had been away far too long. The walk down Market Street yesterday caused her to gape in surprise at the amount of renovations the city had experienced, as well as curse the men who encouraged this change. The stroll to the bay had been a hollow, empty experience, lacking the energy and vitality she had felt during her last visit here. She shot a venomous glance at the Holiday Inn sign in the distance and spat. Change, change, change! Why did this city change so quickly? There was that earthquake to recuperate from, but nonetheless! The breeze hiccuped and shifted direction, sending a gust of night air between her legs. April snuggled deeper into the bearskin and backed into the main room of the apartment.

Across from the balcony doors on the opposite end of the room, a bar stretched the length of the penthouse wall. Several leather stools sat parked underneath its granite top and on one of those stools lay her mink. She let the bearskin fall to the floor and strode nude across the apartment to the mink coat, encasing herself with the floor-length showpiece. Idly, she grasped the crystal flute from the bar and admired herself in the mirror behind the bar. She toasted herself and sipped the drink. Only an hour ago, it was a Champagne Royale. Now, however, the sugar cube had coagulated at the base of the V-shaped flute and delivered the pungent taste of bitters and alcohol. She opened her throat as the fluid drained into her. While most women over forty wrestled with the question of cosmetic surgery, April was not one of them. Her taut skin left none of the usual age lines people associate with a forty-five-year-old woman. Her thick red hair glistened with the luster of women half her age and her tight belly and defined limbs illustrated the benefits of good diet and exercise. She smiled at herself, reflecting back the straight white teeth and show-stopping smile. She was beautiful, was she not?

It hadn't been easy keeping her body in this condition, especially since that fool Victoria had abused it terribly.

With one final flourish, she downed the last of her drink, tossed the flute aside, spun around, and stumbled over the corpse's cold pelvis. She bent down and grasped the mother-of-pearl knife lying next to the body. Although the blood was still tacky to the touch, it seemed like hours ago that April had rammed the knife into the abdomen of Ralph S. Thompson, Jr.

She sat cross-legged next to the corpse and stared at it. In the dim light, Ralph's body looked much older than its fifty-six years. Ralph's thick, once jet black hair now gave way to patches of gray along his temples; flesh lay loose and flabby around his middle and his tight, curly pubic hairs had become a small patch of white around his flaccid penis. April smiled at the thought of Ralph's member, which, only hours ago, had stood stiff and tall while they copulated. She reached out and stroked it, yet still it remained dormant. She held it more firmly and jerked at the flesh, feeling her pulse quicken and her face flush with heat. How dare he not rise to the occasion when she demanded? Did he not realize she was—

He's dead.

A voice from deep inside of her spoke. Dead? With a start, April saw again how the knife had jerked when it plunged into Ralph's flesh. She laughed despite herself and pulled open her mink. She turned the dagger around and placed its pearl handle against her vulva, running it up and down the soft flesh. It felt so much like Ralph! Short but thick and hard. She pushed and the handle penetrated her. The sharp curve of the knife's handle cut her, sending waves of pleasure along her spine. Pleasure was, after all, so much like pain. She imagined the handle to be Ralph, feeling it become him as he thrust into her, sending electric shocks through her body. April bit her lip, warm blood trickling from her mouth as she moved the knife in and out of herself faster and faster, twisting it, thrusting it until she orgasmed with such force that her leg jerked uncontrollably and kicked Ralph S. Thompson, Jr., who was now very flaccid indeed.

Now all she had to do was find and kill the remaining people on her list. Even though He would undoubtedly try to stop her, she would deal with Him when they crossed paths. If only He had joined her when she asked Him, she would not need to worry about His interference. But no matter. She would kill Him, too.

From somewhere within the penthouse, a clock struck 2:30 a.m.. April turned to the sky and smiled.

*   *   *

The digital clock for which Dane spent a fortune at Sharper Image screamed 2:16 a.m.. Damn, he hated this insomnia. The physical therapist had warned him he might suffer from sleeplessness but shouldn't seven months be enough time for his body to acclimate to the new sleep patterns?

"Take a Tylenol PM," Jake beseeched him whenever he caught Dane haunting the condo in the middle of the night.

"Makes me drowsy," he'd reply.

"Isn't that the point?" Jake would mumble in a voice seeped in sleep.

"No. The point is sleep, not walking around WANTING to sleep and being unable to GET to sleep." Dane would snap.

"Whatever." And then Jake would roll over and instantly fall back into his deep slumber.

On nights when the insomnia hit, Dane would sometimes sit and watch his partner sleep. He never tired of staring at Jake, who would snore and grunt while Dane restlessly squirmed in the worn leather of the recliner watching his lover's bearded cheeks puff in and out, keeping time to the ticking of the grandfather clock. He felt a tinge of jealousy, as Dane hadn't slept a full eight hours in a year. On the bright side, however, was the fact that these sleepless nights never seemed to be a detriment to his waking life.

Hoping to find an answer other than drugs, he would ring Mrs. Jeremy (who, oddly never seemed to sleep either) and invite her to a late night rendezvous. "You need a God-damned hobby!" The old woman spat between mouthfuls of Carl's Junior's bacon cheeseburger when he explained the insomnia. "If you're up all fucking night, you think you might want to have some kind of damned hobby. What 'cha do all night, boy? Sit around jacking off?" Her pudgy jowls wiggled as she chewed, her eyes reflecting a twinge of mischievousness.

Masturbation was an option he hadn't considered, and the idea was a great one. So after an afternoon of assisting Mrs. Jeremy on her errands, he'd run over to Castro to pick up an armload of porn before returning home. Sitting on the leather couch beating off worked for a few nights, but the habit lost some of its earlier appeal. Besides, all he really had to do was awaken Jake, who was usually sporting quite a boner at two in the morning. Nevertheless, after he came, he still found himself restless and awake. So he donated the porn to his friend Kevin and went back to prowling the condominium like a caged animal.

He shrank back into the old leather wingback chair and stared down onto the panhandle separating Fell Street from Oak. Usually the grassy knoll provided some entertainment; it was, after all, just around the corner from Saint Mary's Hospital. If the usual clientele of students, addicts, or drunks weren't available, there was always the hospital's steady stream of visitors who walked the park after visiting hours. When the weather was warm, it often serviced those who chose to prowl its dark corners in search of release rather than face the same old bullshit in the bars along Castro or SOMA.

From his carefully chosen vantage point, Dane could see almost everything, from the hesitant, coy movements of a heterosexual couple on their first date to the seasoned queens who wanted nothing more than an anonymous blowjob. When he first started this voyeuristic pastime, he couldn't understand why so many people engaged in sexual activities against the same oak tree. Couldn't they tell it was in full view of the street lamp? After a couple weeks, Dane realized that the park visitors DID know, and that was precisely why they chose its rough bark to lean against. Dane shook his head in amazement, envious of such loose behavior. Was lust for sex outside of his relationship another betrayal of Jake? The relationship seemed so smooth and effortless, and the sex had always been a roller coaster of ecstatic highs to mediocre lows, but Dane had regretted none of it. Until recently.

Dane's leg started to throb along the incision, so he cupped his balls and peeled them from the leather so he could shift position. Since the accident, he hadn't been able to get used to the scar, no matter how many times he looked at it. Running down the inside of his right leg from his groin to his ankle, the red thread of skin remained a constant reminder of the crash a year ago. Maybe that was why tonight's sleeplessness felt so much worse than other nights. It was exactly one year ago today that he pulled away from the coffee house on his Harley and was killed.

Although he'd replayed that night a thousand times in his head, the exact details of the accident remained a blur. He had downed too many vanilla lattes with Jenny, who was rebounding from yet another failed audition. Even after they left the confines of the shop, they remained outside in the cool night air talking; he remembered this much clearly because it had been his idea to get as much quality time with Jenny as he could before she left for L.A. to film a Ford commercial.

It was after this point that his memory failed him. He had vague images of Jenny walking him to the bike, hugging him and then running to leap onto the N-Judah train as it pulled away from the cul-de-sac. He remembered waiting for a woman in a red dress to cross before he began making a U-turn. Somewhere in the distance, he heard screaming, a car honking and a skid. But everything else was a blank until he awoke in the hospital several days later with Jake asleep in the chair next to him.

He grabbed his cup of decaf from the window sill and sipped the hot liquid, feeling it burn as it went down his throat. The most haunting aspect of the accident and subsequent complications was that try as he might, the coma-induced memory loss wasn't complete—his memories returned from the darkness long enough to haunt him.

Desperate to fully recall what he dreamed while in coma, Dane tried journaling the ethereal memories, talking to the hospital-provided social worker and even going to a shrink after being released from SFU Medical Center. Nothing worked. Whatever he had experienced that night would forever remain hidden, reminding him that no matter what he believed, he wasn't fully in control of anything.

The sounds of Ace's claws on the hardwood floors interrupted Dane's musings. After a few seconds, he felt the German shepherd's nose on his leg and he gave the dog the reassuring pat. Not once in the past year had the dog ever come to him in the night. So, there were still surprises in the world! The shepherd, like his master, slept like the dead and on the rare instances Ace awoke during the night, he would never stray far from Jake's side of the bed. It would be newsworthy if either of them stirred during the occasional earthquake. Dane stroked the dog, glad for the company.

He tried reading during these late night bouts of sleeplessness, but over the past year, he'd read countless autobiographies from crash survivors, psychics, loonies and fakers, all trying to explain "life after death." Dane didn't buy any of the bullshit. Unlike the subjects of the books, Dane wasn't interested in saving the world, reconnecting to universal consciousness or being an inspiration to the human race. He just wanted to get a fucking night's sleep.

Maybe the question he should be asking wasn't would he get a full night's sleep but would he leave Jake or would Jake leave him?

Jake grunted. Both Ace and Dane turned to the queen-sized waterbed to stare at the sleeping giant. Jake lay spread—no, sprawled—diagonally across the bed. He lay, legs apart, the sheet barely covering his cock and balls. Dane's gaze lingered. The full moon combined with the glare of the digital clock shed an eerie dark illumination on Jake's body. He could never get enough of his chest hair—the way it led a dark, thin trail to his pelvis. Hey, little boy, want some candy? Just come on over here—

He glanced to the clock again. 2:36 a.m. Maybe he should pop a couple of the quaaludes Kevin had given him. But as much as he craved sleep, a small part of him feared slumber, for recently, during the few hours his body did shut down, horrible dreams haunted him, dreams in which a red-haired woman stalked him from the shadows.

All his life, he had enjoyed vibrant, joyful, colorful dreams that stayed with him long after he awoke. But nowadays, he awoke from catnaps shaking, covered in sweat, infused with a deep sense of fear. For all the meditation, journaling, and therapy, he could remember only portions of the dream; a violent, angry woman dressed in bright red with a name that sounded noble, like Veronica, Vivica…something with a "V." His brain allowed previews of the picture, but never the entire film.

Ever since the accident, his relationship with Jake had deteriorated, his sleep patterns had been destroyed, and the only steady commitment he could fulfill was the volunteer position at the animal shelter. It was as if his whole world had been overturned like a giant Etch-A-Sketch. But through it all, good ol' what's-her-name in the red dress had seared a place for herself in his nighttime jaunts. And he knew that in his dreams, she was killing people.

Dane knew he should tell Jake that these vivid dreams had started again, but he didn't want to concern him. Admit it, he said to himself, you don't want Jake to think you've totally lost it. You're afraid he'll think less of you.

But there was also another reason he couldn't tell Jake about the dreams. He harbored a feeling that was impossible to describe, an inner sense that through the dreams, he was fighting some kind of battle…a battle that was his and his alone. It's personal.

He put his feet on the side of the dog to warm them. Silly trying to hide the dreams from Jake, as Jake, always knew when something was bothering him.

Dane stood up, startling Ace, who leapt to his feet with a low growl.

"Oh, Ace. Sorry, boy." He stroked the dog. Ace looked at him and wagged his tail. It took too much effort for him, though, as he stopped after two swings, padded over to his other master and resettled on the floor next to Jake. Dane returned his gaze down into the now empty park. He suddenly felt abandoned and alone, so he grabbed the small pillow from the window seat that Mrs. Jeremy had made for their housewarming gift and hugged it tightly. The fluffy blue pillow bore the embroidered symbol of a male/male union, with birthdays of Jake and Dane stitched below it. Usually, holding it provided Dane with a profound sense of comfort and security. Tonight, however, it held no such power.

FRIDAY, JULY 7

9:00 AM

JAKE PRETENDED TO COUGH to mask his yawn. When he first accepted the job at the law offices of Larner, Reaves and Ball, the weekly staff meetings had provided an opportunity to observe his colleagues. He tried to validate these dull, futile meetings by comparing his attendance to the fieldwork of a sociologist like Dian Fossey—only his primates held law degrees from Yale, Harvard and Stanford.

He became aware that the other attorneys in the brightly lit room were bobbing their heads in agreement and realized that his daydreaming had caused him to miss an aspect of the weekly summary report from Larner, one of the firm's partners. He applied his well-rehearsed stern lawyer face and nodded, hoping he hadn't agreed to anything too peculiar which, judging from Larner's history, was doubtful. He stifled another yawn. Most of the discussions that ensued during these meetings didn't pertain to him and bored him stiff. As the sole employee of the Real Estate Acquisitions division, the name of which he thought obscenely self-indulgent, he operated in a world of faxes, emails, and overnight couriers concerning obscure pieces of land that held the firm's interest only because of their potential profitability. There were no external stakeholders in Real Estate Acquisitions—he worked only for the partners and was charged with the responsibility to make them as much money as possible. But the position allowed him to work alone and he liked the autonomy. The downside was, of course, meetings like this, which only supported his assertion about high-paying, high-profile jobs: they deserved neither the prestige nor the respect people gave them. Rather than utilize the workday efficiently by finding answers to the questions that troubled their clientele, the attorneys descended to the lowest common denominator of forced competition by trying to outclass, outdress and outjudge each other.

"Doin' the lawyer circle jerk," Dane said one evening after Jake's retelling of the weekly ritual. "The only thing missing is a cup to catch the jizz."

Jake dropped his pen onto the floor so he could duck under the table to disguise his next yawn. Dane's description was right on the money—another uncannily accurate summary. How did Dane do that? It was as if Dane could crawl inside peoples' heads. True, it was one of the traits that Jake found endearing, but it was also infuriating.

Oh, well. What the hell. It's a living, and if Jake was lucky, his tenure here would be nothing more than a minor inconvenience. The income from the brownstone would make it feasible for him to buy a second apartment complex and, with fiscal discipline, a third building. By that time, Jake felt certain that the long-term plan he laid out would be complete and he could quit this monotonous, dreary, happiness-sapping job, take his 401k and run. And, as always, Jake had a plan B if Dane didn't return to work as planned, although it wouldn't be as profitable. Jake always had a plan B. Jake considered people without a plan B irresponsible and idealistic; people without a plan B were called "artists."

The plan was simple yet brilliant. It had come to him in a sudden flash of inspiration the day his old pal Daniel from law school offered him the position at the firm. He appreciated Daniel's faith in his legal prowess, but how could he expect Jake to abandon Montana's massive expanse of gorgeous nothingness? How could he leave the clear skies, clean air, and acres of natural beauty only to surround himself with concrete, noise, and crowds? Could he stand waking every morning to the sight of people and cars instead of green fields and horses? He was a country boy, not a city dweller.

Later that same night, he awoke with a perfectly formulated plan, as if an otherworldly gift of divination had descended upon him in his sleep. According to his calculations based upon the current real estate market, it would take about five years to expand his own financial portfolio to the point of early retirement. All he had to do was identify the properties that held the highest chance of profitability and snatch them up when the firm passed on them, which was sure to happen sometime. It was illogical to think otherwise. Although five years of miserly financial restraint combined with living in a foggy, crowded city filled him with disgust, it was a small price for a lifetime of financial independence in a remote cabin amongst nature's splendor.

Minutes after hiring the intern from the law school, he had the young woman assigned to tracking down statistics on various cities' population growth, pending building contracts (specifically with malls and industrial parks), company mergers, and tax mill rates. Jake had been presented with his one chance to set himself up for life, and the grand payoff was too good an opportunity to squander. Thanks to his job, Jake had spent the past couple of years acquiring an impressive portfolio of land that, on the surface, appeared like risky investments. Jake knew better. He could sense these things. It was this sixth sense that helped Jake surf right through the real estate bust that devastated so many others.

This plan was the only reason that he, despite the agonizing suffocation of concrete, crowds, noise, burglaries, and beggars, bided his time in the City by the Bay. And leaving Montana wasn't even as bad as he had anticipated—because he had met Dane. Despite Dane's idiosyncrasies, his brazen candor not only showed refreshing integrity but implied a quality that Jake craved and cherished even more—safety. He never wondered where Dane stood on issues and never sensed underlying motives for Dane's behavior. Dane was as transparent as they came.

Until the accident.

The changes that confused Jake were the unexpected ones, such as how Dane suddenly stopped looking at him, how Dane refused to be seen naked and how Dane become moody, easily angered and borderline psychotic. Even their sex life, which had always been the best part of their relationship, had fizzled. So, he had decided to give Dane a year to pull his act together. He couldn't even remember the last time they'd had sex.

But after one year, Dane was still a bitchy, confused, solitary mess. And as usual, Jake had a plan B: he would leave. Leave both the city, and sadly, Dane. He patted the pocket of his jacket where, moments before, he had retrieved the confirmation number from his e-ticket. Thank God for ticketless travel! He had hoped he wouldn't need to leave; that miraculously Dane would come to his senses and return to the world of the living. He had hoped that this morning he would see Dane's face in bed next to him, smiling that sheepish grin Jake had fallen in love with. He had hoped the one year anniversary of the accident would be a new beginning for them, just as it would be a new beginning for Dane.

Unfortunately, he awoke at 2:16 a.m. with Dane creeping back into the living room. Jake knew then that if Dane wasn't going to open up to him about the return of the nightmares, he never would. He didn't understand why Dane felt the need to withhold this information—did he think Jake was stupid? Unobservant? More than anything, he needed to know that Dane would turn to him in times of trouble. But Dane believed he must journey on his own. He believed everyone should take personal responsibility and wouldn't have it any other way. The independence was infuriating as it was enticing and was the part of Dane Jake would miss most.

Suddenly the chairs in the conference room squeaked, and the air filled with the vibrations of movement. The meeting had ended and the partners stood gathering their papers and files with forged smiles plastered across their faces. The various non-attorney staff members of the agency, the secretaries, interns and runners, dashed out of the room to their duties while the legal experts stood, hoping for one last chance to impress each other with a useless bit of knowledge. Jake waited until the remaining underlings clamored around the principals and then slid from the room.

Shannon, his secretary hailed him as he strode around the corner to his office.

"Did you hear?"

"About what?" Jake asked.

"Ralph S. Thompson was found murdered this morning."

Jake froze. "Howwhat happened?"

Shannon shrugged. "No idea. The police are investigating. But my roomie's sister's boyfriend works in the hotel where he was found. I suspected you would prefer to hear it now than on the six o'clock news."

"Yes. Thank you." Jake shook his head. "Damn. Damn, damn, damn."

"I've already informed Mr. Larner and Mr. Ball. They're meeting with the legal department over at Thompson Construction this afternoon."

"Well…I guess you can cancel my afternoon, then."

"Done. I've also notified the team the Thompson construction project meeting set for next week may be delayed."

"Thanks, Shannon. Nice work."

"I'll miss him."

"I thought you didn't like him."

"I didn't. He was a sexist pig, but he was your first client after I was hired."

Jake smiled. "You always remember your first, eh?"

"No. Because of his account, I got that holiday bonus. That bonus was the down payment on my condo!"

*   *   *

Minutes later, he pushed through the double glass doors of the building's lobby. He yanked off his tie, shoved it into the pocket of his sports coat and peeled the stifling garment from his back. He unbuttoned the first few buttons of his shirt and let the salty breeze blow onto his chest. This city must have been quite a spectacle when it was first settled. How much the city had changed since his arrival here.

"Hey! You!" The voice jolted Jake from his musings. Jake recognized the nasal, New England twang instantly. Maggie strode up next to him. "Yo! Paul Bunyan!" She slid up to him and clutched his arm. "Everyone else in this city jumps on the bandwagon of snatching up land in the Pacific Northwest so they can retire early and spend the rest of their lives on the Mediterranean. You? You want to move to Maine and build a log cabin. What the hell kind of self-respecting faggot are you?"

"What do you know?" Jake asked.

Maggie thrust a paper at him, and he took it with hesitation. "If you're going to get the interns to fax the paperwork for your personal real estate projects, double check to see if they erase all telltale signs of said purchases from company equipment." She glared at him sternly. "There are those within Larner, Reaves and Ball who would frown upon such use of company property."

Jake took the fax from her and shoved it into his pocket. "Ralph S. Thompson was murdered last night."

"What?"

"Shannon told me. Apparently her roomie's sister's boyfriend found out."

"Jesus Christ!"

"Yeah. My thoughts exactly."

"Well…I guess that pretty well fucks up our week. I was planning to meet with Thompson Construction."

"I suspect those meetings are cancelled, my dear."

"Jesus fucking christ! I was planning on that new condo development as the down payment on my boat. Fuck!"

Jake chuckled. "A real humanitarian, aren't you?"

"The guy was a sexist pig. He deserved whatever he had coming to him. Just wish he had waited until after I got my boat. Fucking dogs!"

"Lunch?" Jake asked.

She rolled her eyes and sighed. "Daniel wants this folio completed by yesterday."

"The insurance fraud gig?" Jake asked quietly, glancing around to make sure they were alone.

Maggie shook her head. "Apartment building liability suit in SOMA. Have to give the appearance of TRYING to wrap it up. You know, I have an idea on the Johnson itinerary if you have a minute and—what are you staring at?"

Jake jumped at her sudden change of intonation. "Nothing."

"Liar."

"Daydreaming."

Maggie giggled. "I hate those stupid staff meetings, too."

Jake nodded. He had been daydreaming, but not about the meeting. He had learned long ago that he had an empathy for real estate. He resonated more strongly with land, but it worked with buildings, too, mostly those of stone. He could feel a slight electric tingle travel throughout his body while he scrutinized a property; the longer he stared, the stronger and more defined the vague electric tingling became. Often, he would discover an hour evaporated while he had stood feeling a building. Jake had learned the difference between a soft tug in his gut (fertile, rich land) and a sharp pain in his ribs (contaminated water). He never questioned the source of this intuition. Questioning a good thing would be illogical.

Such a call had come from across the street where the Holiday Inn stood. From there, a feeling seemed to tug him into the distance, slightly to the north and west of the hotel, where an unusual apartment building cried out to Jake, begging for his attention.

Jake knew this building—Daniel's firm had sold it to Ralph Thompson, Jr. last year. Ralph had particularly loved the top floor penthouse with its view of the bay, Alcatraz and North Beach. Jake had passed that building every week on his way to meet Dane at the Back Alley, but the building had always stood regal and mute. Why was it speaking to him today? His head began to pound, and he forced himself to break the connection.

"When will the papers be ready to sign?" The words poured from Jake's mouth.

"Tomorrow morning, I suppose. Look, Jake, are you sure you're alright? You look...well, frankly, you look like shit." She touched him lightly on the elbow.

"I'm fine." He waved her off.

"Great. I can pawn off the file on you Monday. Say over coffee at 8:00?" She said hopefully.

"No thanks. I hate jogging on a full stomach." Jake rubbed his temples as the throbbing headache spread through his brain.

Maggie pressed the back of her hand to his forehead.

"Meetings always do this to me," Jake brushed her hand away. "I'll be fine. Thanks. Look, I'll stop by your office in the morning. If you don't have time to copy them, I'll have Craig do it."

"Craig?" she asked, confused. "Your new intern?"

"Tall. Lanky. Goofy plastic glasses."

"Oh! That's his name?" Maggie giggled. "How do you memorize them all?"

Jake shrugged. "Names are important. Names contain power."

"Okay! My cue to leave! Deep conversation is not my forte this time of the day. See you tomorrow." Jake nodded and watched her turn towards Market. After a few steps, she spun towards him once more. "Take care of that headache!"

Jake forced a smile onto his face until Maggie turned the corner and disappeared into the crowd. Suddenly, sweat began to pour out of him and his knees wobbled, so he had to lean against the building to keep himself upright. After breathing in several lungfuls of air, he felt stronger, although not better. He dug his thumbs into his throbbing temples—a trick he'd learned in college to help sober him up after a night of drinking and screwing. He steadied himself and had turned back towards the lobby doors when he noticed the woman.

She stepped out of the red Ferrari idling along the curb, its right turn signal blinking madly. Gracefully, she grasped the hand of a husky man and swung her legs from the car. She unfolded herself to reveal a trim, athletic body cloaked in a flowing green evening dress. As she turned and nodded to the man for his assistance, she flashed him a toothy, cordial smile. She was elegant and gorgeous. She had to be a movie star, or model. Nobody that attractive could avoid it. But who was she?

He stared at her, willing her to turn around, wanting— needing—to see her eyes. He stood still as a statue as she ascended the green-carpeted stairs of the hotel across the street. Another man held the door for her, but just as she went to step over the threshold, she stopped and turned.

Goddess was the only description for this creature. Her flowing red hair framed an oval face as it cascaded onto smooth, delicate shoulders that were tan from the sun. Her well-proportioned body graced an emerald dress as if she were 1950s MGM royalty. A mink was draped over her shoulders. Only her ankles appeared below the dress's hemline and the ankles, like the shoulder, revealed a smooth, even tan. Her eyes remained hidden behind oversized, dark sunglasses that faced in Jake's direction.

As an invisible hand grasped his brain and squeezed, he fell backwards against the cold, gray concrete of the building for the second time and closed his eyes. Then, as quickly as it had descended and without explanation, the pain disappeared. He shook his head to clear it of the cobwebs and turned back towards the hotel. The goddess was gone.

"Hey, dude. You okay?" a calm, deep voice rumbled.

Jake looked towards the dark-skinned stranger dressed in a UPS delivery uniform who was staring at him. Despite his contorted face and knit brow, the guy was stunningly handsome.

"Fine. Thanks." Jake said. "I had a headache but—" But what? What had he been doing moments ago?

"I know how that goes," the UPS man said. "But standing outside in the fresh air can really clear one's senses, don't you think?" He flashed a smile at Jake. "Or at least make things more pleasurable to look at."

"Yeah." Jake finally tore himself away from the thick mustache and piercing blue eyes. "I'll see you around." Jake said, forcing himself to walk 8th towards city hall.

"I hope so." The man's voice was cheery.

Jake sauntered up the street feeling as if he could take on the world. He liked good-looking people and not necessarily only those who flirted with him. All of them. He got an odd sense of satisfaction from knowing that such beauty existed amongst the pollution, decay, and evil in the world. Somehow, their beauty made sense—it was a balance struck in an otherwise unbalanced world.

He hit the corner and stood amongst several other pedestrians as they waited for the WALK light. He began to hum a tune he hadn't thought of for years, although it was one of his favorites. Elvis sang it in his mind, although other singers had laid claim to it as well. The green, green grass of home. He smiled to himself, staring into the blue sky. Green. One of his favorite colors. The color of the fields behind his farmhouse in Montana. The color of…what? Jake shook his head as a throbbing pain shot through his temples. Green. Why was he thinking of green? He had the vague recollection that he had seen something green today. Where was it?

By the time Jake reached The Home of the Dead Bovine, all memory of the woman in the green dress had long faded away.

*   *   *

Kevin stood behind the richly polished imitation walnut counter filing the morning's registrations when the trashy redhead in the green dress came plodding down the hotel hallway like an elephant on smack. The hotel required employees to stand next to the computer terminal when working the front desk, but luckily for Kevin, he was not standing at the computer terminal. The lean young black man had just laid the phone back into the cradle after dealing with the arrogant closet homo from St. Louis. Who did he think he was kidding? It was a good thing he wasn't at the counter, too, because he wouldn't have been able to see jack squat from the computer, and as reigning Princess of Preying Eyes, he had a duty to his subjects. That duty was preying his eyes upon the sources of gossip—which, if he wasn't mistaken (and he was never mistaken), this bitch in green was definitely a source of gossip. He straightened his tie, smoothed his sports jacket and peered around the corner.

The floozy thumbed the elevator button wildly, and when it didn't appear quickly enough for her liking, she lifted her arm and flagellated the door with her olive green purse.

"That's it, sugar! Beat them doors! Go on, now!" Kevin muttered under his breath. As if on cue, the woman in green spun away in fury and, having spotted the JUBILEE sign, headed towards the bar.

"How do you know it's a hooker, boss? Maybe a tourist." A thin voice behind him creaked.

Kevin slowly turned to Sean. He gave an exaggerated sigh to illustrate his extreme patience with the blond airhead and spoke very slowly.

*   *   *

"If you can't get into the rhythm of the city, love, I'll banish you to housekeeping." Kevin clicked off his points on the long black fingers of his left hand as he explained. "One: dress is too expensive for the average tourist. Two: much too tight for the Midwest. Three: she's TAN!" Sean stared at him through glassy eyes which screamed non-comprehension.

Kevin was about to open his mouth to chastise the young man's inability to apply simple logic when he happened to glance down at Sean's crotch. From this angle, it appeared to Kevin that the boy had stuffed tennis balls in his jockeys, which, as Kevin well knew, would be not only painful, but totally unnecessary. His impatience instantly subsided and he began to smirk. Big cocks had that effect on him.

"Tan, Sean, TAN! It's JULY in the city! Means she's probably from L.A. I'm guessing the valley. Lastly, my adorable-yet-clueless friend, that girl cannot walk in them high heels. Did you see her wobbling around like a two-bit drag queen? She, my brainless beauty, will bite the carpet in a matter of minutes—watch her and see if I'm not right."

"Betcha two bucks," Sean grunted and winked, pulling the bills from his pocket.

"I KNOW you are NOT gambling on company time," Kevin snapped as he dug two bills out of his uniform. With childlike glee, the two turned towards the redhead and watched breathlessly as she lurched towards the lounge. Her heel caught in the rug and she stumbled but didn't topple; then she regained her footing. The two watched the green extravaganza until she disappeared into the bar, when Sean hastily shoved the four dollars into his pocket.. Kevin was indignant. "Well seeing as your ass won the four bucks, I think YOU owe us a Starbucks. Venti nonfat mocha, please. Light foam, extra chocolate. Go on now. Run."He swatted at the boy's ass as two elderly women in polyester pantsuits tottered up to the registration desk, clutching their patent leather pocket books in their fists. He ducked through the door marked MANAGER ON DUTY before they caught sight of him. Let them wait. They don't have anywhere to go, hell, they're on vacation! Besides, that new girl, Crystle, would be starting her shift any second. He needed to think about the woman in green. From deep within came the overwhelming desire to see her face again—no—her eyes. He was sure he'd seen her somewhere before.

*   *   *

April clung desperately to the bar stool. Under the green dress, her heaving chest felt tight as her heart thundered against her ribs. The disheveled velvet gown clung by its left shoulder strap, revealing a boney, pale right shoulder. She knew decorum required her to pull the strap up onto her shoulder, but right now April didn't care about the damned dress.

The dark-haired one was near. She had looked directly into his eyes. She clenched her fists until her crimson nails dug into her flesh.

Why did that man have to show before the next phase of her plan was in place? April's eyes scanned the bar for any sign the dark-haired one had followed her into the lounge. She felt sure he recognized her, yet he made no attempt to contact her. Why? What was his plan? Did he have one? Had he failed to recognize her? Did he sense her presence just as she had sensed his? Should she kill him now?

No, she decided. She would advance with her plan. She had labored for too long to make compromises now. Much better to continue on schedule and not be misled by presumption. She pulled herself erect, adjusted the dress, uncurled her hands and laid her palms on the bar. After a moment, she felt her heart begin to slow and her breathing become shallower, more rhythmic and natural. The dark-haired one was not Him, was he? While He had the power to stop her, this one did not. This dark-haired man was merely His…what? What was it like what sodomites called their "special friends?" The thought of Him caused April to clench her teeth and swallow her rage. She was such a fool! She should have killed Him when she'd had the chance; when she regained consciousness in the hospital and He lay next to her, body reeling from trauma, it would have been so easy to lean over, cover his mouth and nostrils, and squeeze.

This speculation wasted precious time. If she was to find Bethany, she couldn't allow herself the luxury of retrospection. He would be dealt with, along with the dark-haired one, but it would not be now.

"That's an awfully sad face." A cool, deep voice breathed into her ear. "Let's see if we can't brighten you up."

Startled, April looked up. The stranger standing next to her had a tight, muscled body. His blue eyes, dark hair and firm skin broadcast potency and vitality. He stood close to her, the curious yellow canvas jacket unfastened to reveal a mustard yellow shirt with pink flowers. He smiled, revealing a line of pearly white teeth. Ah! She loved men with good teeth. She might just accept this handsome man's flirtations. It would be the perfect distraction. "Can I buy you a drink?" He asked in a cool, low voice that sounded like clear mountain water.

"No, thank you. I'm fine." She responded, her gaze lingering on him a second too long for polite conversation.

"Yes, you are. But are you also thirsty? Mind if I join you?" Then, not waiting for an answer, he slid into the stool next to her. "What are you drinking, Miss...?"

"I'll have a Champagne Royale," she said pleasantly, enjoying the musky smell of his skin. She ran her manicured hand through her thick hair. "My name is—"

Victoria Lemark a voice screamed from within.

April shuddered as an icy finger ran along her spine, moved into her neck and sent tentacles of fear creeping up her scalp. April had satisfied her vengeance last night; her purpose had been fulfilled once the dagger plunged into the old man's gut. It was time for April to die and be laid to rest alongside Victoria.

"Are you alright?" The voice sounded tight with concern. "Whoa!" The stranger cried as he stood and reached an arm across her shoulders. "Steady now."

"Thank you," she responded with a weak smile. "I don't know what's come over me. A little light-headed, I suppose." She laid one hand on the bar and wrapped the other around his hairy wrist.

"Do you need to sit down? In a chair, I mean?" He asked, nodding towards one of the small café tables to his left.

She shook her head, making sure to brush against his hand with her breasts. "I'll be fine, really. I haven't eaten in a long time. Maybe a snack will help."

The stranger looked down at her hand, which grasped his. And with a sudden gentleness, he twisted his arm so that their hands locked, fingers intertwined. "Let's order something," he said, smiling into her flushed face. He nodded towards the bartender. "A bar menu, please."

"How fortunate," she said with a nervous giggle, "that you were here." She flitted her eyes away from him coyly as he grinned.

"You still haven't told me your name," he whispered. He patted the stool next to him, motioning for her to join him.

She looked into his eyes for a long moment before responding. "It's Lily," she said. "Lily Dayton." He took her hand and tenderly kissed each finger, ending with her thumb.

"Nice to meet you, Lily Dayton."

FRIDAY, JULY 7

1:00 PM

MRS. JEREMY STOOD in a fucking long line at The Home of the Dead Bovine just to get a God-damned cheeseburger with no onions, extra mustard, and pickle. Waiting for one of those greasy things was a necessity, though, as they loaded those fuckers with onions and everyone knows onions on burgers is just stupid, as Americans already suffered from acute halitosis.

She impatiently looked around, scouring the crowded restaurant for a vacant booth she could lay claim to if she ever got her fucking order. Finding them all occupied, she scanned the dining room to locate the poor schmuck she would evict so she could sit down at a cramped, God-forsaken table. When she spotted a familiar face, she did a double take. Could that be Jake? She clutched the red tag with the yellow 53 printed on it and shoved it into her cleavage. She waddled over to the table, leaned on her good foot and her cane and raised her double chins at the man who stared out the window.

"Ain't no glory holes here, boy. Move along!" she bellowed, drawing disapproving looks from the young yuppies sitting to her left.

Jake jerked in surprise as he snapped out of his daydream. "Jesus Christ!"

"No. Just me. He knows better than to eat here," she croaked, "and so should you! You're not going to ask an old lady to sit down, or are you just afraid my fat ass won't fit in the chair?"

Jake leapt up to lift his sports coat from the chair opposite him and motioned for the old lady to sit. As she sank into the chair, he realized how much she had aged since he last saw her. Could it be that long? Her once meaty build now strained under the weight of her girth. Her thick glasses betrayed her failing eyesight, and the red rash on her hands proved that eczema still bothered her. As he swung back into his seat, he savored her small triumphs—her cheeks had returned to a healthy pink and her hair looked thick and well groomed. And as always, her emerald eyes still twinkled with mischievousness. When Dane had introduced Mrs. Jeremy to him three years ago, the woman refused to carry the cloth cigarette case Dane had purchased for her, opting instead to shove the sticks of tobacco down her cleavage. The habit meant nothing to Jake until the day the three of them lunched at Hamburger Mary's, and she spent five minutes with her hand shoved down her bra struggling to retrieve one.

"What's that for?" Jake said, gesturing to the cane.

"What the blazes do you think it's for? I'm old. Sometimes I don't walk so good." She glowered at him and Jake quivered. Even though she was an old, fat lady, she did an excellent job of doing what few people ever did—intimidate him. It was like Catholic school all over again, only this time he didn't have the desk to hide behind. Sometime in the future, years maybe, he would read one of her potboiler romances and see himself in her book as he is now, a frozen caricature immortalized in print. Why did he give her this kind of power? What was it about the woman?

"How the fucking hell are you, Jake Lucas?" She smiled and grabbed his hand warmly.

The table on Jake's right fell silent the minute the woman uttered the vulgarity. The Yuppie Princess scowled at Mrs. Jeremy and pursed her lips in disgust.

"Do you have a problem?" the fat woman snapped at the young woman's heavily made-up face. The Princess shook her head and clucked her tongue in protest before swatting the toddler's hand, causing it to drop its french fry.

"I'm fine, Mrs. Jeremy. Tired. I just got out of a meeting…a long, boring meeting. If only Shakespeare's advice had been followed: 'First, we must kill the lawyers'."

"Well, you know, stud, he's not immoral for nothing," she said sternly.

"Immortal," Jake corrected.

"Well, that, too." She said with a smirk. "Oh! My number! They called my number! Be a stud and go get my burger and buns, will you dollface? That's a boy." Jake jumped to his feet and dashed to the counter, marveling again at the power this woman had over him. As Jake reached for the tray and nodded to the pimply faced worker, he heard Mrs. Jeremy's voice through the din of the restaurant bellowing."AND GET MUSTARD, TOO!"

Jake threw a handful of the plastic packets on the tray. As he approached the table, he could hear Mrs. Jeremy talking to the Yuppie Princess. "Don't you just hate running out of fucking mustard?" The Princess rolled her eyes and began clearing her table of the debris with quick, sharp jerks of her arm. Jake laid Mrs. Jeremy's plastic tray onto the table in front of her.

"Pass the salt, dear," Mrs. Jeremy said as Jake sat down. She loaded the french fries with salt, and then stuffed the burger in her mouth as far as it would go before biting down on the juicy meat. "Mmmmm! This is good. Really hits the spot. Where were we?" She mumbled over the food in her mouth.

"You were telling me how you were."

Mrs. Jeremy swallowed and paused long enough to wipe the grease from her chin. "Well, I got the family back another generation."

"Really? I thought you were stuck in the 1600s someplace."

"Early 1800s. I WISH it was the 1600s. I finally plugged that gap between my mom and her step-brother by writing to one of my sisters-in-law who lives in Maine. God, what a bitch!" With a fry dangling from her mouth, she glanced to the toddler. The genderless tyke stared at her, eyes wide with terror. Mrs. Jeremy chuckled. Jake grimaced; he knew what that sound meant. Mrs. Jeremy waited until the Yuppie Princess turned her back on the kid before leaning over and whispering in the kid's ear.

It shrieked in glee and clapped its chubby little hands. "Mommy! Fuck off! Fuck off, Mommy!" the little voice sung loudly. The Yuppie Princess spun wildly about and gasped in shock at the laughing child. The kid took the movement as encouragement and cranked up its volume to a near scream. It began to sing, "Mommy, Mommy, fuck you fuck you! Mommy, Mommy, fuck you fuck you!"

Sputtering in anger, the Princess gathered the last of her things and shoved them into the humungous cloth bag at her feet. "No go, Mommy! Want stay!" The Princess grabbed the child and dragged it out of the Home of the Dead Bovine, leaving the echo of "fuck you fuck you" reverberating in their wake.

When they were gone, Mrs. Jeremy looked at Jake blankly. "I just love pissing off those Yuppie bitches. Makes my fucking day."

"How do I live without you?" Jake asked laughing.

"Good question. How is my boy, anyway? Taking good care of him?" The pause that ensued warned Mrs. Jeremy to let the issue drop. And Jake felt relieved when she took the warning. "So, that no-good, slut of a sister-in-law told me Uncle Ferdinand—"

"Ferdinand?" Jake asked incredulously.

"Better name than my Aunt Fanny. Can you imagine being called a fanny all your life?" Mrs. Jeremy asked, rolling her eyes.

"Could be a compliment," Jake said, eyes twinkling.

"Tramp," the woman responded with a slap on his hand. "Now, where was I?" She scratched her thinning gray hair. "Oh! Ferdinand! Yes. Anyway, as soon as I can trace back to Ferdinand directly, I'm ready to start the next phase of my father's side of the family. Or, as I prefer to call them, the Trashy Whites of America."

"Still needlepointing? Or have you given up?" Jake asked, passing the salt.

"Oh, I still dabble. That's the thing old ladies do best—dabble." Her eyes rested on his for just a moment before she let loose with an earth-shattering belch that echoed through the restaurant. The entire dining room fell silent and looked at her. She ignored them.

"You're a wreck, old lady," Jake said, trying to sound untroubled by the attention.

"That's why you love me. Now help an old lady home."

*   *   *

"That's the problem with today's parents—they hide their kids from reality. So the kid swears. So what? Fuck 'em, that's what I say. Fuck 'em all." Mrs. Jeremy spat vehemently and jammed the Camel 100 back into her mouth.

Jake reached the corner first and jabbed the walk button before turning back to Mrs. Jeremy and waiting patiently for her to continue her tirade.

"The point is, my boy, life isn't safe. It was never meant to be. See, that's God's whole point—to see how you survive in a place that's NOT safe!" She paused long enough to take another drag from the cigarette before continuing.

"Do you meet uncertainty with fierce determination, or do you lie down like a pussy and let fear walk all over you?" She paused for dramatic effect, which had no effect on Jake at all. "So you can take all your federal regulations and labels on food and FDA-screened bottled water and shove 'em up your ass. Shit's gonna happen even with your electronic fences and home security systems. Bad things. Terrible things. Things that aren't fair. That's just the way it is."

He nodded. Jake knew once she started one of her tirades, there was no stopping her. When the light changed to WALK, Jake hooked his elbow about Mrs. Jeremy's, and the two walked slowly across the busy street, the woman flipping her middle finger to anyone who even slightly hinted at impatience. Time was the one thing he had plenty of, and she wouldn't be rushed.

"So anyway, I get this call from Abbey. Remember Abbey? The editor they assigned me for the last book? Although fuck knows why, she's such an elitist. She sends me these messages in the edits that piss me off. Pick up the pace! Do you fucking believe that? I go back to the third chapter and put the two lead characters on an island instead. You know how all those old dried up snatches just love a desert island romance! Anyway, I'm trying to decide if they're going to do the deed now, or if they decide to wait and have the interlude interrupted by something. I don't know what, but something that will 'pick up the pace.'" She snorted loudly and flicked the worn butt into the gutter.

"If I have them wait, I can do the whole safe sex shit, too. Get that idea in there. Then, the hero can really give it to her when they're rescued," she said, more to herself than to him.

"I thought you did that with *Green-Eyed Love Spy*." Jake asked, confused.

"Dear, I do that with ALL of them! How do you keep them straight, anyway? I tell you, the old days were better. You had time to PLAN what you were writing. I could really develop a CHARACTER. Now, I pump out one a month. There's no time for any of that creative stuff anymore, it's all about the numbers, demographics, percent of sales volume, blah, blah fucking blah. All those old biddies say they like the romance but I know better. They're only waiting to see how much the prince pays to poke the virgin." She said with a disgusted wave of her hand.

"*Romantically Poked*. Good title," Jake mused.

"The story of a troubled rancher in the Old West where his daughter is in love with the cowboy of her dreams, who turns out to be transgendered F to M with an illegitimate mulatto son. How's that for PC trendy?" She nudged him playfully.

"It's a hit. Retain the movie rights," he said with a nod.

"In the ads, we'll say COMING ATTRACTIONS and spell it c-u-m-m-i-n-g," Mrs. Jeremy suggested, slapping him lightly on the arm. "Enough about me. I need gossip. How's Dane? How are the two of you doing?"

"Questions! I'm under cross-examination, I see. You should have been a lawyer," Jake thought, choosing his words carefully. "The purchase of the property in Maine went through."

Mrs. Jeremy stopped, tugging his arm with such force he spun around to face her.

"You're getting ready to run, aren't you? You motherfucker—" She snapped, glowering at him.

He held up his hands defensively and interrupted, "I am NOT getting ready to run. I—"

"Why didn't you call me to discuss this, Jake? I thought—"

"Why?" Jake's voice rose. "What am I going to say? That I think my boyfriend is losing his mind? He's treating me like shit, has depression to the point of catatonia and I can't take it anymore. Is that what you want me to tell you, Mrs. Jeremy?"

He stared at the old woman gaping at him and instantly felt his stomach open. He had no right to speak to her that way. He never had disrespected her before and never thought he would.

She began shuffling again, gripping his arm tightly while trying to light another Camel.

Jake let the old woman clutch his arm and forced himself to walk slowly, matching her stride. He felt his face flush as the embarrassment washed over him. How could he lose control like that? He was not the type to let his emotions get the best of him, so why now? He shot a sideward glance at the old woman who shuffled alongside him. Mrs. Jeremy always had this kind of effect on other people, didn't she? She had some inexplicable, innate ability to look into a person's eyes and nudge their deeply hidden insecurities and fears. She was a walking spark, wandering around the city igniting fire kegs of emotions in everyone she met. But Dane loved her beyond reproach, ergo, so did he.

"I'm constructing a three-bedroom log cabin from a prepackaged kit. I'm hiring a couple of journeymen to help me complete the project. If nothing else, we'll be able to sell the property for five or six times what we paid."

She coughed and squeezed his arm tightly. "You haven't told Dane you're going."

"We haven't discussed it yet," he countered.

"Don't fuck with me, Jake Lucas. You only 'discuss' when you know the outcome of the discussion. You may be shrewd, but I'm old. Old people are wise."

"So I've heard. You're right," he said quietly.

"Damned right."

"You are older than I am."

"I don't know what to advise you, dear." Mrs. Jeremy sighed, sounding uncharacteristically sympathetic.

"I want Dane to have the freedom of choice."

"When people say that, they really mean they want their own freedom," she challenged.

Jake stopped and looked at the woman. "He's having the dreams again."

"Did he tell you—"

"I'm capable of making observations all by myself," he snapped more harshly than he intended. When he started walking again, Mrs. Jeremy tugged on his arm and pointed behind him. He spun to see what she pointed at and noticed with some embarrassment that they stood in front of her apartment building. Jake snapped out of his reverie and noticed the telltale signs of her neighborhood: the pungent smell of wok cooking, the lilt of Chinese speech and tinny dings of bicycle bells in the distance. "Dane gets up at night and sits by the window."

"With the action the panhandle gets, I'd videotape it," she laughed.

"Please don't make light of the situation."

Mrs. Jeremy nodded.

"I don't like what it's doing to Dane."

"You don't like what it's doing to you," she countered.

He looked away, hurt. "That is unfair and untrue."

"No, it's not." The hefty woman waddled to a nearby cement stoop that served as a threshold for a small restaurant. "Come here. Sit."

"I need to be going home," he said coldly, looking at his watch.

"In all the time I've known you, Jake Lucas, you've used that line twice. Both times when your mother came to visit. Come. Sit." Jake consented. He lowered himself next to her. The matron wrapped a flabby arm around him. "Is getting out of San Francisco really going to solve things?" He shrugged. "Jake. They may follow."

"What may?"

"The dreams."

"This is not one of your metaphysical bogeymen. This is an explainable event!"

"Then explain it, smartass." Mrs. Jeremy shot back. "You tell me. Why does a young man, devoid of alcohol, drugs or previous mental problems—"

"It was a motorcycle accident! Lots of people have accidents!"

"Yes, but how many of them become clairvoyant afterwards?" She waited for an answer that never came. "We've heard of seeing angels, ghosts and the bright light, but—"

"He's not seeing the future," Jake scoffed.

"Jake, honey. Listen. He was clinically dead for four minutes. They thought he was dead at the scene, for fuck's sake! Dying does a number on you. I learned a long time ago there's no such thing as accidents. Everything happens for a reason. He died and came back for a reason. The question is, why?"

Jake turned to her coldly. "He's having nightmares, strange dreams brought about by a terrible accident that took his life. It has no further meaning. People take the normal and force it to look abnormal. I don't want to talk about this anymore."

"Fine, honey. That's fine." She grabbed his arm and pulled herself to her feet.

"I'll call you more often. I promise. I'll tell Dane you said hello," he said as an afterthought.

Mrs. Jeremy watched Jake walking down the hill and rubbed the goose bumps that had sprouted on her forearms. Damn, it was suddenly so cold! When did the chill hit the air? The old woman wrapped her sweater tightly around her shoulders and started up the cold, barren cement stairs towards a hot cup of tea.

*   *   *

Lily Dayton slipped out of the large bed, silently cursing her wretched, fleshy body. How did she ever allow herself to become so dense? What had she been doing, eating nonstop for months? She thought back onto the last few months of her life, digging into her memory for a hint of an explanation, but found she couldn't remember specifics about the last couple of days, and nothing at all before that. She lay in bed searching for the lost time and felt her whole body shiver and twitch uncontrollably. What had happened to her? Where had she been? A void opened in her mind and she felt herself falling into the dark abyss.

She had not taken a thrill from life in many years, yet lately she seemed to be making up for lost time. Ah, if only she had come back to the City by the Bay years ago! Oh, well, what can she do about it now? It was enough that she had accepted her destiny and abandoned poor, pathetic Victoria Lemark, who didn't dare risk so much as a nickel in a slot machine, much less a lifetime of misery in exchange for the possibility of…what? Redemption? When this corner of the city had buckled from the quake, mousy Victoria could do nothing but watch with breathless fascination from her hovel in Los Angeles's San Fernando Valley as picture after picture of the destruction flickered across her television screen. Ignoring her job at the JC Penney catalog call center, she sat frozen on her faded couch, straining to see familiar faces as the cameras broadcast their sensationalistic journalism, seeped in phony displays of compassion. The narcissistic reporters had ceased to be of any interest to Victoria, eliciting not awe, but disgust as their "spontaneous" banter reeked of forgotten scripts and unbelievably bad acting. On her second day of television obsession, Victoria moved as far as the kitchen, for hunger reared in her belly, forcing her to retreat into the cupboards for soup, where she held the cans between her knees, cranking the ancient can opener as she absorbed more facts about the quake.

Then, a miracle occurred. In that moment, with Campbell's chicken noodle soup splashing over the sides of the tin can, staining her already threadbare carpet, Victoria received her first subconscious glimpse of her future: she knew she must leave Los Angeles and move to San Francisco. Victoria, cowering on the secondhand couch, didn't know why she must go, but she knew she must—a deep, mystical yearning she couldn't ignore had called to her. Without this happenstance of psychic awakening, April may have never been able to burrow out of the depths of time and be born again.

But this momentary insight was only a spark. Victoria didn't have the guts to walk out on her job, her apartment and her obligations. Like a drone programmed only to serve, she stayed in the smoggy Los Angeles hills, trying to deny her psychic awakening, toiling like a serf for twelve more years until April accepted the fact she would have to kill the pathetic Victoria, which, of course, she did.

Now, weak Victoria Lemark was gone, replaced by she, who had spent these past several years in the City by the Bay, learning about her gift and growing more powerful. Then one year ago today, she, too, had her own spiritual awakening. One year. How time flies!

As she stood, the world around her swam and shifted, causing her to grope the wall for balance. What was wrong with her? Glancing to the bed, she looked down onto the slumbering, naked man and smiled. He was so handsome! She remembered him from somewhere…where was it? She racked her memory, desperately trying to pull shreds of history from her mind, but found only the same cold emptiness. She remembered him…yes…a face in a dimly lit room where he sat holding a glass of bourbon. She stifled a naughty giggle. She simply must stop this naughty behavior now that she had begun exacting her revenge—a bit more tact and diplomacy would be crucial, lest she make some grave mistake and reveal her hand too early.

As she stared down at the bronzed body, a dam in her mind suddenly opened and visions of the past flooded into her. Of course! How could she be so forgetful! He had been sitting next to her in that lovely saloon downstairs. Later, after he offered her that ghastly champagne, which she had swallowed with great difficulty, he suggested returning to his room. She knew she ought not to do so and shook her head coyly, but her token resistance shattered under his hypnotic eyes and dazzling white teeth. His masculine bravado tickled her fancy to the point that she simply nodded and followed him into the elevator. She never could refuse any man with dark skin. Back on the plantation, there was this one—

STOP! The voice in her head screamed.

Lily clasped her hands to her ears, trying to drown out the voice. The pressure from its stubborn insistence to be heard built within her, causing her head to throb and her eyes to water. She gasped for air as the tentacle of pain seared down her neck and into her gut, constricting around her lungs. Fear washed over her. She felt as if the pressure would consume her from the inside out. She hobbled to the bathroom, feeling the heavy weight from within pulling at her with every step. Once inside the tiled room, she swung the door closed with her elbow and flicked the light switch. Harsh white light ricocheted off the sterile white walls and she bent over the sink, forcing air into her lungs and struggling to maintain consciousness as waves of nausea flowed over her. After three deep breaths, she felt the pain diminish and a minute later, she stood clearheaded, staring into the mirror at a body she still did not recognize.

She poked the loose flesh gathered around her midsection and with a disgusted sigh, pulled at the tiny pinch of fat circling her hips. These breasts, so small and flat compared to what she remembered, looked malformed and shapeless. Who was this woman staring back at her?

She froze as her memory returned to her.

Flashes of the past flowed into her mind, playing in her head like a moving picture show. The plantation, richly decorated and warmly lit from the fire, ebbed into her consciousness. Then, a vague memory of a large glowing book sitting upon a wooden dais within a huge white structure. The warmth of the structure's white light caressed her body as she looked around and saw herself reflected in the thousands of mirrors that surrounded the Book. Yes! She remembered now. She had awoken within the crystalline structure as if awakening from some long, horridly dark dream, only to gaze once more onto the green grass, the brilliant sunlight and—

—and "Him." The other. The motorcycle rider. She jerked upright as the full memory settled into her consciousness. When she had awoken in the crystalline shrine, it was as if awakening into Eden. Warmth enveloped her, white light bathed the stone building and a peaceful contentment filled her soul. Then she saw that man gaping at her with that insane horrified expression, standing mutely as if paralyzed. She recognized him, too. Oh, yes she did. Just one look at that vapid, stupid expression was all it took for her to remember who he was. He had been there when she first gazed into the Book.

Now she was forcing herself to awaken fully. She willed herself out of the crystal shrine and into her slumbering body. She was becoming conscious again. Yes. She awoke and began to hatch a plan for vengeance. She looked once again at the body in the mirror and vowed that when the revenge ended, she would get herself new breasts. Nowadays, many women did that without shame. When she was Victoria, she'd read about it in the newspaper. She smiled. It would be fun to have her original body back.

She searched the floor of the bathroom for her clothes and put them on. *Why was it that so many men enjoy the shower before making love?* Her shoes were not under the pile of clothing, so she turned her attention to the small clutch lying on the counter and began to re-apply her makeup. Here it is, almost four o'clock in the afternoon and she still had plenty of work to do before the day expired.

She emerged from the bathroom with the stealth of a cat. The man stirred on the bed. What was his name? The only response from him was another deep grunt and congested snort as he rolled onto his stomach. As he shuddered, he spread his legs slightly, allowing her to see a glimpse of his thick manhood pressed between his body and the mattress. She adjusted the green dress and gazed upon his trim physique—the strong back muscles, the smooth olive skin, the perfect mounds of flesh.

How do men cope with those things between their legs? Aren't they bothersome? How do they sit down? Should I not kill him? The throbbing ache pressed against her temples again and her vision blurred from the pain.

NO! The same small voice cried from within. *Kill only the guilty. He is unable to connect this body to the woman who killed Thompson.*

Lily rubbed her forehead, wishing this insipid little voice would shut up. Oh, how that prissy Victoria bothered her! On the bedside table near the too-good-for-a-hotel brass lamp, sat his briefcase, made of expensive worked leather. Beside it lay an ornate letter opener. It wasn't expensive by any means, and she had seen hundreds of more exotic styles. Once, her Daddy brought her a pearl-handled letter opener with onyx studs along the base. What had happened to it? It couldn't be more than a few weeks old. After all, Daddy only recently returned from the war, stiffly dragging his useless leg through the summer dust as she clung to the bag slung over his shoulder. Lily remembered that day quite well, as did all the other Negroes on the plantation.

DAMN YOU IF YOU KILL HIM! The voice bellowed. Its force sent a searing dagger of pain into her brain and Lily reeled from the attack. In adolescent defiance against the arrogant voice, she snatched up the letter opener and twirled it in her fingers, examining it in the sliver of light sneaking into the room through the crack in the thick pleated curtains. The letter opener felt as sturdy and deadly in her fingers as a pistol. She glanced back to the naked man. Yankee Pig! Damned, infernal Yankee Pig! It was his kind who barreled through the countryside, burned the crops, slaughtered hundreds of innocent people and maimed Daddy.

He snorted and tossed onto his side. Startled by the sudden movement, Lily jumped slightly, driving the point of the letter opener into her left palm. With a wince, she drew her hand away, secretly enjoying the intense pain. Fascinated, she rotated her hand and watched the blood ooze its way down her palm and drip onto the carpet.

LEAVE HIM BE. HE IS INNOCENT, Victoria's even voice cried. LEAVE.

No! Lily cried back. I'll ram this into his heart and be done with the Yankee. I'll watch the monster die to repay the horrendous way he's treated the Dayton family!

The voice of Victoria did not respond. Well, that's as it should be! Lily Dayton's family stood out amongst the entire state of South Carolina as a proud, Southern family. All four of the Daytons prided themselves on their hard-won reputations, which were earned by years of conducting themselves in a Southern, genteel way; each was gifted with a generous soul. Why, to this very day, a huge oil painting hung above the fireplace as bold and vibrant as any statue: Father, a large man of independent means, strong jawline and full head of hair, ruled the plantation with the strength and grace of a colonel. Mother, who was equally as fierce, had long, straight hair that framed her delicate face, and stood at his side with a hand upon his shoulder. Seated upon the floor on either side of Father sat she and her younger sister, Jennifer.

Lily faltered as the vision of the picture rushed back to her—Jenny...Jenny? Her sister's name was not Jenny, it was Bethany. Who was Jenny?

YOU ARE NOT LILY DAYTON!

Lily felt the blood drain from her, turning her flesh to ice. No! No! She was Lily Dayton. Lily Dayton of the South Carolina Daytons! I'll kill this Yankee scum and be done with him! She yearned to plunge the flimsy weapon into his heart; she ached to see the blood flow from him, staining the sheets of the bed.

YOU ARE VICTORIA LEMARK. I AM VICTORIA LEMARK. I AM GETTING ALL CONFUSED BY THE VISIONS I SAW IN THE BOOK.

Victoria? Victoria Lemark? Yes...that name sounded familiar. Faded pictures flashed through her mind—a red car, a motorcycle, a man dressed in leather. They came at her quickly, flooding her mind with unwanted, yet familiar sights that filled her with both disgust and comfort. She reeled as if she might faint.

She retreated from the bed and let the letter opener fall to the floor. She bent down, scooped up her purse and sped to the door, turning to look at the naked man one last time. He slept soundly in the fading sunlight, legs spread wide and a slight smile on his lips. As Lily exited, closing the door quietly behind her, he snorted loudly.

FRIDAY, JULY 7

6 PM

"I'M TELLING YOU, DANE, you never know about these things," Jenny continued, hunched over the cutting board, hacking the hell out of the celery. "I mean, you were REALLY banged up in that accident. Did you talk to Mrs. Jeremy?"

"And say what? 'Hey! Long time, no see! By the way, I dream of a woman who murders people'?"

Jenny halted her attack on the celery and stared at him blankly. Then, she responded as if addressing a child. "Yes. She'll TOTALLY believe you. You know what a freak she is about that psychic mojo stuff."

Dane shot the short brunette a condescending glance. "Not comforting."

"You know what I mean," Jenny sighed, slipping another piece of celery into her mouth. "Look what happened when you told her about those, you know, freaky "feelings" you were getting. She called you telepathic and wet her pants with glee," Jenny said, crunching loudly.

"Not telepathic. Clairvoyant. You're not helping," Dane muttered.

"You know, you DO sound like that TV show, the one with the psychic woman who…OH! YOU KNOW!"

"Jenny, hand me the carrots, will you?" He took the bowl from her and continued as he shoved baby carrots into his mouth. "It seems so silly by the light of day."

"Hey! I'm hungry!" Jake bellowed from deep within the condo.

Dane sighed. "He wants the Friday night let's-get-together-thing, yet we do all the cooking. What's wrong with this picture?"

"We can cook. THEY can't," she said, winking.

He shoved a carrot into the freshly made dip and held it to Jenny. "Taste this. I think it needs more."

"More what?" she asked, eyeing the carrot suspiciously.

"More. Just more. Shut up and taste it." He shoved the carrot at her and she pushed him away.

"I can't. I'm too hungry. I forgot how to swallow." Melodramatically, she draped her hand across her forehead and folded onto the kitchen floor.

"Patience is a virtue, my sweet," Dane reminded the lump on the floor.

"So is virginity, but I'm not doing that again, either. Hello there, Ace," she said as the dog nudged her.

Dane held out the carrot, and Jenny kneeled and gently ran her tongue along the stubby vegetable, licking up the white dip. She parted her lips and sunk her mouth over the carrot until her lips met with Dane's fingers. Slowly, she closed her mouth around it and pulled her head back, sucking up the cream.

Dane sighed. "A little stubby. Too much work, too little reward."

"Hungry out here. Starving." Jake bellowed again.

"Go," Jenny said, nodding towards the other room and gesturing to the bowl of dip. "Wait. Let me double check that." She snatched a celery stalk from the plate on the counter, dunked it into the dip and munched. "No. The official answer is no, it doesn't taste funny. Take it to that man before he blows a fuse."

"Better just a fuse," Dane smirked. "Help. Balance." Jenny rushed to him and centered the platter of vegetables atop the crook of his elbow. Then she gently placed the bowl of dip in his right hand. "Thanks honey." He maneuvered his way past the slender woman as the phone rang.

"GOT IT!" Jenny dashed with insane velocity to snatch the phone from its cradle, and then Dane found himself face to face with Jake.

"Ah! Good," Jake smiled wryly. "Plates?"

"They're coming! Christ! Can't you get them?" Dane snapped at him.

Jake looked as if he was trying to refuse to yield to anger. "Yes, but you told me to entertain."

"Are you entertaining?" Dane grilled.

"I deduce so," Jake responded quietly, backing away from him.

"Then keep tap dancing or...whatever you're doing," Dane murmured, trying and failing to make it sound like a joke. Why is he snapping like this so much lately?

"I shall. I consider myself lucky I'm not being torn limb from limb in a mad rush for food." Jake snatched the appetizers away from Dane and abruptly strode back to the living room.

"WHAT DO YOU MEAN you GAVE that BITCH a call back?" Jenny screamed into the receiver. "I have THAT ROLE! It's MINE! I…what? Oh. That. Well…" she shot an awkward glance at Dane as he passed, so he planted a quick kiss on her forehead and began searching the cupboards for the paper plates. "Yes, but…no, but…yes…NO!" Jenny's voice hit a feverish pitch. Jenny's conversations made Dane proud he knew her. Regardless of what the woman said, it always seemed to Dane that her conversations carried the urgency of a MASH unit.

Jenny pulled a gum wrapper from her hip pocket and motioned for a pen. He scooped one from the pencil holder and palmed it to her. She wrote frantically on the wrapper. "Okay…okay…if you can. GET ME THAT CALL BACK. Yes, Amy. I don't care. Call me at THIS number when…OKAY!" She slammed the phone down and issued a low, long growl that culminated in a hysterical scream.

"It was good for me. How about you?" Dane inquired as he peeked into the oven. Jenny paced the middle of the kitchen with her arms folded across her chest.

"You will NOT believe what they did! They're giving my role to that BITCH Kate! God, I HATE her! She's a FAT, stupid SLOB!"

Dane closed the oven and leaned back to gaze at his short, petite friend. "How in the world can you be up for the same role as one who's plump and un-jazzercized?"

"The director wants a 'real person.' What kind of bullshit is that? Like SOME of us are REAL people, and the rest are—what?—made of papier maché? Shit!" She grabbed a stray carrot and shoved it into her mouth. "What he's REALLY saying is that he can't make up his FUCKING mind if he wants Olive Oyl or Rotundo, the Amazing Whale. I HATE this business. I should have stayed in RETAIL. Then, I'd only be dealing with pregnant yuppies and idiots." She collapsed onto the counter as Dane placed the baked potatoes on a serving platter.

"Damn! I forgot! Run those out there, will you?" Dane pointed to the stack of paper plates on top of the refrigerator. Jenny grunted, grabbed the plates and slithered into the other room with a sigh.

Dane watched her schlep down the hallway and smiled. In the two years since they'd met in the gallery he managed before the accident, they had grown inseparable. On the long nights of insomnia, he often wished she were less of a morning person and more of a night owl so he could call her at two in the morning. He did that one time and she berated him through the phone lines at a blistering temperature. He never called her after eleven again.

The summer they met, Dane had worked harder on the Georgia O'Keeffe look-alike exhibit than any other exhibit in memory. It was after the third frantic, restless night that he finally felt his fatigue tug at him. He stood staring at a three-painting piece, debating whether he should lower the canvas on the left, when a slender brunette with large brown eyes wandered into the room. Jenny, absorbed in a two-toned desert scene, had been walking backwards. Dane couldn't remember why he didn't move out of her way—perhaps it was the fatigue, the surprise of a woman walking backwards or merely fate—but within seconds, Jenny had plowed right into him, spraying Diet Pepsi flying on the walls and Dane's duct tape rolling across the floor as the girl bounced off him and into a tall vase of roses. He made the instantaneous decision to let the girl fall, opting instead to save the wobbling vase. So, he got his flowers, she got a wet ass of Diet Pepsi and they both got a shot of adrenalin. Rather than bitch and scream like most of the gallery's high-visibility clientele, Jenny erupted into gales of laughter, flashing a smile full of straight white teeth. She asked him to lunch, her treat, to make up for her clumsiness. The tab for lunch ran $24.97, and the friendship was worth a hundred times that.

A siren tore through his reverie. Glancing nervously out the tiny kitchen window, he saw the ambulance drive past, bypassing gawking tourists and bored locals. A year later and sirens still gave him the creeps; the sound heralds either pain or death. Maybe Jenny is right—he should talk to Mrs. Jeremy. God knows she won't think he's insane. She's the one who's really into this crazy-ass dream stuff. She'll probably say the nightmares are a Freudian image of sexual frustration brought about by his lack of masturbation. Either that or they're some psychic harbinger of the end of the world. Whichever answer she gave, he knew he'd feel better for having heard it from her.

"What the hell is this?" he heard Kevin ask Jenny. "I know Mr. Jake Lucas has got to have himself some china plates. I am not eating off cheap ass paper plates."

Jenny snapped her fingers three times. "You'll be eating off of my cheap ass BUTT if you DON'T."

Dane smiled. One of the few things in life he could count on was that Jenny would always run defense for him.

*   *   *

Lily Dayton stood frozen in fascination as the ambulance rushed past. She loved watching the speeding vehicles spewing their funny red light. They looked rather festive, didn't they? As a young girl in the field, she had witnessed one of the Negroes cut himself quite severely when he became reckless with the sickle. She had became so obsessed by the pretty green of the leaves changing color under the thick red blood that she didn't even hear his screams of pain. The flies had descended upon the wound in a thick cloud. No ambulances then.

She looked down the street at the flow of strolling people. The night's cool breeze whipped in from the bay, encircling her with its chilly torment. Lily knew this wind well. It carried the icy, sharp sting of Him. She backed further into the doorway, hid in the shadows and frantically searched the street for Him, trying to pinpoint his whereabouts by intuition alone. Was He watching her from a dark corner? Perhaps He had passed her without her even seeing Him? She knew she felt Him, somewhere, but where? After a moment of fruitless searching, she stepped out from the doorway with guarded apprehension. During the few weeks since her and April's return, she'd worked diligently with April to pinpoint the area of town where they felt Him the most frequently and strongly. Lily vowed to be on the offensive tonight; the sighting of His…"special friend"…had intensified the need to act quickly.

She never knew when knowledge of Him would come in handy. Who knows? She may need to kill Him prematurely. Although that would be unexpected, it would also be a welcome relief, for then she wouldn't be a slave to the constant torture of feeling His presence.

"Excuse me, do you think you can take a step backward, young lady, or do you own the entire fucking sidewalk?" Lily turned to the rough, gravelly voice that spewed cigarette smoke. The old fool! How dare she talk like that to a Dayton like that?

LEMARK.

Nonetheless, Lily stepped back from the curb and into the doorway of a three-story Victorian. She let the fat old woman pass, shuffling as she struggled up the curb and onto the sidewalk. God! What had happened to the world during her absence? In her time, only the strong survived.

"HELLO! ARE YOU DEAF?" the woman screamed at her. It took Lily several seconds to realize that the fat old woman was still speaking to her.

"No," Lily spat.

The old woman shuffled past her, muttering under her breath. As she came abreast to Lily, she looked up and shot her a double take. She squinted her eyes and leaned closer, making Lily back away with apprehension. "I know you, don't I?" The woman asked softly.

"No, I'm sure you don't." Lily said disdainfully and turned her head away. But Lily couldn't deny the feeling of recognition. Was this fat creature connected to her? She closed her eyes and tried to concentrate, but the woman continued to stare. Better to ignore the type of riffraff who reeked of stale cigarettes than to encourage them with attention—besides, the familiar sensation she felt was probably only His close proximity. Sure enough, after a moment of showing her complete indifference, the old creature continued hobbling down the street. Lily breathed a sigh of relief. She had no intention of putting up with that...thing.

She turned towards Golden Gate Park and the section of town she knew He frequented and began to walk in quick, long strides.

* * *

Mrs. Jeremy clutched her cane as she shuffled along the uneven sidewalk. She knew how badly her legs had deteriorated—she didn't need any overeducated prick of a doctor to tell her that. She was officially a tottering old lady, no doubt about it; her ancient, creaky muscles told her that. But the ache in her left ankle also sent her another message: something nasty hovered nearby. Oh, yes, her body may be on a fast slide down to hell, but she wasn't so far gone she couldn't read simple signs. When her left ankle snapped coming down the stairs ten years ago, she had come to accept its limitations because she knew it was the price she had to pay for the ability to sense danger.

God never closed a door without opening a window.

Mrs. Jeremy lit another Camel and scanned the streets, trying to read the body language of the few people gathered on the corner. She saw nothing abnormal: a couple of punked-out drunks, a young couple necking in the doorway to an apartment building, an elitist, red-headed snobby bitch who stood with her nose in the air, thinking she owned the damn sidewalk. As a chill passed through her and she pulled her sweater tightly around her body, she thought about the snobby red-haired bitch with the stern mouth and glassy eyes. Was the girl stoned? She sure had that faraway look that addicts get. Mrs. Jeremy wasn't sure about the bitch's exact nature, but every fiber of her being told her there was something fishy about that dame. But for the life of her, she couldn't figure it out. Damn! Maybe she's losing her touch. In the old days, she would have been able to read the woman's aura better. Maybe all her ankle was telling her is she should have worn a heavier sweater.

*   *   *

Jenny watched Dane prepare the potatoes. Leaning against the counter, she admired, then envied, his skill with a knife. She herself remained clueless as to the workings of her own stove, a cluelessness she often defending by citing early childhood trauma. With disdain and anger, she thought back to her upbringing, her white trash family and her mother's shitty maternal talents. Her mother, a tall, lean woman with several missing teeth who chain-smoked Camels, had harassed Jenny constantly about her failure as a child, and then later, her failure as a woman. So, Jenny never caught onto what she referred to as the requirements of femininity: cooking, sewing, cleaning and catering to men.

Jenny had learned at an early age not to argue with her mother. Her mother called her in from the backyard one hot summer day. "Your grandpa's bringing some friends of his here after their huntin' trip," the woman croaked. Jenny had waited while her mother lipped a Camel and struck a wooden match against the side of the door. When she touched the flame to the tip of the cigarette, Jenny shifted from foot to foot, anxious to get back to playing in the yard. She had spent the entire morning carving little roads for her Matchbox cars into the mound of dirt behind her house and was ready to place the cars in their rightful positions.

"Now, I want you to get into the house and peel some of those potatoes." Her mother finished with a great exhale of blue smoke.

"Why?" Jenny asked innocently enough. She didn't like the idea of her smelly grandfather and his dirty, smelly friends sitting around the kitchen smelling up the room.

"Cuz," her mother continued irritably, picking tobacco out of her teeth, "we got to fix those men some food. Not that you're much use — you can't cook worth a shit. The least you can do is peel them spuds."

"I'm not a good cook," Jenny said with a smile, "You're better than me."

"Move!" her mother bellowed, plucking the cigarette from her mouth.

"Let the men fix their own food. I'm not their slave," Jenny replied brazenly.

What followed was the worst beating she'd ever gotten. Not only did she wind up peeling the potatoes, but she ate them standing up — sitting down was much too painful. For the next ten years, her mother used this incident as reason to spew inane nonsense about how Jenny should behave, think, and act to be a better woman and, thus, be able to keep a man. But inside, Jenny wasn't listening. Jenny was dreaming of her future as the head of her own production company. She would be an actress, work for a production company named after herself and make all her own decisions without a mother to berate her or a man to legitimize her. Working the average job from nine to five had never felt humane to her — it resembled indentured servitude.

Thus, her legacy would forever be the ability to burn water. All you need is a microwave and a microwavable plate to cook. But watching Dane handle the kitchen knife stirred the jealous streak she normally kept under control. The curve of his brow and set of his thin lips made him seem far more intense than his abilities suggested.

"What?" she asked, sensing his mental distress.

He sliced another potato. "Thinking."

"About?"

"Do you think I'm crazy?" he asked flatly, with a pained expression.

"No. Well, no more than the rest of us," she said honestly. "Now if you were to ask me if I thought you were obsessive, overdramatic and anal-retentive, I'd say yes."

"My life…I don't know, it's like a giant puzzle where the pieces are just missing."

She took another sip of wine. "A picture puzzle or one of those small ones of cute kittens?"

He ignored her question and whined. "Somewhere along the line, my life was stolen and sold to an unsuspecting six-year-old with a future, leaving me in total, utter despair. I want my life back. The life where I'm happy, Jake's happy and everyone's happy except for the shitty people we hate who don't deserve happiness in the first place. I want my Kodak commercial."

"I'll drink to that," Jenny said, helping herself to another stray carrot.

"I always knew the honeymoon would end, but not so…explosively," he sighed.

"Is that a word?" Jenny asked, munching.

"I guess—HEY!" Dane turned to her just in time to see a carrot fly at him, but not in time to duck. It bounced off his nose and fell to the floor where Ace descended upon it with abandon.

"I hate the part where the green leaves attach." She reached across the countertop and grabbed his wrist. "Come here," she said lovingly. He leaned forward to extend his cheek for a kiss.

With a firm hand and sharp stroke, Jenny pulled back and smacked Dan across the face. "Get over yourself. You should have died in that accident. Scratch that—you should have STAYED DEAD in that accident. When you didn't, we all thought you'd wind up one of those guys who sits in front of the 7-11 in a wheelchair begging for money."

"Sorry to disappoint you," Dane whined.

"Don't get pissy. If my agent calls me back, I've gotta run because if that cunt Jane gets there before me, I'm gonna kill myself. Listen," she continued as Dane returned to stirring the vegetables. "Something DID happen in that hospital. The coma. It wasn't a coma, but it was. It was like…SOMETHING ELSE, you know?"

"No."

"That was rhetorical!" she said, slapping him again, lightly this time. "Your life signs faded, like you were waves on a shore…the lights on the machines got DIMMER, like the hospital was running low on electricity and just needed a boost. It was weird—very, very weird. Now, it's not illegal to see a SHRINK you know, it's like, very TRENDY, and I think you need to do it.

"Stop ragging that you can't sleep and when you do, blah blah blah, Get off your butt and DO SOMETHING. Anything. And," she said, taking his arm, "about Jake. The only thing I know about relationships is this—sometimes it's in anger that the truth comes out."

The phone rang, causing Dane to jump slightly in surprise. "I'll get it!" Jake yelled from the other room. "Hello—hold on—JENNY! FOR YOU!"

"TELL HER I'M ON MY WAY!" she yelled to Jake. "I'm your friend, Dane. I love you. Help yourself. Please. I've gotta go beat that bitch because she's gonna boff the director and take this role, I can tell."

"Nobody's going to screw anyone," Dane replied.

"Be serious. This is show business."

He grabbed her and pulled her close. "Break a leg. You deserve it."

She brushed her lips softly against his and departed, grabbing her $300 only-at-Neiman-Marcus leather coat from the chair. As she moved to the front door, Jeannette intercepted her. She held up her hand in self-defense. "I really want this role, Jay. You know that!"

"We just got here!" Jeannette whined, running her calloused hand through her buzz cut. "I can't believe Amy set up an audition on a Friday night."

Jenny pressed her fingers against her lover's lips. "It was my idea. The producers are flying back to L.A. tomorrow, and I want one more shot at this. I'll meet you back here—I won't be long."

Jeannette considered Jenny's plea with a grim face. In a final act of defiance, she crossed her muscular arms and said sternly, "Call if you're going to be too late."

Jenny nodded and hugged Jeannette, who refused to embrace her, but allowed Jenny to wrap her arms around her neck. "Careful! My nipple rings!" Jeannette whined, backing away from Jenny and rubbing her breasts. Jenny blew her a kiss, threw open the condo door and exited with a flourish, leaving Jeannette holding her palms against her own hefty chest.

From his vantage point in the kitchen, Dane watched Jenny fly through the doorway and disappear into the hall before snatching the overpriced silver serving platter he bought Jake last Christmas and setting it on the counter. Setting the potatoes on the platter, he turned to the window and stared down onto Stanyon Street until the red VW Bug pulled away from the curb and turned the corner. With the hollow feeling of defeat ebbing through his body, Dane realized he felt abandoned being left to face Jeannette alone without the protective shield of Jenny. He sighed, grabbed the bowl of chips and headed into the living room as he heard Kevin's voice boom through the condo.

"So this bitch breezes through the lobby like she owns the joint, right? Not enough she beats an elevator, but now she's acting like Miss Thing in MY hallway. But as she approaches the lounge, she slows down and begins to wobble...such a pedestrian word! But it's the truth—the girl WOBBLED. Just like one of those toy wibbles."

"Weebles," Sean interrupted. Kevin looked at the blond and rolled his eyes.

"Excuse me. WEEBLES. Thank you, Toymaker Tina," Kevin shot back. Sean smiled at his victory and scooped up some chips from the bowl. "She wobbled like a WEEBLE and grabs the wall. Then, she does this," Kevin demonstrated, his lithe, ebony body tenderly twisting upwards, like a bird ascending. "I swear, she looked like she was having a bad acid trip."

Kevin nudged the boy. "Baby, hand me some Lay's."

"I think they're Pringles," Sean said, eying the chips.

"I'll eat those. There's very little I won't eat," he said, patting Sean on the head.

"The worst. The absolute worst! That dress. Girl, I could have hung from a coat hanger with more grace," Kevin wailed, popping the Pringles into his mouth.

Dane slid onto the wingback chair with Jake, squeezing him into the corner of the cushion. Jake adjusted so Dane could sit, although their legs remained intertwined. "So I suppose you redesigned it for her?" Dane offered.

"Hell, no! Everyone knows green isn't my color," Kevin mused.

"Green?" Jake asked suddenly, sitting forward in his chair.

"Beautiful color. Takes a certain panache to wear green, don't you think?" Kevin said.

"I liked her eyes," Sean said, leaning against Kevin's leg. "Pretty eyes."

Dane felt Jake stiffen.

"You saw her eyes?" Jake whispered hoarsely. Sean nodded and munched a few more Pringles.

"What?" Dane laughed and elbowed Jake.

"What, what?" Jake mumbled, avoiding his gaze.

"You okay?" Dane asked under his breath.

"Yes," Jake said.

"What's with the cross-examination?" Dane started.

"I'm fine, Dane. Drop it," Jake snapped. Dane pulled away from Jake and turned to Kevin, who pretended not to notice Jake's abruptness. Sean, as always, smiled vacantly and nodded at the room to nobody in particular. Dane glared at the boy. What did Kevin see in this bozo, anyway?

"I need some more ice," Jeannette's voice boomed. Dane had forgotten the abrasive clod was still in the condo, but now that she spoke, he had no choice but to address her.

"I'll get it!" Sean burst forth, leaping to his feet. He pointed to the kitchen. "In the freezer, right?"

"Wow. Good guess," Dane began.

"Dane, dear—" Kevin interrupted.

"Don't, Sean," Jeannette said, turning to Dane with a sinister glare. "It's not your house. Let our host get it."

Dane held the stare as long as he could, but as usual, Jeannette bested him and he blinked first. Taking the move as further proof the woman was some kind of self-lubricating demon, he snatched the ice bucket from the coffee table and stomped into the kitchen.

"I was supposed to do that!" Sean moaned from the other room.

"Oh! Sugar! Don't pout! Come here and rub my feet. It's just as important as the dyke's nasty ice," Kevin said, sliding off his loafers.

"Play nice," Dane yelled on his way into the kitchen.

"What are we playing?" Sean asked, taking Kevin's foot in his hand.

"Later, baby," Kevin replied as he lay back in the leather sofa.

Dane slammed the ice bucket onto the counter. He was unaccustomed to dealing with emotion in its raw form and he disliked indescribable feelings, but he just couldn't put his finger on the reason Sean annoyed him so much. Maybe it was genetic—he'd always wanted to be blond. At least Sean was better than the last man Kevin latched onto. Dane had managed to adjust to Kevin's fondness for befriending the lonely and downtrodden, but all of his boy projects looked the same: blond, thin, fair skinned and vapid. The turnstile of young men wasn't all bad, as Kevin always left the men in a better spiritual place after the affair ended. Even so, something about Sean bugged him—a mysterious, uncomfortable oddness.

The night Kevin had hired Sean as a part-time desk clerk, he'd barreled into the condo bubbling with excitement. As Kevin launched into his patented monologue, Dane glanced out the window to hide his yawn. When Kevin segued into describing the boy's interview at the hotel, a vision formed in Dane's mind. Like an aged photo, frayed at the edges, Sean's figure stood prominent, yet blurred; obvious yet unidentifiable. As abruptly as it appeared, the vision faded and left Dane with a cold chill that puckered his skin. Later, Dane and Jake had sat naked in front of the fireplace laughing at Kevin's never ending optimism for finding lost love.

Two days later, he'd met Sean. He instantly hated the blond airhead. There was nothing specific about Sean, but the young man made Dane's arm bristle in a way he didn't enjoy.

Now the kid had done something to Jake. Yes, Jake tried to hide it, but Dane knew very well Sean's comment about the woman in the hotel had hit a nerve with his partner. Why? Dane emptied the ice into the bucket. Green. Sean's comment about a green dress was what struck Jake. Didn't he dream about a green dress last night, before stumbling into the leather chair and scaring Ace to death? Shit, what was it? Dane flipped through the still frames in his head, but came up with nothing tangible. He hated these ambiguous tentacles of memories that seemed to monopolize his mind lately. It was akin to the feeling he got when he stood in the Alpha Beta, thumb in his pocket, trying to visualize the grocery list he'd left at home. If he concentrated hard enough, he could almost see the counter, the pen—

"My ice! My ice! My kingdom for ice!" Kevin's voice screamed, pulling Dane back into reality. The ice bucket dripped condensation into a tiny pool of water that had accumulated on top of the countertop. How long had he been standing there holding it? What the hell?

"The iceman cometh!" Dane announced as he mopped up the small puddle and scooped the ice bucket into his hands. He glided into the living room, forcing a smile onto his face in hopes of concealing his consternation. Jake sat frozen on the chair where Dane had left him. Dane palmed an ice cube from the bucket and reached into Jake's shirt, but even a daydreaming Jake was more swift. He grabbed him by the wrist and glared at Dane venomously.

"Are we eating or not?" Jeannette bellowed.

"That's what I'm trying to do, woman!" Kevin snapped back.

Jeannette stomped towards Kevin and Sean, and stood towering over them, her face wrinkled in disgust.

"You've nose hairs, girl," Kevin chirped happily.

"Eat shit," Jeannette snapped.

"Dane! Do you need any help prepping our feast before that dyke thing rips us limb from limb?" Kevin asked, his eyes never veering from Jeannette's.

"Better feed 'em," Dane sighed, nudging the unmoving Jake.

Jake nodded back and let Dane's hand fall. "I'll start with Jeannette before she kills Kevin."

"Dig in, guys!" Kevin took a place at the table. Then, looking to Jeannette, "and girls. Women. I mean women! Jesus, Mary and the donkey, I am never going to be politically correct, am I?" Sean tittered with childlike glee and fed Kevin a spoonful of diced carrots, while Jeannette rolled her eyes and heaved herself into a chair. Jake shuffled to the table without a even backward glance to Dane.

It was going to be a long night.

FRIDAY, JULY 7

7:45 PM

JENNY FELT CERTAIN someone was following her. Ever since leaving Dane and Jake's, she had been consumed by a relentless itch under her tongue, deep within the tender tissue of her soft palate. She had never been a believer in New Age bullshit, but she had come to believe in the power of her tongue; that whenever that area of her mouth itched, something bad was lurking about. It was a strange form of intuition, but one on which she had become strangely dependent. Running from audition to class to rehearsals often lasted into the late hours of the night and took her to seedier parts of the city. She couldn't remember how she'd become aware of her oral early warning system, only that she was now aware of it. Like a relationship that begins innocuously and develops into an emotional foundation, her itchy tongue had become a part of her and had often coerced her into taking a different route home or ducking into a store for a drink when she wasn't thirsty. She had taken it on faith that this mysterious power had saved her life in ways she would never know. But isn't that what faith was about—trusting something to be true without proof? And tonight, even though she traveled streets glowing brightly with incandescent lamps, Jenny couldn't deny that her tongue itched like crazy, and it made her jumpy.

She shook off the shadow of doom and tried to concentrate on finding the address of the building for the audition. She slowed her ancient VW Bug to a crawl and inched over to the right a bit more, allowing other drivers to pass—she hated it when she was forced to follow a slowpoke and felt no reason to inflict the suffering onto others—and found the address her agent had given her. She rode the brake as she searched for a parking spot on the busy street. Just ahead of her, she noticed a Lincoln with out of state plates pulling into traffic, so she turned on her directional and waited for it to clear the stall. Behind Jenny's VW Bug, a yellow cab honked and pulled to the curb.

Within minutes, Jenny parked and threw open the driver's door. Damn! Why couldn't she have gotten here just minutes earlier? As she stepped onto the curb, she remembered the new headshots from last week's photo shoot were still on the passenger's seat. Grumbling, she unlocked the car, grabbed the photos, slammed the door shut and collided with a woman in a beautiful green dress.

"I'm so sorry!"

"No bother. I'm fine."

'Excellent!" Jenny shouted over her shoulder at the woman. Why did she have the feeling she had seen that face before?

The double glass doors of the dingy office building loomed before her like a gaping mouth of a terrible beast. She knew that somewhere inside this building was a group of pale, self-absorbed men who knew nothing about the art of acting but would have the power to determine if she got this gig, thus enabling her to boast a hefty profit, or if she would crawl back to her agent begging for another used car dealership commercial.

She sighed. What was the worst that could happen? She had survived worse humiliations than crawling back to her agency — like the time she played the invalid in the nursing home training film and had her diaper changed thirty-seven times during a nine-hour shoot. She had never thought about wearing adult diapers in her life and after that shoot, she not only gained a new respect for the incontinent, but vowed to send gift certificates to all the attendants at the home where her grandmother lived.

Damn this itching in her tongue!

She shook out the butterflies. Damn, she needed this job! The last gig she did was the furniture store commercial and that was almost three months ago. If the ad had been a national, the residuals could float her for a bit, but it being a small, local outfit, any further income was off the radar. She sighed and stared up at the building. It sat squat and dirty between two newer, taller post-earthquake office structures. Why would they hold the audition here? It looked half empty, judging by the many darkened offices behind the streaked windows and cracked glass. Perhaps the building was one of the shoot locations, or the producers had bought it as investment property, or any one of a hundred reasons.

She bit her tongue and tried to scratch the itch with her teeth. Don't worry! Just go in there and don't suck! She plastered her audition smile onto her face, gathered her leather coat around her shoulders and stepped forward, colliding with a short woman carrying a purple bag.

"Oh! I'm sorry," Jenny began.

The short woman snorted and clutched the Gucci bag tighter, puffing her cherry red cheeks comically. "They're here you know. They're here! They came back!"

"Oh," Jenny smiled weakly, "how nice. Well, have a good night."

"Sometimes when they come back, they're angry!" The squat woman hissed through brown, rotting teeth. She ran one of her dirty, calloused hands through her thin oily hair and cackled a high-pitched laugh. Jenny tried to sidestep the short woman, but before she could pivot a few feet, the woman heaved her overloaded shopping bag over her shoulder and shoved past Jenny, hurrying down Market Street in an erratic zigzag.

"Okay, Jenny," she said to herself. "Take two. This time, don't trip over the set dec." She lifted her chin, gathered her leather coat around her, looked both ways and stepped forward. She opened the glass doors and sauntered through, doing her best Liz Taylor imitation. She practiced her charming introduction and coy head tilt, making sure she threw her hair back in a way that was both professional and sexy.

Behind her, the woman in green followed her.

*   *   *

"Here, want a toke?" Kevin wheezed, holding out the roach clip.

Jake waived his turn, as did Dane, so Kevin handed the joint off to Jeannette, who held it aloft as she ran her hand over her silver crew cut. The whiff of weed brought back memories for Dane, most of them embarrassing snippets that supported his decision to say *au revoir* to drugs forever. He felt proud of Jake's anti-drug stance and secretly envied the guy for having such strong boundaries. Dane knew firsthand how adamantly Jake derided pot, coke, even poppers, ever since their first month of dating when Jake had discovered ecstasy in Dane's bedside table. The pills had almost ended their relationship on the spot.

He glanced up and noticed Jake watching Kevin with a soft glow of contentment Dane hadn't seen in quite a while. Good. *Laissez les bons temps rouler.* Across from him, Kevin and Sean leaned against each other, more out of laziness than romance. Off to the side, somewhat removed from the circle of furniture, Jeannette sat cross-legged with her eyes closed, swaying to Vivaldi's *Four Seasons*. Dane smiled and leaned against his partner, soaking up the peacefulness of the moment. When he and Jake had moved in together, he felt sure his personal sacrifices—what he smoked (pot, never cigarettes), who he screwed (not as many as he had hoped) and the foods he ate (too fatty and rich)—were all things he could eliminate from his life. He felt sure that finally, after years of living only for himself, he was ready to make the compromises that a relationship required. He felt confident that he could forsake the cruising, toking, and partying without a second glance. Now, sitting on the soft rug, watching his chosen family relaxing after a good meal confirmed that he had made the right decision. It was true then, what Jenny had told him: When the obsolete parts of our lives get tucked into the past, we have killed off a portion of what we were, but not who we are.

"You don't believe me, do you?" Jeannette accused Sean, her voice dripping acid.

"Well, I dunno. I guess," slurred the blond with a shrug.

"You guess that you don't believe me?" Jeannette asked, confused.

"Well, no. I mean, yes," his voice trailed off. Sean's voice had began to quiver with the first joint. Now, it was so quiet and weak it was almost gone. Almost, but no cigar, Dane mused.

Jake sat lethargically, with one hand resting on Ace and the other on Dane's head. He glanced at the firelight playing on Dane's face and felt a tremendous urge to fondle the man's hair. He refrained.

Uncharacteristically, Jeannette held the reins of tonight's conversation. "I'm serious," she said sternly. "We were on our way to see Holly when—"

"Who?" Sean asked

"Holly. Holly Near?"

Sean remained stone-faced.

"The Womyn's Music Festival?" Sean coughed and shrugged. Jeannette rolled her eyes in contempt. "Never mind. Not the point. We were standing in Stormy's apartment and she says to me, 'Oh! You're Jay!' As if she knew. I said, 'Yeah.' Just like that. 'Yeah.' That's all."

"You always were a wit, dear," Kevin wheezed, passing the joint to Sean.

Jeannette continued icily. "So she looks at me and goes, 'I thought you'd be thinner.' Who's holding?" Kevin ripped the roach clip out of Sean's grasp and handed it to Jeannette. "Thanks. Where was I?"

"The bitch's apartment," Dane offered, hoping he was correct.

"Right, this bitch's apartment," Jeannette said, placing the clip against her lips.

"Whose bitch?" the blond asked, his glazed eyes surveying the room.

"Do you want me to tell you this story?" Jeannette snapped.

"More than life itself," Kevin said through a yawn.

"So, I just look at this bitch and say, 'Oh, it's the clothes. I look so much thinner without the sweatshirt.' So Stormy sort of gives me one of her looks, you know, the death look?" Dane grunted vaguely. "So I told Stormy to fuck off and I started stripping."

"You what?" Kevin asked, suddenly engaged.

"You heard me, Queenie. You bet your ass. Oh, sorry, seems you already lost your ass." Jeannette chuckled, glancing as his rear.

"So I finish, stand there buck-ass naked, and all the women start to applaud when Jenny comes out of the kitchen with the wine. She…" Jeannette paused while she searched for the proper word. "Eeeked."

"Eeeked?" Sean slurred.

"That noise she makes. Not a scream. Not a squeak. An eek. I'll show you," she began to purse her lips.

"NO!" Dane yelled, startling Ace. "Please. No eeking."

"What happened? Uh? What?" Sean begged through half-closed eyelids.

"We went to the concert. Jenny never took anything I said as a joke again." Jeannette said with a firm nod.

"Have you decided what to do?" Jake whispered, a quiet somberness invading his voice. Jeannette shook her head slowly and finished off the joint. "It doesn't have to be a big deal, you know," he said tenderly.

"So I should let her just fuck men?" Jeannette snapped.

Dane rolled over on his side to face her, but he felt Jake's firm hand of restraint. Jeannette had always bonded with Jake more intensely, so Dane fell back into Jake and let the big guy handle this conversation.

"Monogamy is monogamy. Period." Jeannette said fiercely. "She could be with me, and, you know, thinking about a guy."

"Honey, I do that all the time," Kevin shot back, then to a hurt Sean. "Except with you, baby."

"Jeannette," Jake began slowly.

"What's that?" She interrupted Jake and pointed out of the bay window into the Panhandle below.

"THAT is what happens when two tops fight over a navy blue hanky, right pocket," Kevin said, watching intently. "Not a pretty sight. Don't watch. I'll tell you when it's over."

"Men! Fucking H Christ! Sex, sex, sex! Doesn't sex mean anything more to you guys? I thought after all that's happened," Jeannette muttered in disgust.

"To support the ideology of 'freedom,' we have to accept the fact that people are free," Jake said, using his educator voice. "Whether or not you support what they're doing in the park is irrelevant. The point is we fight for the right to live in a country that allows people to exercise free will. That," he gestured to the park, "is their free will. Want to take THOSE civil rights away, too?"

"I am not fighting for equality just so guys can go screw in the park!" Jeannette shouted.

"YES YOU ARE!" Jake shouted back. "Now stop shouting. We cannot say 'do what you want as long as I agree with it.' Unless it's a fascist state."

"Or a conservative right-winger," Kevin chirped.

"Don't help, please," Jake said to Kevin. Then, to Jeannette he added, "Just as you cannot tell Jenny that you love and trust her, then act as if she will cheat on you."

"I don't really," Jeannette stammered into silence. She sighed and shrugged.

"Then what is it?" Jake prodded.

Jeannette looked to the floor. "What if she likes him better?"

"What if she does?" Dane said, sitting up. Suddenly this conversation seemed much more interesting. If only he had some chocolate. "If she does love some guy better than you."

"Her ex's name is Jeremy," Jeannette spat.

"Really?" he asked sarcastically. "Thanks for telling me." Jake nudged him gently, and Dane changed the pitch in his voice to sound less condescending. "It always seemed so dull."

"You have no idea," Jeannette continued as if she hadn't heard the sarcasm. "An accountant. Excuse me—FINANCIAL ADVISOR. Parts his hair on the side, for fuck's sake."

"Oh, he does not STILL do THAT!" shrieked Kevin. Jeannette nodded.

Dane continued, "What if she does discover she loves Jeremy more? Do you want her to stay with you regardless? Knowing you've placed second?"

"At least she'd be with me," Jeannette said quietly.

"Where would you be?" Dane asked.

"So, Dane," Jake said in a cool, toneless monotone, "If I said to you, 'oh, Dane, I'm leaving because I love someone else,' you'd just say 'okay?'"

Dane's blood ran cold. What did that mean? Was this code for 'I'm kicking you to the curb?' Dane cleared his throat. "I...I don't know. I hope your happiness outweighs my feelings of insecurity." Jake stared at him, expressionless. Dane thought he saw Jake smile right before the man turned away.

Jeannette nodded and blurted out, "I know Jeremy loves Jenny. I know she loved Jeremy, too. I also know Jeremy doesn't like me at all, but I'm trying to accept Jeremy because Jenny loves him so much."

"I'm confused," Sean said dreamily.

"Of course you are, dear," Kevin responded, patting the blond's arm.

Jeannette opened her mouth to say something, but quickly closed it. After a moment's hesitation, she said quietly, "I'm losing who I am." Jeannette looked directly to Jake, who nodded in silent understanding.

He stared at her a moment and said with a strong determined voice. "You're Jeannette. Nobody can take her away from you."

"Yeah, you may be someone else tomorrow," Sean whispered.

Jeannette ignored Sean and continued staring unblinkingly into Jake's eyes. "I don't know, Bo, I still need more," Dane felt Jake cringe at the sound of his old nickname. Jeannette gave had given Jake the term of endearment during Jake's promiscuous period when he first moved to San Francisco. She meant it to be a shortened version of Boner, but for some reason, Jake thought that word repugnant. Although they all tried to edit the word from their vocabulary out of respect for Jake, whenever they gathered, someone always let it slip out. Usually it was Jenny. Dane thought it strange that tonight the slip went to Jeannette. "Do you believe in fate, Bo? I mean, Jake?"

Kevin's face lit up. "Do I ever! Girl, let me tell you about the cruise on the Golden Gate. Did I ever tell you about—"

"Yes," the group answered in unison. Kevin looked hurt, so Dane stretched out his sock-covered foot and stroked the man's forearm. It was a stretch, but Kevin accepted the gesture and responded by grasping Dane's toes and squeezing them lovingly.

Jeannette turned her attention back to Jake. The two of them sat closer to each other now, leaning into the other as if to create their own reality within, yet separate from, the rest of the circle. "How do I know if I'm giving too much, Bo? Am I compromising my own selfness by being with her, even though the divorce isn't final? Or is it just another quirk, like eating crackers in bed?"

"I don't equate eating crackers in bed with marriage," Jake snapped.

She shook her head furiously. "You know what I mean, Bo. When you love someone, or at least when I love someone, I put up with a lot of shit and sometimes I think, 'what a doormat.' But sometimes, when I'm giving and giving and giving, it doesn't feel like I'm being a doormat at the time. What am I saying?" Jeannette groaned with frustration.

"That history repeats itself," Sean whispered. When silence greeted the blond, he continued through a sleep-laden voice. "We talked about this last time. You're all going in circles. We're living one big circle."

Kevin patted the boy's arm. "He's tired, so you can ignore him. As a matter of fact, ignore him anyway. What were you saying, Jay?"

Jake reached out and grasped Jeannette's knee. Without looking at him, she laid her hand over his and squeezed back. "People change, Jay. They change. What was okay yesterday is tomorrow's rotten deal. We grow and we change. If you're repeating the same mistakes, just make different choices and," he paused for effect before continuing, "realize other people have free will to make different choices, too. That's their right."

"Like the fuckers in the park," she laughed.

"Like the fuckers in the park," Jake nodded back.

"Arrgh!" Jeannette groaned, throwing her hands into the air. "I can't believe I'm taking advice from you! Look at you! You have Mr. Perfect right here, with the perfect education, and you're getting out of this rat race anyway, so what do you care?" Too late she realized her mistake and covered her mouth in a comical cliché. Her eyes grew wide and began moving back and forth between Jake and Dane. Jake jerked up his head and shot her a reproachful look.

An eerie silence descended.

"She knew about it?" Dane growled accusingly at Jake. "You told Jeannette before you told me?"

"Come on, sweetcheeks, we're going!" Kevin said urgently, yanking Sean to his feet.

"How many others did you tell before you happened to mention it to me?" Dane looked to Jake. "Oh! That's right—you STILL haven't mentioned it to me!"

"Bo, I'm sorry," Jeannette pleaded, grabbing for Jake's hand.

Jake waved her off with a curt. "It's done." He spun around and confronted Dane with a cool stare and icy tone. "You're jumping to conclusions."

"Well! What a swell party!" Kevin crooned musically. "Thanks, guys. Dane, delicious as always. Jake, handsome as always. Jeannette...well, you're something as always. Come on, doll, this way. Night!" He sputtered as he shoved Sean towards the front door. Jeannette quickly followed suit, her face flushed with embarrassment and her lips forming a silent I'm sorry.

After the company fled, Dane sat staring coldly at Jake.
"You're not blinking," Jake quipped, hoping for a laugh.
Dane didn't oblige.

*   *   *

Jenny loosened her scarf from around her neck, hoping to alleviate the feeling of suffocation and avoid the panic attack she felt mushrooming inside her. The meeting room was impossibly small. An oval walnut table consumed most of the floor space, and six walnut chairs ate up the remainder of the room. Jenny forced her plastic smile to remain fixed on her face and grabbed the table in a vise-like grip. Bet your ass that's not fake lamination, she thought.

Jenny surveyed her audience from her place of honor at the head of the table; four pudgy little faces sitting atop four pudgy little men, all of whom had stuffed themselves into light blue suits for the occasion. Jenny focused on the munchkin to her immediate left. This one looked like a maverick with his maroon tie that almost glowed with defiance amongst the three red ties the other producers wore. Jenny smiled wider, hoping the bile would stay in her belly when she finally fainted from heat stroke. The four pudgy men smiled back at her and Jenny noticed that beads of perspiration had grown above their brows as well. Jenny felt relieved to know she wasn't the only sweaty person in the room.

"Jenny! Good to see you again!" Maroon Tie said in a thick New York accent. "Sorry to bother you on such a wonderful summer's night, but we're on a tight deadline."

"Oh, no bother!" Jenny said just a bit too cheerfully, wishing she could remember any of these men's names. "I just finished eating! You saved me from dessert!" She hated herself for speaking in exclamation marks whenever she felt nervous. She knew it reeked of amateurism but couldn't seem to force her voice to relax.

"Well, too bad we didn't know," Maroon Tie exclaimed. "We would have asked you to bring it to us. We haven't eaten yet." He chuckled heartily and patted his middle.

"May I suggest a great Italian place?" Jenny asked, hoping to hell she could remember if it was on Stanyon or Oak. Why was she suddenly forgetting everything?

"Oh, no. We always dine at the Mark," Maroon Tie responded with a smirk and a wink. She smiled back. Right now she wished she had the money to park her car at the Mark. "Want some coffee before we begin?"

Jenny giggled and threw her head back, hoping her hair wasn't plastered to her temples. "Oh, no! Not this late at night! I'd never sleep!"

"Oh, now, Roy!" one of the cloned blue suits said to Maroon Tie. "You're the same way!"

Jenny forced a placid giggle. Roy! Maroon Tie's name is Roy. Roy. She had to remember. Roy Rogers. Trigger.

"Well, enough chitchat," Roy said. "Jenny, these are the panel members you met previously." He gestured to the three Blue Suits.

She spun towards the clones and flashed her million dollar Salem/Winston/Michelob smile. "Hello, guys! Thanks for asking me back!"

"Our pleasure, little lady," Blue Suit Clone on the right replied in a thick southern drawl. He pulled out a small pack of cigars and proceeded to unwrap one. "We're just havin' the hardest dang time of it, don't you know. Why, both of yous—that little lady, Jane and you—are such pretty little actresses! Ain't that the truth." He inserted the cigar into his mouth and rolled it back and forth across his lips.

"Well," Roy began with the plastic smile still glued to his face, "you know we're very happy with the reading so far, but we just aren't sure which way we want to take this role. Considering you're new—"

"Excuse me, Roy, but there must be some mistake. I have worked in the business almost twenty years. I was a model for years before doing stage and voice over work." Jenny forced herself to sit back. Her breasts looked bigger when she thrust her chest forward.

"I meant to feature film," Roy corrected himself. "We want to give it another go 'round anyway. Right. fellas?" He glanced to the others at the table. "You just give us your best, alright?"

Three days ago, Amy had forwarded a draft copy of the sides to both her and Jane for preparation. The script was a piece of crap from start to finish. A mildly amusing romantic fantasy centered on a mis-identified Angel. She liked to think of it as *Touched by a Desperately Sought Susan*. Unfortunately, nobody got the joke except Dane–thank God for Dane.

"So," Roy continued, all business, "you need to be funny. Can you do a James Cagney impression?"

"No!" Blue Clone on the left screamed, "We need the rooster first!"

"Well, we'll get to that," Roy replied. "First, James Cagney. Then, we'd like to see you do a rooster, please." Jenny clutched the sides and intensified the smiling façade. "And if you don't mind," Roy said flatly, "stand on one leg. Remember, the girl loves her job, so you've got to ENJOY this!"

Jenny sighed and started to work.

*   *   *

The only thing Jake hated more than playing the Lawyer Circle Jerk was enduring Dane's Silent Treatment. Over the years, the playing of the game changed slightly, but the not the rules: one of them would state a problem, they would both SWEAR not to allow the discussion to descend into a fight, and then their discussion would spiral out of control into a raucous argument. In the final stage of the Silent Treatment, Dane would gather his bucket, rags, and various cleaning supplies and begin to sanitize the condo while ignoring Jake completely. In the early stages of their relationship, Jake found this passive-aggressive behavior endearing; he rarely had to do housework. But tonight he was in no mood to play by the rules. He stared into the kitchen for a couple minutes, gauging the level of Dane's anger before stepping into the ring.

"I understand you're upset," he began gently. "I did what I thought best. It's been a year already, you realize. I knew the anniversary of the crash would weigh on your mind." He stood his ground, forcing his voice to remain even and nonjudgmental.

"So you decided what I needed was a break from the city," Dane said politely, detaching the heating coils from their plugs.

"Good. Then we do understand each other," Jake replied, somewhat confused. This calm, rational voice was not Dane's normal response.

"What I DON'T understand," Dane said, throwing the steel wool into the cleaning bucket, "was why you don't hear me when I speak. I said I wanted to be HERE. I need to be HERE."

Jake sighed, knowing now that they were headed straight
downhill. "You're not thinking rationally."

"Imagine!" Dane spat sarcastically. He began drying the
stovetop violently.

"I'm being honest. You're being sarcastic." Jake sighed and
turned from the doorway.

"Jake Lucas, don't walk out on this conversation." Dane threatened.

"I won't argue," Jake responded flatly. "Not this time."

"Yeah, you will," Dane commanded. Jake turned to stare at Dane
for a moment before jerking open the refrigerator and pulling out a
beer through the maze of leftovers and condiments. "You want to be
honest? Fine. Let's be TOTALLY honest. Tell me the real reason you
bought the property when I distinctly told you it wasn't a good idea."

"I know the nightmares started again," Jake stated simply. He
watched as blood rushed to Dane's cheeks.

"They're worse than last time, only this time around you refuse
to tell me about them. Why? You think I won't believe you? Dane, I
believe you. And I believe they're being caused by anxiety, possibly
PTSD. You've got to get out of the city for a while. You can't learn
how to deal with this trauma by yourself. I thought you'd have
learned that by now." Jake paused for a moment, watching Dane put
the last of the coils into their plugs, and waited. "You're obviously in
denial about the severity of your situation."

"Oh, god, Jake! Nobody's in denial about anything!" Dane shot back.

"See what I mean?" Jake said, sipping the beer. "You're not
accepting the limitations this accident has forced on you—physically
or mentally. It's fucked up your life, Dane. Arguments?" Dane
turned to stare out the kitchen window into the dark July summer.
"And because of that," Jake continued softly, "it's fucked up mine, too."

"You still haven't answered my question. Why did you buy the
property?" Dane's voice was steady.

"I told you. For you."

"For me?" Dane asked.

Jake nodded.

"Jake, where IS this fantastical property with the magical
healing abilities?"

"Maine," Jake replied, peeling at the label on his beer bottle.

"Maine?" Jake remained silent as he pulled the label off the brown glass. "Why the hell would I want to go to Maine? Why not Montana, or Idaho, or Brokeback Fucking Mountain?" He stared into Jake's unblinking eyes.

"What difference does that make?" He mumbled. He could feel Dane gaining the upper hand.

"Why did you buy the property, Jake?" Dane persisted.

"I'm your lover. I have a vested interest in your recovery," Jake stated without emotion.

"With the emphasis on 'vested interest.' I swear, ever since this real estate phase of yours–"

Jake slammed down the beer and stormed away.

"Hey! Don't leave! We're arguing," Dane yelled at Jake's back.

"Which is exactly why I'm leaving," Jake yelled over his shoulder as he continued down the hallway, grabbed Ace's collar and called for the dog.

"Ace needs to go out?" Dane's voice was low and controlled.

"Yes." Jake snapped the clip onto Ace's collar as the dog spun in excited circles.

"Thought so," Dane agreed.

"You know, Dane, I'm doing this for your own good," Jake said, spinning towards the door.

"Spare me the bleeding heart routine. It's not butch. Besides, I'm better at it than you are," Dane challenged.

"I'm not putting up with your potshots," Jake said, jerking open the front door. Ace strained at the leash, tugging at his master. "It's not okay."

Dane grabbed the door, yanking it out of Jake's hand. "What's not okay is that my lover bought cheap-ass property on the other side of the country and plans to sell it at three times the price and make a mint, but—here's the catch—he does it for his poor, brain-damaged partner–"

"You're not brain damaged."

"–who is losing his mind and needs to be saved!" Dane continued.

Jake paused, then stepped back into the condo, pulling the anxious Ace behind him.

"You're not brain-damaged," Jake said, sounding genuinely sympathetic.

"Good. I don't think so either. Why, Jake?" Dane pressed.

"Why?" Jake asked, locking eyes with Dane.

"Why did you go behind my back and buy it, regardless of what I said? Don't you see how that makes me feel?" Dane asked. "I mean there are LOTS of reasons you could have mentioned to me: the property's near the new mall that's going up, you got an inside scoop from the construction company or you want to keep building your real estate portfolio." His voice was angry, but hurt was creeping in.

Jake's eyes grew, looking as if Dane had just punched him. "How did you know about the property?"

Dane shook his head. "How could I not know? Jake. For fuck's sake! Your office is like my second home. I spend as many hours there as you do—you don't think I meet people? Make friends?"

Jake's face unfroze. For a moment he betrayed his weariness and resignation. "It is for me—for us." But then his cold, stoic lawyer face regained control.

"No." Dane said shaking his head. "It's your land. Your retirement. It's great, really great, God knows, because I don't have a retirement plan. I really think the reason you bought the property is because you want out." He let the impact sink in before adding, "You want out of us."

"I don't want out," Jake said, avoiding Dane's eyes.

"This is our home, Jake. This city. I told you that I need to face...whatever it is that's happening to me HERE. I need to be in San Francisco."

"Why?" Jake asked quickly, his eyes wide and pleading.

"I don't know. But I have to be." Dane averted his eyes. "I just have to."

"Fine." Jake said with a resigned shrug. Get dressed. We're going out."

Dane froze. "Just like that?"

"Yep. Fight over. Let's go." Jake opened the door again, sending Ace scooting excitedly into the hallway.

Dane stammered. "But we haven't resolved anything."

"I can't win with you, you know that?" Jake said with a heavy sigh as he pulled the dog back into the condo.

"I didn't know it was a game someone could lose," Dane said.

Jake shook his head and leaned wearily against the wall. "Your ambiguity has reached new heights," he muttered, feeling indignant.

"Jake, we've gone around this bush before," Dane spoke carefully. One of the occupational hazards of being a lawyer is wordsmithing to a level of absurdity. "You have trouble acting as a unit with your partner. You enjoy the Lone Ranger role too much."

"Drama queen." Jake tried to sound lighthearted, but Dane seemed to take it like a slap in the face.

"It's the same bullshit as always with us, isn't it? I assume you want to control me, and you assume I want to control you." He didn't know who he was saying this for—Jake or himself.

"God, you can be annoying," Jake countered with a smirk. Ace and I are going out. I need my sweatshirt." Jake strolled into the bedroom, Ace following on his heels.

"Jake, do you want to put aside this illusion we're the perfect gay couple and just split up?" Dane asked quickly. "Yes or no. Fifty-fifty chance of getting it right."

"Is that what you want to do?"

Dane shrugged and looked out the bay window. No action in the park tonight. Maybe later.

"Because if it is, Dane, you're going to have to make the first move." Jake turned and walked back into the bedroom.

In the bedroom, Jake found his wool camping socks under the covers of the bed and decided to change into them. Pulling on his favorite Nikes, he lowered himself onto all fours and crawled into the closet. Sure enough, Ace lay pressed into the corner, lying atop the dirty laundry pile. When Jake stuck his head into the closet, the shepherd thumped his tail against the floor. Why was it dogs always knew when a couple fought? It must be that canine sixth sense. The dog leapt up and out of the closet, dragging Jake behind him.

"I'm taking Ace down for a stroll now." Jake's voice sounded strong and forceful. "I want you to walk with us. Please?"

"I don't think you're brain-damaged, Dane." He paused for a moment, his mind scrambling for the right words. "I don't know what's happening to you, but I do know that it's been a stressful year for both of us, actually. You're...different. You're not the same person you were before the accident."

"You aren't present in this relationship with me anymore. You're off somewhere distant where I can't go. I don't like being alone together anymore. I'd rather be really alone." Jake played with the leash through his fingers.

"I want you back, but you've got to come back on your own." He patted Ace, who whined and tugged for the front door. Jake took a couple steps behind the dog before returning his attention to Dane. "I really do believe getting out of here for a while is a good idea. Who knows what the dreams are. The mind is a strange creation."

Dane let the comment sink in for a moment before responding. "Call if you're going to be late."

"Okay," Jake mumbled.

"One more question." Dane said.

Jake stopped mid-step and was gripping Ace's leash tightly. He waited.

"If I refuse…if I want to stay in the city, are you going to Maine alone?" Dane stared at Jake's back for a long time before his partner answered.

"I'll call if I'm going to be late," Jake said without turning around.

Dane listened to Jake's footfalls down the hallway, the door open, and then close again. Then the condo became very silent. He stood gazing out into the park again, scrubber in his fist, his mind whirling. Had he really suffered some kind of nervous breakdown? Following the accident, he pursued physical therapy, legal recourse and medical follow-ups. But he only attended the suggested mental health counseling a couple of times, claiming he didn't need it; friends sufficed for the role of therapist. Maybe that had been a mistake. Maybe it has been important to see a therapist. Maybe he had internalized his fear without realizing it. Had he somehow pushed Jake away without realizing it, too?

He threw the scrubber into the sink. Dane could think of one person who would know—one person who always had answers for anything in inexplicable. It was 10:30 p.m.. Should he call first? She may be asleep. No. Go before you lose your nerve, he thought to himself. He stripped off the rubber cleaning gloves, ran to the coat rack and grabbed his jacket before speeding out the door and onto the street below.

*   *   *

The cool water felt good on her face. Jenny leaned against the porcelain sink of the women's restroom, feeling the water run through her fingers. The stream echoed off the tile walls of the empty room, acting as a soft melody to calm her frantic nerves. She glanced at her watch: almost three hours had elapsed. Three hours! If she hadn't wanted to steal this role from Jane so badly, she would have given up two hours ago. She cursed the Blue Suits under her breath. In all her years in the business, this was the first time she had given a three-hour audition. Waiting in line at a cattle call? Yes. Shuttling from agent to screen test? Or course. But sitting in a hot, sweaty, smoke-filled room for three hours with a bunch of mad lunatics who wanted her to cluck like a chicken and look "really, really scared?" That was a first. They wanted really, really scared? Great. Lock them in a room full of lip-syncing diva wannabes. Nothing was scarier than an inept drag queen lip-syncing a song she hadn't memorized. Now that was an experience they would remember forever.

Jenny laughed to herself and threw more water onto her face. Maybe she wasn't too old to get back into modeling. Since the baby boomers had hit forty, the need for older models was rising. And thanks to the Big and Beautiful movement, she could bypass the nicotine and coffee that used to be required.

The door swung open and Jenny spun sharply, feeling her heart pound in her chest. Wasn't this building closed to the public at this late hour?

"I'm sorry, did I scare you?" the stranger asked. She was an average-looking woman, about the same size and build as Jenny. Did the Blue Suits have a third actress in mind? No, it couldn't be. It was down to her or Jane, wasn't it?

"Actually, yeah. I thought I was the only woman in the building." Her heart pounded and she felt perspiration break out on her forehead. Shit! She needed to lay off the slasher flicks; they were making her way too jumpy.

The woman giggled. "I know that feeling! Scary, isn't it?" The smile struck Jenny as insincere. She'd worked for years with actors and models, so she could spot a phony smile from one hundred paces. This woman was a phony; of that there was no doubt. "I thought I was the only woman here, too! Imagine! Who knew?"

"Who knew?" Jenny threw her own fake smile in return. This is what a professional phony smile looks like. Take that!

"It looks like we're alone. Seems so, yes?" The woman smiled again.

"Yeah," Jenny responded half-heartedly. "Sure does." Jenny looked into the woman's eyes and felt herself swoon with light-headedness. The eyes! From somewhere in her past, Jenny recalled the intense glare of that pair of eyes, but for the life of her, she couldn't remember where. She had met this strange woman before, though, of that she was certain. Another audition perhaps? Goose flesh spread along her arms and Jenny felt chilled. Something about the woman wasn't right. She could feel it.

On her fifth birthday, Jenny's newly single mother loaded her and her little sister into a beat-up Plymouth and took the girls to McDonald's for a Happy Meal. Money had been tight for since her father had left and even a small indulgence like McDonald's felt like an extravagance. As Jenny stood on the sidewalk watching her mother pull her sister from the back seat, Jenny happened to glance at the front of the restaurant. A man stood outside the black bars watching the children play. He looked like her father—tall, thin, thick mane of hair flowing onto his shoulders, so she thought it was him. But only for a moment. In that instant of her lingering glance, the tall stranger turned his head and caught little Jenny's eyes. Although his appearance hadn't changed in the few seconds she gazed at him, the simple act of seeing his eyes had changed everything for her. Her arms broke out in goose bumps and she felt cold all over. Then her tongue began to itch again.

At that moment she knew. She could feel that he was a bad man. Very bad. She hurried through her Happy Meal, gulping down her small Coke and refused a trip to the playground, much to her sister's chagrin. She lied to her mother for the first time in her life, claiming she'd rather go home to play Chutes and Ladders than play on the playground. When her mother pulled out of the parking lot onto the street, little Jenny stared out the back window. The man's dark eyes followed her until the car pulled around the corner.

The next day, the newspaper had a picture of the bad man on the front page, next to a picture of a little girl. Although she couldn't read, Jenny knew he had done something evil to that girl. When she asked her mother, the only reply she received was a warning not to talk to strangers and a face full of smoke from her mother's Camel.

Jenny quickly shoved her paraphernalia back into her purse. The faster she got out of this room, the farther away from the stranger's intense eyes she would be.

"They call you Jenny Ricks now, don't they?" the strange woman asked, her voice carrying a high-pitched, professional edge. It reminded Jenny of the tone people take when they speak to a doctor or a lawyer.

"Yes," she replied, avoiding the woman's eyes, shoving the last of her stuff into the handbag.

"I'm Lily. Lily Dayton." The woman's rehearsed voice reverberated through the restroom.

Jenny glanced to the woman out of the corner of her eye. She zipped up her purse and threw it over her shoulder. "Hello."

"You don't remember me, do you?" The strange woman giggled.

Jenny stared at the woman's feet, doing her best to avoid the awful eyes. "No, I'm sorry. Have we met before? Maybe at an audition?"

Lily tittered nervously, and her mouth contorted into something halfway between a smirk and a smile. "It was a long time ago. Very long. I guess to you I was a nobody."

"Oh, don't say that!" Jenny said, taking a step towards the exit. "Everyone's a somebody. Well, nice to meet you again, Miss Dayton."

Lily stepped towards Jenny, blocking Jenny's escape. "We were sisters, you know."

"Excuse me?" Jenny said, stepping to the left.

Lily mirrored her, keeping her body between Jenny and the exit. "See? You don't remember...Bethany."

"I'm sorry, I think you must have mistaken me for someone else." Jenny smiled weakly. Her heart pounded in her chest and she felt sweat break out along her hairline. She bit her tongue to alleviate the terrible itching, but even her sharp teeth didn't help. Every fiber of her body screamed RUN. Jenny felt suddenly claustrophobic and her lungs collapsed, forcing her to struggle for air. There had to be some way past this crazy bitch. Her eyes scanned the room for another means of egress, but the window to her left was useless—too small and high off the ground to be of any use. Thankfully, the door to the hallway sported a large, translucent square of glass in the center. If she had to, she could break it. Jenny pulled herself to her full five-foot, eight-inch height and pushed forward.

"Oh, no, I'm not mistaken. Not this time." Lily sauntered to the door and deftly turned the lock. Jenny heard a soft "click" as the bolt slid into place. "You always were the vain one. Even to the last."

Jenny stared at the dark brown eyes. "Look, lady, I don't know what your problem is, but maybe professional help is the answer."

"Professional help?" Lily smirked.

"Sure. Why not? There's plenty of help in the city. Now, if you'll excuse me–"

Jenny nudged Lily, trying to shove her way past the woman. To her surprise, Lily shoved back. "Look, Lily, I'm sorry you're upset at your sister or whoever."

"You," Lily whispered.

"Whatever," Jenny said. She felt her heart pounding deep into her throat. "But you have me confused."

"I AM NOT CONFUSED!" Lily hissed violently, her eyes narrow and hard. "You always thought that, didn't you? You always thought you were so much better than I was. That's why you took him. That's how you took him."

Jenny stared at the woman, momentarily forgetting about her fear. "What? Who?"

"Well, vengeance is mine, sayeth the Lord," Lily spat, breaking eye contact for a moment as she turned to reach into her satchel.

The moment gave Jenny a chance. She grasped Lily with both hands and shoved her to the side with all of her strength. Lily slipped on her heels and fell against the wall, her satchel sliding from her shoulder and falling onto the floor, spilling its contents. Without stopping to look at the paraphernalia spilling onto the cool tile floor, Jenny pushed past Lily, spun the door lock and grabbed the handle.

The door was lighter than she thought and her violent tug sent it crashing into the wall, bouncing back into her, sending a burst of fire down her right shoulder. She leapt over the threshold and into the hallway of the building. She turned left, back towards the conference room where the Blue Suits undoubtedly still sat, puffing cigars and debating the fate of the actresses. She tottered unsteadily on her slight heels and grabbed at the wall for support, clawing along them like a demented cartoon character. There! Up ahead on her right! Light shone from under the door of the conference room! She turned towards the door when her feet slid on something slippery and she felt her legs slide uncontrollably beneath her. She tried to keep her balance, but the skirt proved too confining. Jenny felt herself weightless for a moment as her legs vaporized beneath her, then a stab of pain down her left shoulder as she crashed onto her back on the linoleum floor.

Behind her, she heard the bathroom door fly open, its mass bouncing off of the walls of the ladies' room once again. The crazy bitch was after her! Jenny turned onto her side, feeling warm liquid spread across her shoulder—had she tripped over the janitor's cleaning bucket? Her left hand pressed onto the floor to lift herself and her fingers made contact with a thick, syrupy stickiness that engulfed her fingers. Jenny turned her head and stared into the dead, blank eyes of Roy Maroon Tie.

She screamed and rolled away from the corpse. Frantically, she looked around her. She lay in a pool of blood. She pushed herself into a seated position. Roy and the Suits must have been on their way out for dinner when they were attacked, as all the pudgy bodies lay atop one another in a heap, as if they had been playing a deadly game of tackle football. Their pasty bodies lay unmoving in a pond of red that spread across the entire hallway.

The sound of a sharp "click click click" brought Jenny back to the present. Lily was still following her. Scrambling on all fours, Jenny crawled through the sticky liquid towards the elevators at the far end of the hall. As she reached the door to the conference room where she had watched Blue Suit shove the turd-like cigar into his mouth, she clutched at the door's knob and pulled herself to her feet. Come on! Come on! Open up! Her wet fingers slipped uselessly on the knob.

Suddenly, she felt a blow to her back and the knob vanished beneath her fingers as she flailed forward, trying vainly to regain her balance on the slippery tile of the hallway. Her head gave a loud "crack" as it hit the floor. Pain shot through her, but Jenny forced her eyes open. The world swam dizzily out of focus. She crawled her way toward the elevators and away from the mound of dead Suits and the stalking crazy bitch. Crazy with panic and fear, she planted her leg beneath herself and forced herself to her feet, ignoring the pain that pulsated in her shoulder and streaked through her head.

"Is that any way to treat your sister?" a voice whispered hoarsely behind her. "Especially one to whom you owe so much?" Lily's foot caught Jenny squarely in the back, sending the small woman crashing chin first onto the floor.

When her head stopped spinning, Jenny realized she must have bitten her tongue, as the flesh in her mouth felt thick and unwieldy. Before she could process the idea, she felt arms under her armpits, grabbing her roughly and dragging her backwards. Jenny struggled feebly, her legs spasming as she tried to regain use of her limbs. At least they weren't broken, she thought. Then Lily threw her onto the floor and grabbed her hands. Jenny tried to lash out, wanting more than anything to shove a fist into the crazy bitch's face, but the throbbing in her shoulder proved too much for her and the arm refused to function. Within seconds, she felt Lily's agile hands fastening bonds around her wrists, then her ankles.

The crazy woman grabbed Jenny by the feet and dragged her towards the door to the conference room. As she heard the slight "click" of the doorknob turning, Jenny knew they were bound for the cramped audition space. "HELP!" Jenny screamed into the emptiness, but to her horror, the only sound her body emitted was a gurgling jumble of words, followed by a trickle of blood and spit that spilled over her lips and dribbled down her chin. Her body fell onto the plush, soft carpet and then a giant pressure squeezed her lungs as Lily knelt on her chest.

"I would hush if I were you, sister dear," Lily snarled, her face inches from Jenny's. Through the blood trickling down her forehead and into her eye, Jenny watched horrified as Lily dug into her satchel and emerge with a roll of silver duct tape. She struggled frantically and to her surprise, felt the bonds on her wrists loosen.

"Look, you bitch," Jenny wheezed through the blood in her mouth, "get the fuck off me!" Jenny summoned all the breath she could and hocked a huge wad of bloody phlegm into Lily's face.

Lily pulled back, sliding off Jenny's chest and onto the carpeted floor of the office.

With a heaving grunt, Jenny sucked in a lungful of air, pulled with all her might against the restraints and felt her hands break free of their constraints. Lunging to the side, Jenny curled her fist and smashed it into Lily's face. She felt it connect with bone as a sharp crack filled the air.

Lily screamed in pain as she rolled onto the floor, clutching her nose, blood spewing through her fingers.

Jenny pulled herself up into a sitting position and crawled crab-like backwards towards the door. When Lily regained her senses and began to scamper after Jenny, her nose was swollen to twice its normal size. Despite the broken nose, it was obvious Lily would overtake her in a matter of seconds. Well, damn it, she was a trained actress with stage combat certification, and she'd be fucked if some bitch in heels would take her down. She sat down and pulled her legs back into her chest. Lily crawled faster. When she was almost on top of Jenny, the lithe woman thrust her legs into Lily's chest. The crazed woman flew backwards, her legs kicking comically behind her.

Jenny screamed. She could feel her hands tingle as blood flowed back into them. Ignoring the dull throb of her shoulder, she climbed to her feet and limped down the hallway as fast as she could.

The kick came from nowhere, the force of it throwing Jenny onto her injured shoulder. She screamed in agony as the shoulder joint ground bone against bone. She looked up just as Lily jumped at her. Jenny rolled out of harm's way, and Lily slammed into the floor like a wrestler on late night television. *It would be funny if it wasn't so fucking scary,* Jenny thought.

Lily rose unsteadily to her feet, her eyes narrow slits that glared at Jenny like a cat stalking a mouse. As her right arm hung limply at her side, Jenny pushed herself to a kneeling position with her left arm, then to her feet. For a moment the two women stood wobbling, staring at each other; bloody, aching and panting for breath. Then, with an ear-splitting shriek, Jenny kicked Lily in the knee cap. As the crazed woman clutched her knee, Jenny thanked God she'd spent her childhood with older boys. She cocked her functioning arm back and sent a powerful round house punch to Lily's face. The woman collapsed in a heap onto the floor.

"HELP!" Jenny screamed as she hobbled down the hallway towards the elevators. As if in response, a weak "ding" sounded. Ahead of her, the lighted numerals above the elevator doors flashed "four." Which floor was she on? Wasn't this the fourth? Damn! She didn't remember. She hobbled faster, pushing her aching body towards the escape. Suddenly the doors before her opened and the warm glow of the elevator's interior welcomed her. Jenny threw herself towards it.

But a hand grabbed her hair from behind and yanked her backwards. She reached behind her with her good arm, hoping to connect with the interloper.

"You hurt me, sister!" Lily hissed, wrapping her arm around Jenny's windpipe.

"Fuck you!" Jenny whispered through the growing pressure on her neck.

"Hey!" A man's voice resonated through the hallway, "I'm calling the police!"

From the corner of her eye, she saw a green-clothed man pushing a mop bucket standing before the doorway labeled STAIRS. He held a cell phone to his ear.

"HELP!" Jenny screamed.

"Yes, I have two women fighting in the hallway of my building. I need the cops now!"

Jenny felt a jolt of pain shoot down her side as Lily shoved her at the janitor. The force of Lily's shove caught Jenny by surprise, and she collapsed at the feet of the dazed man.

"Hey! You! Stop!" the man yelled. Jenny heard erratically paced footsteps echoing in retreat. She suddenly felt very tired. Her world shimmered and began to go black.

"Lady," the janitor said, "are you okay?"

"I don't know," Jenny managed to say. She reached to scratch a tickling on her scalp, but her hand came away bloody. She wretched and a thin line of bloody spit oozed from her mouth and spattered the janitor's work boots. Then she collapsed onto the cold floor, unconscious.

* * *

"So, she disappears upstairs with that guy who, I swear, had teeth bigger than a breadbox," Sean said, fluffing the throw pillow. "And she came back down about an hour later. Alone!" He winked at Jake who sat staring at the young blond, amused by his attention to detail. The boy sounded more like a reporter for *The Star* than a hotel clerk.

"And?" Jake prodded.

"And what?" Sean insisted, punching the pillow one last time before tucking it behind the small of his back. "Isn't that enough? You just watch. She's going to be a regular." He looked up as Kevin emerged from the kitchen with Jake's scotch on the rocks. "Oh! A drink!"

"For our guest!" Kevin insisted, pulling the tumbler away from Sean's prying hands.

"Look, honey, why don't you run along and take your bath? Jake and I need to chat."

Sean began to protest but Kevin patted the boy's head. "Please?"

Without another word, Sean slid off the couch and slinked down the hall to the bedroom without another word.

"Okay, boy," Kevin said, his voice taking on a harsh edge, "this is no social call. What's up?"

Jake looked at Kevin with eyes filled with fatigue and pain. Few could boast experiencing this side of Jake, and even Kevin hadn't seen it for a long time.

"How do you sober up so quickly?" Jake asked, deflecting the question with sarcastic flippancy.

"Years of practice. What is it?" Jake's wry smile faded and he stared into the tumbler of scotch. "Oh, fuck you! I know you are not coming into my house in the middle of the night to watch your ice cubes in my scotch. You only drink scotch when you're about to go all gooey and emotional. Now," the lithe man said as he slid onto the leather couch and picked up the discarded pillow, "unless I recollect incorrectly— which I never do—we left your place about an hour ago just as you and your beloved motorcycle man were winding up for battle."

Jake swallowed a bit of scotch. "Can you beat around the bush a bit more and give me time to choose my words?"

"The only bush I'm beating is that young stud's in there. I suggest you, dearest, drop the diva bullshit and get it out so I can get it on." Kevin crossed his arms and sat back into the cushions, waiting.

Jake nodded. He much preferred building up his courage before exposing his vulnerabilities to someone, even to a good friend like Kevin. Dane called this habit "ritual stalling" and would always say in that uber-dramatic way of his, "Jake, it's not getting any better between now and two minutes from now." He looked to Kevin, who patiently withdrew an emery board from his shirt pocket and began filing his nails. "I think Dane and I are breaking up."

"Hallelujah! Pass the collection hat, this boy hit the jackpot!" Kevin screamed with glee.

"Try to be a little more depressed," Jake spat, gulping the scotch.

"Honey, this is a fight that's long overdue. Ever since you two been goo-gooing each other, you have never had a knockdown, drag out catfight. That is not normal, my dearest, not normal at all. Two people in love have got to fight sometime. If they don't fight, it means they're not listening to each other. That or they don't care about each other's feelings enough to listen."

"Well. Silly me to worry," Jake mumbled, rolling his eyes.

"You two ain't ever gonna break up! Everyone knows that. Except you two, of course, but that's normal. People grow. People change. Do you love your relationship enough to let him change?"

"I want him to be happy," Jake said, fumbling for words.

"That wasn't my question." Kevin threw the emery board at Jake's head.

Jake dodged it. "I want what he wants."

"Oh, Jesus, Mary and the Donkey! Will you two stop playing the perfect homo couple and rejoin the human race? Please?" Kevin gesticulated wildly, his voice going an octave higher. "Stop treating him like a child who needs to be protected from everything! His independence attracted you to him in the first place. So let him BE independent. People be like a dog struggling on a leash: the minute that leash come off; they don't know how to be free."

Jake considered this. He certainly understood how Kevin could make the assumption that people seemed to be happier when they were free to choose their own fate. But did he really want a partner who felt compelled to be in a relationship? Wasn't it better to be with someone who chose to stay of his own free will? Jake rubbed his temples. He had a massive headache.

"Now, enough about you. Let's talk about me. Remember that woman Sean was talking about when I made my grand entrance?" Kevin asked as Jake drained his scotch.

"Wonderfully done by the way." Jake smiled.

"Thank you! You're such a doll." Kevin exclaimed with a melodramatic swoon. "Well, I've seen her around the hotel before. And since she's your friend–"

Jake held his hand up to stop Kevin. "Mine?"

"Yes. The woman in the green dress. The Weebles wobble but don't fall down woman," Kevin said, imitating her awkward walk.

Jake struggled to keep the blank expression on his face. Green dress. Green dress? He remembered something about a woman in a green dress, but what was it? He thought back to the conversation in the living room less than an hour ago. At the time, he remembered the woman clearly, but now she seemed distant and vague, like a potent dream that had lost its vibrancy in the light of day.

Suddenly a mental image of the hotel on Market came to mind. Ah, yes! The woman he saw getting out of the car, her long legs sliding out from behind the door as she stepped to the curb, dark glasses hiding her eyes. Yes, he remembered the green dress woman. Beads of perspiration broke out across his hairline. He raised his eyebrows to Kevin. "What about her?"

"She was seen with what's his name. You know! Man. Rich. Famous. He was known for his sexual...kink." Kevin snapped his fingers as if the act would magically produce the name.

"Ralph S. Thompson?" Jake asked with growing interest.

"YES!" Kevin said, clapping loudly. "Ralph. Anyway, San Francisco's finest stopped by the hotel to ask a lot of questions about her. She was with him the night of his murder. Isn't that just the cat's P.J.'s? And yours truly saw her!" Kevin beamed with pride.

Jake tried to refocus his attention to Kevin. "They're after her for suspected murder?"

Kevin shrugged. "Don't know. Just for questioning, I think." He leaned into Jake's face with excitement. "They say she disappeared without a trace."

Sean's voice whined loudly from down the hall. "Honey! What's taking you so long! I'm cold!" A broad grin spread across Kevin's face, and he leapt to his feet.

"Duty calls. Night, sweetie. Night, Ace." Kevin quickly pulled Jake to his feet and ushered him and Ace out the door. As Kevin closed it behind them, Jake stood on the doorstep in the night air, wondering how in the hell a famous man like Ralph S. Thompson, Jr. had found himself with a woman so commonplace she couldn't be found.

*   *   *

Mrs. Jeremy shivered as she stood in the flickering candlelight. It had nothing to do with the open windows through which the cold night breeze blew; hers was a chill that froze the bones. It was the shivering felt by children who tell ghost stories in the dark around a campfire. Or by people who walk through a cemetery during a full moon, the ones who whistle in the dark while they glance over their shoulder to make sure it was trees casting those odd shadows and not something more sinister.

She pulled her shawl around her, walked away from the kitchen window and peeked through the multicolored beads that separated the kitchen from the living room. She had been making herself some Swiss Miss when the lad showed up at her door. When he declined her offer of cocoa, she breathed a sigh of relief. Although she would have given it to him, she only had one package left and wanted it for herself. She could have brewed coffee, but how could coffee compare to the hot chocolaty goodness and those cute little marshmallows?

She drank alone and listened to him spin his tale about strange, vivid dreams and haunting, albeit fleeting, faces. When the boy finished, she wafted her sage stick around the living room, lit her white candles and started to work. She looked at Dane, who was lying on a pile of pillows on the living room floor, his chest rising rhythmically as the candlelight threw tentacles of shadows across his body. He looked as comatose as when she had visited him in the hospital one year ago today.

She cursed herself for not following up on her instincts. She knew very well the effect a coma had on people's psyches; Marshal had often told her stories about clients who experienced profound spiritual awakenings while sleeping in the between realm. She knew something was afoot with Dane other than simple nightmares! Why hadn't she gone directly to Dane with her suspicions once the boy regained consciousness? Hadn't she told him about her suspicions that night in the hospital? Hadn't she tried to warn the stubborn buffoon to pay heed to the possibility that the Dane who had overcome death would be a different man? Of course Jake wouldn't listen to her; he always ran from anything he felt was too "mystical" for his Midwestern sensibilities. Damn him! Like her dead husband always said, "Some of us run from this world into dreams, while others run into themselves." He was right, too, the old fart. People who embrace logic tended to lose their souls without realizing that while they might survive with half a brain, they'd die without a dream.

She couldn't blame the boy. She'd learned long ago the hardest of hard-nosed assholes, the bitchiest of bitches, deserved pity more than anyone; for they felt the most intense fear. Unlike the rest of humanity, the assholes and bitches of the world had perfected the art of transforming fear into a battering ram to destroy what they didn't understand. Jake's dis-ease was the worst of them all—he feared the power of his own emotions. Jake reminded Mrs. Jeremy of a Vulcan who believed that by limiting emotions, he could limit pain. Fool! Pain is the only reliable lover anyone ever has. In his flight away from pain, he ignored the blessing that accompanied pain: love.

She forced herself to breathe. After her third deep breath, she let Jake's condemnation fade away. Looking at Dane lying on his back in peaceful repose while the soft light flickered over his features, she wondered why Jake couldn't love this man. Not on Jake's terms, full of rules and logical reasoning, but on Dane's terms, illogical, unstructured and erratic as they were. And so handsome! When she mentioned removing his clothes, he balked so she didn't press the issue even though she believed journeying should be done sky clad. She acknowledged his embarrassment, but God! She wanted a glimpse of that ass.

When he had pounded on her door over an hour ago, he was angry, full of questions and expected immediate answers. "I need you to do whatever hocus pocus you do, Mrs. Jeremy. I need to know what is making me crazy." His voice was tinged with panic and his eyes were ablaze with determination. How could she refuse?

"Nice to know there's no pressure," she quipped, then, seeing the hurt expression on his face, instantly regretted it. "Dane, boy, sit down."

He did, although he would have fallen over onto his hiney if she hadn't steadied him. "If you want to understand what it is you do not know, it can be done. But nobody journeys under hypnosis who doesn't want to go. Understand?"

He nodded his head, but his eyes betrayed him. "Oh, boy. Think of it this way: it's your mind, so you'll be in complete control at all times. You'll feel relaxed, like you're floating, you'll hear sounds around you, and you may even feel an itch. You'll know your physical anchor is here, but your mind—your spirit—is elsewhere. You'll see pictures in your mind that will feel like a daydream or a hallucination."

"So no acting like a chicken?" he joked weakly.

She rolled her eyes. "Bullshit! Absolute bullshit! The fact is," she continued, "people go in and out of hypnosis every day. It's nothing more than an altered state of consciousness. But you must get out of your own way and allow your mind to remember." She took his hands in hers. "It's nothing more than suspending the busy, everyday mind and letting the subconscious out to play."

He nodded his head and followed her directions to the letter, falling into a deep trance much more quickly than she thought possible. But as soon as she told him to move backwards in time and come up out of the darkness, he remained silent. That had happened about ten minutes ago and he had remained silent ever since. She vowed to give him a couple more minutes before she brought him out of the regression. She had turned back into the kitchen to make a cup of tea when she heard him speak.

"I'm afraid," Dane murmured softly in a drowsy voice.

"Why? What do you see?" Mrs. Jeremy asked, moving through the beads into the living room once more. Taking care to step over the ashtrays where the incense burned, she finally arrived on her footstool next to the boy and plopped her heft onto it, grabbing the pen and notepad.

"I'm afraid." His voice sounded thick and heavy in his throat.

"I'm here. You are safe. Stay a minute and look around, then tell me what you see." Damn Marshall! Damn the fucker for dying, anyway! Why couldn't he be here helping her? He was a superb past life regression artist, while she was merely adequate. Want your Tarot cards read? Curious about numerology? Needing a Runes reading? She was your person. Marshall was the shaman of the family. He instinctively understood what each client needed and fulfilled their request, whether it be with energy healing or herbs. They were a team in their day, weren't they? Fuck, how she missed him.

She blinked several times to clear away the tears that had formed in her eyes. She looked back down at Dane, wondering where to go next. She didn't have to wonder for long, for after a brief moment, Dane spoke in a manner that reminded Mrs. Jeremy of the men she met in 1962. The men who begged her to eat something called "acid." By the time the Summer of Love arrived, she was best friends with the substance, but in 1962, she had only stared at the men dumbly. She refused, asking them instead, to allow her to observe them and their reaction to it. They agreed and for the next chunk of a day, she watched them scratch themselves raw, mumble about the giant hairy legs on the walls and listened to them talk. My! They babbled incessantly about everything and nothing at the same time. She had never seen or heard anything like it. Until now.

Dane began to spew forth a running commentary that rivaled the ramblings of those acid-tripping men.

*   *   *

Dane emerged from blackness to a blur of color and shapes. He panicked, feeling a burning icicle of fear grow along his spine. What the hell?! He blinked furiously to clear his vision and the scene swam slowly into clarity. As soon as he registered where he was, he felt a bone-chilling coldness creep through him.

He stood in the hospital emergency room where he died. The stark white room contained two gurneys, each containing a prone body surrounded by a clutch of medical personnel who moved at a frenetic pace. They frequently shook their heads in a worrisome fashion while gesturing to one of the two bodies. Dane strained to see the body lying on the table closest to him and totally ignored the second one. As one of the doctors stepped away from the gurney, Dane looked down into the face of the patient and froze in his tracks.

He stared down at himself. The leather jacket and flannel shirt lay to his side while the tattered remains of his blue jeans hung in shreds around his legs. His face bore deeps cuts from where the shattered face shield sliced his skin. Dried blood streaked his forehead.

Nobody took notice of him as he stood gazing down at his battered body. Suddenly the computer next to the second gurney began to beep loudly. Dane looked over to see four green lines shooting horizontally across the tiny screen. The doctors abandoned his body and dashed to the aid of the second patient. Looking down at himself, Dane remembered what Jenny had said to him in the kitchen earlier that night: "You died that night. By rights, you should have stayed dead." He suddenly felt dizzy and weak as the world around him began to spin, giving way to darkness once more.

He walked through the dark, unable to see, hear or sense any of his surroundings. It felt to Dane as if he walked through black syrup, lacking dimension or any sense of direction.

Suddenly he found himself standing in a dimly lit room where he could see the vague black outlines of two beds to his right. Dane looked around for the source of the illumination but could see no lamp. He turned to the bed closest to him and stepped towards its dark shadow. As he walked, the eerie illumination followed him. Where was the light coming from?

With a sudden flash of realization, Dane understood the luminosity was originating from himself. Looking down, he saw a glowing silver thread that extended out of his belly button to cross the room and hit the opposite wall. Like a dayglow leash, Dane mused. Fascinated, he followed the glowing string's path towards the wall. When he reached the spot, Dane paused for a moment to wonder how he would get to the other side of the barrier.

Instantly, Dane was standing in the hallway of the busy hospital. Medical personnel rushed up and down the tiled hall looking hard and focused, paying him no attention. A nurse laden with syringes and bottles emerged from a door to his left and scurried towards him. Before Dane could sidestep her, the woman plunged headlong into him and passed right through his body. As she did, she shuddered slightly, as if chilled, and continued on her path. The silver strand of light floated in the air down the length of the corridor and out the window at the end of the hall. Dane followed. As he walked, the glowing leash flowed back into his body; injecting itself into his skin.

He paused at the window, looking out over the city. He could see the thin thread of glowing silver shooting up into the night sky, becoming brighter and more pronounced the higher it went. Usually, if the bay was devoid of fog, the stars shone brightly out over the ocean. But with the exception of the sparkling silver cord, tonight's sky looked faded and dim, as if a sheet of cheesecloth separated him from the heavens. THERE! To his left, one pinpoint of light shone brilliant and crisp against the sky. It wasn't a star; that much was obvious. Instead, it reminded him of when he was young and had watched Batman on television—the light hanging from the heavens looked exactly like the Batsignal. Holy crow, Batman! Dane laughed to himself.

As Dane wondered what to do, a loud noise pierced the quiet. Up until now, all the sounds Dane heard had sounded muffled and distant, as if he were floating underwater and had to strain to catch a snippet of the world above him. The sounds that now caught his attention were clear, crisp and loud: bells. They reminded him of his youth, running up the concrete stairs into St. Peter and Paul's Church on a Sunday morning as the bells tolled for the beginning of Mass. Where were they coming from?

Maybe I should have gone to church more, Dane thought. Maybe then I wouldn't be here. I could have converted to Judaism like Uncle Fred.

The bells sounded again and this time Dane was able to pinpoint their origin. The sound came from outside the hospital building. He scanned the night sky, not knowing what to look for, but hoping that when he found it, he would know. Directly across from where he stood sat the east wing of the hospital. From his vantage point, Dane could see into the third floor window of the hallway near the elevators and, as if he had Superman vision, the patients' rooms. From the second window to his right, another glowing thread of illumination ran from the window into the sky, where it disappeared into a second circular glowing ball like the one that hovered above him.

Jesus! Dane exclaimed, wondering about its significance. The bells rang a third time; this time chiming so loudly and clearly that Dane felt as if they were inches from his ears. They chimed more harshly than before; the sound was like a warning bell. Dane thought of the elementary school he attended when he was about ten or eleven. Mrs. Hall, the English teacher, sounded a huge Chinese gong at the end of recess. She said the children heard it above the din of the playground and it saved her the extra work of calling them in. She named it her "calling gong."

Dane looked up to the sky and stared at the two glowing threads that ran into the black night. The calling gong. To call them in.

He leaned against the window and wasn't surprised when he felt not the cool hard surface of glass, but soft, thick gel, which he passed right through. He now stood outside the building and hovered in the air. *Okay, Dane* speculated, *how do I move?* Suddenly his body shot upwards a few inches. His first response was to flail his arms to keep his balance, but it wasn't necessary—his weightless body remained unaffected by gravity. With another thought of "up," Dane felt himself floating upwards again, only this time, he altered course and headed towards the point in the sky where his thread met the darkness. He felt like he was floating in a vast pool, just like he had done on hot summer days when he was a kid.

"Don't go too far, Dane!" his mother's voice called to him in his mind.

"I won't, Ma! Just a swim around the hospital."

"Well, okay, but you just ate."

"Don't worry, Ma, puke floats."

Above him spread the infinite black void of the night, punctuated by the intense sphere of white from the Bat Signal. He shot through the air, headed directly for the circle of illumination. As he swam upwards, he stared at the blinding brilliance of the Bat Signal Star and saw a glowing figure of a woman swimming above him. She was aimed towards her own Bat Signal Star. He was closer to the light now, perhaps a hundred yards. He could see the woman above him clearly; she, too, wore a hospital gown and a wrist band. She was so close to him that Dane could see her long, flowing red hair billowing behind her like a cape as she closed in on the white sphere above them. Just as she reached it, she turned and looked over her shoulder at him.

Their eyes met. Her emerald eyes seemed larger than normal, more intense and penetrating, like a person who had risen from the dead. She smiled at him, waved her hand politely and kicked her feet like a champion swimmer. She passed into the floating sphere and disappeared into the light.

Dane was only feet behind her and as he reached the glowing ball, he, too, kicked with such force that he could feel himself shooting through some kind of threshold and—

*   *   *

He gasped as he fell back into his body.

Mrs. Jeremy jumped, startled by the outburst, sending her pen and paper flying from her lap and skidding across the carpet. The dainty china tea cup on the side table wobbled briefly, then fell to the floor and shattered.

"I'm here, dear! I'm here!" Mrs. Jeremy said gently as she struggled to lower herself to the floor.

Dane reached out, gasping for air as his lungs awoke, his body flailing blindly as he sought the old woman's hand. When he connected with her, he rolled onto his side, clutching at her wrists like a small child. Only when he felt her warm arms close around him, did he allow himself to calm down, forcing his breathing to slow and deepen. He blinked quickly several times, willing the darkness to clear from around his eyes. Finally, points of light twinkled into view. With a sudden jerk of realization, Dane understood that his vision wasn't impaired, but rather the twinkling was the candles flickering in a dark room. With a sigh of relief, Dane folded into Mrs. Jeremy and let the woman wipe the sweat from his forehead.

"Welcome home, son," Mrs. Jeremy said quietly as she stroked his head. "Thirsty?"

*   *   *

While Mrs. Jeremy brewed fresh tea, Dane talked. He related the whole story with a desperate edge to his voice, stopping and starting often, as the vision was quickly fading from his mind. As a boy, Dane had kept many of his dreams and feelings to himself. His parents had never believed that his frequent feelings of déjà vu held any meaning whatsoever; to them, life's little mysteries could be explained away with a sweeping generalization or clichés. For them, dreams were only dreams and Dane's dreams—no matter how visceral they were—held no mystical meaning. There was nothing in Dane's household that couldn't be explained away with a guttural guffaw, a wave of the hand and another cigarette. So when Mrs. Jeremy nodded and gestured for him to keep talking, Dane lost himself in the telling of the tale.

When he finished, Mrs. Jeremy refilled his coffee cup, sipped her tea and sighed. He stared at her, waiting for her to talk. Finally, she did.

"It's decaf," she said, pointing to the coffee.

"Thanks," he answered. They both sat mutely for a moment contemplating their drinks.

"Mrs. Jeremy, it wasn't a hallucination or a dream. It felt–"

"Oh, Jesus H. Fucking Christ, boy, who the hell do you think you're dealing with?" she said.

She set her cup down with such force Dane thought she would shatter it. Her eyes furrowed and her voice cut through the air with a sharp edge Dane had only heard a few times. Dane had seen her angry before, and he didn't like it.

"You know damn well I believe you. Stop being naive." She waddled to the sink, turning her back on him. "It obviously was an after-death experience. How much do you know about those?"

"I've read of near death experiences?"

"Near death? Bullshit," she spat. "How can you see the other side when you're not dead yet?" She poured another mug of tea. "People die, see the beyond and come back. They may only be dead a minute, but they were dead. They just don't want to admit it, or they want to gloss it over with that typically American sugarcoating."

The woman spewed forth such bitterness, Dane was taken aback.

She leaned over to him and stared at him intensely. "You died, boy. You were dead for almost four minutes. Not something that happens every day." She turned to look at him, her look changing to a softer, gentler gaze. "So you've never read Edgar Cayce?"

Dane shook his head. "Arthur Ford?"

Again, he shook his head.

"Jean fucking Dixon?"

All Dane could do was stare blankly at the old lady and shrug. "I don't know where to start, boy." She sighed. "This isn't my specialty. Marshall always did this kind of thing."

"I saw on *Oprah* these people who, you know, died and came back," Dane began slowly. "They talked about bright lights, voices and stuff like that. I didn't see anything like that."

"I have no fucking idea what the hell happens when we kick the bucket," Mrs. Jeremy whispered. "But I doubt everyone sees what Oprah sees."

"Not her, but the people on the show," Dane corrected.

"Whatever," Mrs. Jeremy said, throwing up her hands with disgust. "But Marshall always said dying is like a road trip. Lots of different ways of getting there, so you have to decide which way you want to go."

"A road trip?"

"Yeah, a God-damned spiritual road trip," Mrs. Jeremy asserted, scrounging around the cupboard for a cookie. "Everyone knows who they want to see when they die, what they want to hear or some freakin' idea of the other side—white fucking clouds or pudgy little angels. So that's what you see."

Dane shook his head with conviction. "I didn't see that."

"I know. That's why I said you need to decide which way you want to go," she said, sounding irritated. She spun back towards him and spoke slowly, as if to an idiot. "You just got in the car to go to the store and wound up on the interstate."

"Are you stoned?" Dane asked seriously.

"I wish I were. I think that sphere you saw—"

"—the glowing one. That's when I woke up."

"I think the real story starts when you get into that hole." She froze, cocked her head to one side and burst out laughing. "Ain't that ALWAYS the story—getting into the hole."

Dane didn't laugh, so she shrugged, coughed and continued in the same authoritarianvoice. "I think whatever you saw after you dived into that light is the thing that keeps you awake at night and makes you see—." She stopped.

"Her," Dane finished the sentence. "You think the woman I saw that night is the same woman I've been seeing in the dreams?"

She looked at him with a sideways glance that could only mean one thing: no shit.

He nodded his agreement. "Me, too."

"And the real interesting story," she continued, as if infused with a new energy, "is why you two went into that light together. She saw whatever you saw, boy. That's why you're seeing her in your dreams." She closed in on him so their eyes were inches apart. "You're connected to her, now, Dane. Best find out how." She winked at him.

He stared back. He had figured that one out on his own. "Great. Redheads everywhere today! Must be the summer."

Mrs. Jeremy looked at him inquisitively.

"Oh," he explained. "Kevin saw a red-haired woman in green at the hotel, I see one in my dreams and now here . . ." he sighed. "Why can't it be, I don't know, Hugh Jackman?"

"You're not that lucky," she giggled back. "Neither am I, son. Neither am I. Now help me put out these candles before we burn this rat-trap fucking place to the ground."

*   *   *

Ten minutes later, Dane was stepping off the front stoop of Mrs. Jeremy's apartment building and heading back towards the Sunset district. He could have jumped on the N-Judah, but the cool night air felt so comforting on his skin he wanted to walk. Besides, after what just happened, he wasn't going to be able to pace the floor tonight. He slung the backpack over his shoulders and marveled at its weight. The books and folders hadn't looked this heavy when Mrs. Jeremy shoved them into the pack, shooting him a stern look of authoritarian dominance.

"Read the "past life regression" process stuff first," she said, shoving him out the door with his load.

He took a right on Market and meandered down the brightly lit avenue teaming with people even at this late hour. Lily. Did he know a Lily? He thought back over the past year and tried to recall the names of the cadre of nurses, doctors, therapists and assistants, looking for a Lily. Why couldn't he get that name out of his head?

*   *   *

Mrs. Jeremy waited for Dane to turn the corner before fetching her scotch. She poured herself a tumbler and gulped it, not caring how it burned her throat. She poured another. This was a big 'un, as her father used to say about any circumstance that required his full attention. "A big 'un, girl! Get yourself ready 'cuz a big 'un is a-comin.'"

"Holy shit on a skewer," she mumbled to herself. The boy wasn't joking about these nightmares. He had seen something big that night one year ago and had a bona fide run-in with some kind of supernatural force. He had faced a big 'un. Oh, Marshall! Where were you when you're needed? She couldn't help this boy—she knew so little! This was the realm of shamans and spiritualists. She gulped down the scotch, wondering about this woman with the red hair. Group karma? Possible. But the hairs on her arms signaled something more sinister.

SATURDAY, JULY 8, 2006

2:16 AM

THE BLACK MURKINESS *engulfed him and he felt its cold grip stimulating every hair on his body, barely noticing how the dark swallowed all light except the soft silver glow emanating from the spiral cord from his midsection. He felt tired, exhilarated, dizzy and horny all at the same time. He felt free, as if any worries he had been carrying were suddenly exorcized. He blinked and the darkness gave way to an intensely bright noonday sun shining down onto an expanse of deep green grass that resembled a golf course with the exception of the mustard yellow daisies that spotted the lawn.*

Dane had never liked playing golf, but he enjoyed accompanying his friends on their quest for the perfect game because he loved the warmth of the sun shining down on him and the feel of the soft turf beneath his feet. He looked around and saw how the sky, grass, water, and trees shimmered with a golden light, translucent and crystalline. As he stood marveling at the beauty of it all, a huge maroon dolphin glided past him, playing tag with a dog. He inspected the dog. It was perhaps the ugliest dog to walk the planet: large, but with ears so tiny they were nearly invisible, long thin legs and thinning white hair that revealed pink skin in several spots along its back. It looked more like a furry albino spider than a dog.

Buster? Dane wondered, looking closely at the pathetic beast. Buster, the huge mutt he'd loved as a boy. Buster had lived a full and energetic life, and died the summer Dane had left home for college. What was Buster doing here? What the hell was the dolphin doing here? He waved to the dog, but Buster was engrossed in his game of tag. He smiled as the dolphin nudged Buster on the rump with his snout, turned and swam away playfully. Buster spun around, noticed Dane and hesitated for a brief moment, as if debating a reunion with his old master. The eye contact was brief, but Dane could feel a nod of recognition from the dog, which made

him feel as if he were twelve years old again, the age he'd been when he and
Buster had spent a summer exploring the woods at camp. Buster had no
desire to reminisce, however, for after a second's hesitation, he turned and
ran after the dolphin, who was now accompanied by a huge deep sapphire
sea turtle. It was pure Warner Brothers and Dane wanted more.

When the sky suddenly went black, Dane felt the earth beneath his feel
shake and roll. A cold wind sprang up from the horizon and assaulted him
with a fierceness that made Dane stumble backwards a few steps. Regaining
his balance, Dane braced himself for the earthquake he knew would be
coming. He'd lived in California long enough to know an earthquake when
he felt one. But as suddenly as the shaking began, it ceased. The darkness,
too, dispelled and Dane found himself alone again, staring out into the
swirling mist. Buster, dolphin, and turtle had all vanished.

But within seconds, the mist cleared and Dane saw new surroundings.
Beneath him now was golden tile with white pinstripes that pulsated with
electricity. With each beat of his heart, Dane saw the threads of white in the
tile glow vibrate with unearthly energy as steady and rhythmic as if it were
alive. In the middle of the empty room stood a single piece of furniture—a
wooden dais—upon which sat a sphere of white light. Dane knew, somehow,
that inside this sphere of light was a book. He strode towards the lectern. He
had seen this all before, but couldn't recall where. The room, the tile, and the
glowing sphere made him feel comfortable and safe here. He felt as if he had
arrived home.

As he stood staring at the podium, a woman materialized before the
wooden dais. She hunched over the glowing sphere, her hands caressing the
golden ball with loving gentleness. Her red hair billowed behind her as if a
strong wind were being generated from within the sphere. She slowly
turned her head in Dane's direction until her emerald eyes met his gaze.

When they did, he felt an odd chill roll across his body, sending
gooseflesh over his skin. Her eyes! He felt the heat of them as they bore into
him, drilling through his skull and into his brain. He could almost feel her
looking into him as if his skin had turned translucent. He stepped hesitantly
towards the table, for now he was afraid of the woman. It was if her presence
was a harbinger of evil. He reached out to the podium tentatively and pulled
himself to it until he stood shoulder to shoulder with the red-haired woman.
He looked down into the sphere.

Jenny's lifeless head stared up at him, the soft glow of the sphere
providing a golden halo, giving it a holy, angelic look.

*   *   *

The lock turned in the door and Dane awoke abruptly as Jake entered the room, leading a leaping and playful Ace, who trotted off in search of his water bowl the minute Jake released the clasp on the leash.

"Hi," Dane said sleepily, forcing himself to regain control of his breathing.

Jake jumped back in surprise. "You scared me to death."

The two stood staring at each other for a moment until Ace suddenly bounded up next to Jake, rubbing against him like a cat. Jake broke the awkward silence.

"You were sleeping," he sounded awkward and unsure, a timber in his voice Dane had heard only a few times.

"Dozed off," Dane answered honestly. "Too much good weed. What time is it?" Already knowing the answer, he couldn't prevent himself from wanting it verified.

"Two sixteen," Jake said looking at the clock and confirming Dane's suspicions. "Want something to drink?"

"No. Have you heard from Jenny?" Jake shook his head and went into the kitchen, Ace close on his heels. "She usually calls after an audition. Even if it went a couple hours, she should have been done by ten or so."

"Did you call her cell?"

"A million times. And a text. And an email."

Jake strolled back into the room with the last of the Samuel Adams.

"Remind me to get more beer tomorrow," Dane mumbled as Jake sat down in the chair opposite him. "Look, I'm going to get dressed and head over to Jenny's. Something's wrong."

"I'm sorry," Jake said quietly.

Dane nodded. "Me, too. I know you want what's best for me. I also know you're worried."

"It's more than that."

"Please." Dane waited until Jake took another swig of beer before continuing. "I know you're concerned about the dreams and whatever the hell else is happening to me. So am I." Dane let out a small smile. "And you're right about something else, too."

"What?" Jake teased, cupping his hand to his ear. "It sounded like you said I was right."

"Smart ass," Dane snapped. "I am different. I mean, ever since the accident. I've...I'm not content being who I was anymore. I want to know more about–" he shrugged with noncommittal honesty, "life, the universe, everything. I can't help wondering why I'm not dead, why I never learned to scuba dive, why I don't buy flowers more often. I love fresh cut flowers."

He fell silent for a moment and Jake let the silence linger.

Finally, Dane said, "I'm different and I'm sorry I'm not who you want me to be."

"I don't want you to be any way," Jake said, peeling the label from his bottle.

"Please," Dane said rolling his eyes. "We all have these little scripts in our heads we want our lovers to play out. Admit it."

"You give me credit for more creativity than I actually have," Jake said quietly.

"How come this fucked-up society tells us we need to make room in our hearts for love, family, and friends, but doesn't say a word about making a place for confusion, pain, and grief?"

"You sound like a demonic Hallmark card," Jake said concerned. "Dane—you of all people know you have a place for pain and confusion. I think you have a monopoly on it."

"Thanks," Dane said sarcastically.

Jake called Ace over to him. "Don't mention it. I love those parts, too."

"You tolerate those parts," Dane corrected. "But, hey, there are parts of you I barely tolerate, too." He turned to look at Jake, and then said very quickly. "Have you ever had real strong déjà vu? Not the run of the mill, spooky kind, but the kind that makes you feel like you're rehearsing a play and know the next line?"

Jake stared at him and said, "You've been talking to Mrs. Jeremy, haven't you?"

"I'm not talking about Mrs. Jeremy," Dane said, his voice coming out much stronger than he expected.

Jake stood up so quickly, Ace slid from his leg and skidded onto the floor. "I am! God, damn it! Every time some quirky little thing happens, she makes it into some Stephen King novel."

"Jake, calm down," Dane said, raising his voice.

"What do you want to do, Dane? Sit around have nightmares that keep you up all night and refuse to see a doctor? Or have the fat little woman tell you how you're suddenly a possessed demon or God knows what? Or do you prefer just sitting around the house like you have been doing?" He towered over Dane now, his eyes boring into Dane like a laser.

Dane looked away and tried to remain calm. "I'd like to find the answers."

"Then see a shrink. See a doctor. Do something! But don't sit around making this accident something it's not. It was a terrible traumatic event, but that's all." He spun away from Dane and stepped to the bay window.

"Do you want to come with me to Jenny's?" Dane asked.

"I don't know what you want anymore." Jake paused a moment before turning from the window and talking a few steps toward the bedroom. He stopped suddenly and spoke from the darkened doorframe. "I stayed with you at the hospital, called your insipid parents, argued with the condescending doctors and juggled schedules with the physical therapists! And I did it all gladly." He lowered his head and continued, "I don't know how to help you, Dane, and you're not helping yourself."

Dane snorted in disgust. "I'm not helping myself, or I'm not helping you?"

"Both," Jake whispered. "Both."

"You know," Dane laughed. "I think we've hit that point when all the annoying things we once thought were cute are now irritating."

"Well," Jake said with a chuckle, "we can't break up. We'd have a custody battle on our hands." He squatted and rubbed Ace's belly as the dog tumbled over onto his back and spread his legs. "Look, he's imitating Daddy Dane."

"Funny," Dane sighed humorlessly. "You've decided to go, haven't you?"

"Yes,"

"When?"

"Tomorrow," Jake said, walking up behind the chair and placing his hands on Dane's neck. "I can come back."

Dane knew he should say something reassuring, sympathetic, or romantic, but the words wouldn't form. The two stood in silence and looked out onto the park for several minutes, each waiting for the other to speak. When the ring of the phone cut through the night, they both jumped in surprise.

*   *   *

From somewhere down a dark tunnel, Jeannette heard a phone ring. By the time her marijuana-induced fog cleared enough for her to think about answering it, the machine had already picked up. She opened her eyes and looked to the LCD alarm clock: 2:16 a.m.. Who the fuck was calling at this hour? She grabbed the receiver and yanked it under the covers.

"Jenny?" She croaked. Her throat, dry and cracked from the alcohol and pot, felt like sandpaper.

"Hello .. Jeannette?" A hesitant feminine voice asked.

"Who is this?" Jeannette asked, hacking so loudly she saw spots in front of her eyes.

"Jennifer Mills. We met at the solstice party last year. I'm the night nurse at USF Med Center."

"Yeah," Jeannette said, barely remembering the wide-eyed young lady with one green eye and one blue. "Do you know what time it is?"

"Yes. I'm calling on business, Jeannette." Her voice suddenly became thick, as if she was about to cry. "It's about Jenny. The rules say we can only call family. I didn't know she had a husband. I figured I'd better tell you, though."

*   *   *

Jeannette got from her warm bed in the Richmond District to the hospital in exactly 22 minutes. She could have easily cut a couple minutes off, but she had gone to bed naked and felt obliged to throw on clothing. She jogged through the door of the ER, and the smell of disinfectant assaulted her, reminding her of why she hated hospitals—they held sick people. What asshole thought of the idea of shoving a bunch of people with compromised immune systems into a confined area with diseased patients? It made no sense.

"I'm glad you're here," the husky voice startled her and she spun to look into the red, puffy eyes of a young, clean-shaven man with pronounced cheek bones and a large nose. "I asked the nurse to call you as soon as I remembered. I should have thought of it earlier, I'm sorry."

"Nathan, shut up and talk to me," she snapped at him. "How is she?" she asked, avoiding his pleading eyes that were begging her for support.

"Stable. She's hurt real bad, Jeannette," he began to shudder and tears rolled down his cheeks.

"Nathan!" Jeannette said, slapping him lightly on the face. "Not now! Fall apart later. What happened?"

"She was downtown, I think. An audition," he hiccupped.

"I know that," she snapped. The bastard didn't even know what his own wife was doing! "She left me to go for the callback. Where was she attacked?"

Nathan shrugged. "Inside the building, I think. The janitor found someone beating on her."

Jeannette stared at him, dumbfounded. "Beating on her?"

He nodded.

"Why?"

He shrugged.

"Who?"

He shrugged again.

"I'm sorry, I don't know, Jay." He began to cry again, heavy heaving sobs.

"DON'T CALL ME THAT!" Jeannette yelled hysterically. She backed away as Nathan slumped towards her, but she couldn't escape his long arms as he collapsed onto her, sobbing uncontrollably. "Do the police know anything? The attacker? The motive?"

He shook his head into her shoulder.

She grabbed him and yanked him to his feet, glaring into his tear-streamed face. "Nathan, think! Why would anyone want to hurt her?"

He shrugged again.

"Was she robbed? Don't you FUCKING find these things out?"

"Don't yell at me! I don't think as quickly as you."

He looked like a child, Jeannette thought. A big, goofy child.

"You mean you just took the call, came here and then waited for me without finding out anything?"

He nodded sheepishly.

"The police didn't talk to me much, just asked for her address and vitals. The hospital only wanted to know the insurance information." He struggled to control his crying and began wiping the tears with his sleeve.

"Why didn't they call me first?" Jeannette screamed accusingly.

"I'm her husband," he said quietly.

Jeannette froze in place, stunned by his brutal honesty. Without another word, she turned and walked towards the doors separating the waiting room from the actual emergency room.

"Jay–Jeannette! You can't go in there," Nathan said, walking towards her. "It's family only."

"Goodness knows I'm not her family," she whispered.

* * *

Nathan sat in the oversized recliner next to Jenny's bed on the third floor of the east wing, looking out at the city as the morning mist crawled slowly over the Sunset District. He sipped his coffee in a daze. Down the hall in the waiting room, Jeannette, Dane, and Jake sat huddled in a circle from which he felt excluded. Once again, they gathered like the famed musketeers rising out of history; the only things missing were the swords. And, once again, he was on the outside looking in.

Nathan leaned his head against the cold window wishing to hell he had a cigarette. Jenny had embarrassed him into quitting just four months ago—recent enough to yearn for nicotine, yet ancient enough to warrant the yearning for a habit instead of an addiction. He glanced to his left to see the young nurse's aide exit Jenny's room and rub hand sanitizer into her fists.

He had married Jenny in a fit of elation, as he had longed for her since the first time he met her three years ago. That night when she said she loved him, he looked into her eyes and believed her with all his heart. He had been hauling saddles for his cousin, who was then only a newcomer to the rodeo world. Walking from the Ford F-280 that they used to transport the equipment, he wasn't looking where he was walking and plowed right into the small-framed Jenny, nearly breaking her nose with the saddle horn. He looked up, horrified, only to see her laughing uproariously as the blood oozed through her fingers and dotted the front of her denim shirt, which was already soaked through with sweat. He couldn't help but notice that she wore no bra.

Their courtship had been intense and brief; he carefully clipping her play reviews from the paper and framing the good ones while burning the bad ones with his Zippo. He brought her old movies and she stole fresh daisies from the park for him. He had always known about her relationships with women; it wasn't a secret to anyone who knew her. Far from being repulsed or jealous, he felt nothing but awe at Jenny's bravery and openness about her sexuality. In the long haul of life, what did it really matter? They never talked about it, as her sexuality was like using the bathroom. Something she did but never felt the need to explain.

Four and a half months after the honeymoon, Jenny miscarried. The pregnancy had been an accident, but the loss of the baby changed Jenny, making her moody and depressed. Why she had turned to Jeannette was still a mystery and a sore point to him. Was it because their love threatened his masculinity? Yeah, partially, he admitted. He felt confident in bed and out, so what was it that Jeannette offered that he couldn't? Maybe their marriage was never meant to be. Maybe Jenny never loved him. Maybe he was a fool. How long was it from the time he knew their marriage ended until he physically left? Three months? Four? He felt like rushing to the waiting room, bursting into the circle of friends sitting huddled around each other and demanding they include him in their vigil. He needed to hear someone else say that everything was going to be alright.

But he drank his coffee in silence.

The marriage effectively ended on a Wednesday. Wednesday was the worst and most wicked of all days—he had always joked that if the world was going to end in a blaze of nuclear destruction, it would be on a Wednesday. He had felt particularly irate and moody all day without explanation and wished the construction site he was assigned to would just go away. By the end of the relentlessly monotonous day, when he stepped through the door of the studio apartment they shared and saw Jenny sitting in the stiff backed chair (why hadn't he chucked that thing like Jenny wanted him to?), he was unprepared for what was to happen. He knew the marriage was not going well; he knew that Jeannette was more than a friend. He knew the whole relationship felt like a fucked-up job interview; when your guts quiver and shake and your legs become rubbery, but you keep moving forward out of necessity. But he held onto the belief that everything was going to be alright.

Then Jeannette walked out of the bathroom.

Once he saw her face, stoic and grim, he could no longer deny the obvious. Jeannette wore her faded jean jacket and boots and looked very butch and intimidating. Stern, actually—yes, that was the word. Stern. They had met at a rodeo, Jenny explained to him later. At least Jenny was consistent.

"Hi," was all Jenny said. It was all she had to say.

"Hi," was his witty comeback. He stared at Jeannette looming over the scene and wondered if the death of his marriage would hurt more or less because of her. He tossed his briefcase onto the floor, stripped off his jacket and threw it over the chair. Time stopped. Nobody breathed. The air felt thick and sickeningly heavy. He turned to the two women. "This is it?"

Jenny nodded. There were no tears in her eyes, only a soft, sad look of pity.

The absurdity of the scene washed over him: their lush, large wedding with enough food to feed an army, their heated arguments about money, their shared pain after the miscarriage and the self-consciousness of his own foibles. He walked to the window and looked onto the parking lot.

"I made a list of all the bills that I've paid already," Jenny said, "and I just went to the market."

"I'll get by," he said quietly. "Thanks, though."

"I know that."

"It's okay," he interrupted not looking at her.

"Would you please let me finish a sentence?" she demanded.

"Why?" he asked calmly. "I don't want you to leave. I love you. I need you."

Jeannette snorted. "Need her?" Jeannette snapped. "For what? You can find yourself a maid."

"Jay!" Jenny cut her off.

"Jenny," Nathan said quietly. "You know I love you, right?" Jenny nodded, avoiding his eyes. "I don't know…I want you to be happy but I don't want you to leave."

"I know."

"Don't go," he pleaded.

She shook her head and whispered. "I have to be true to myself."

"What am I going to do?"

"Deal with it," Jeannette snapped.

Jenny cut her off with a look. "I don't know," she said. She locked eyes with him and with a nod of his head, it was done.

Just like when he and Jenny parted, Jake and Dane appeared on the scene like a posse in a spaghetti western. Only this time, they appeared with stale donuts from an all-night convenience store. He sighed and continued to stare out the window, forcing himself to remember a happier time. Jenny had taken Nathan to meet Dane and Jake immediately after the engagement. She called it her "past meeting her present to decide her future," and the three of them had laughed while Nathan tried to figure out what the joke was.

Nathan saw a shadow out of the corner of his eye and turned to the face of the beautiful red-haired woman with piercing green eyes spinning away from the doorway. "Yes? Can I help you?"

"I'm sorry," the woman stammered, stepping back to the doorway, "I didn't see you sitting there." She paused as if to decide if she should enter or not. "Is this Jenny Rick's room?" she asked.

"Yes," Nathan answered. "Can I help you? Are you a friend of hers?"

"In a manner of speaking," the redhead responded. "I'll…thank you, but I can't stay. Please, no, don't disturb her," she said when Nathan stood. "I'll call on her later."

*   *   *

"Hey! Do you mind keeping the noise down?" the high-pitched voice squealed.

Jeannette pulled herself out of the daydream and glanced around the hallway. Everyone had left the hospital after assuring themselves that they could do nothing further to help, but she had disappeared only long enough to use the pay phone to call in sick to work. Afterwards, she stood out of sight until she heard Nathan telling the nurses he was headed home to shower and change. As soon as the doofus was gone, she crept back to Jenny's room and stood on the threshold, unable to bring herself to enter.

"Over here," a voice to her left said.

She had been so preoccupied with Jenny that she hadn't even noticed the small, frail man in the room directly across from Jenny's. Somehow, during her ruminations, she must have drifted into the middle of the hallway, for now she stood looking at Jenny's still body from several feet away. She turned to address the man. Although not much more than twenty-five or twenty-six, his emaciated body was covered with the thin skin of a person three times his size and the huge brown spots that usually accompanied old age. She stared at him mutely for a moment, stunned by what she saw.

"You have been standing half in and half out of my room for almost fifteen minutes," the man said in a strong, shrill voice. "For Christ's sake! Just come in already! Worrying is not going to make her wake up sooner—she's in coma."

His eyes twinkled with the mischievousness of youth. His wide smile revealed a set of dazzlingly white teeth and infectious smile. He slapped the bed to invite her to join him on the sheets.

"I don't know," she said, hesitating at the intimate gesture.

"Please!" he laughed heartily. "This is San Francisco! People always go to bed with people we don't know!" Then, he squinted at her suspiciously. "Unless you're like, from Iowa or somewhere?"

Jeannette looked at him before breaking into a laugh.

"I can tell these things. Gilbert," he said, extending his hand. "Gilbert Sullivan—no shit. So please, no jokes. I've heard them all anyway. My mom was a crazy ass opera fan."

Jeannette slithered into the barren room. There were no cards, no flowers, and no gifts decorating the room, merely the sterile white sheets of the bed and the pale blue privacy curtain. Her eyes rested on the gaunt man who smiled brightly at her. His smile touched her with its sincerity, and she felt herself grinning back at him. His white teeth seemed to glow in the muted artificial fluorescents, and she felt an odd tug of sympathy for this stranger who retained a strong aura of pride despite his illness. She felt like Gilbert looked: beaten, tired, and fucked up.

"And you are?" Again he let the question linger.

"Jeannette," she muttered.

"Do you have a last name, sweetie, or is it like Cher, Madonna and Di?" he asked, crossing his arms over his chest.

"Fisher. Jeannette Fisher." She sat down on the bed and he gripped her hand with a grip tighter than she thought possible.

"She'll be okay, you know. I heard the nurses talk about her. Nothing that won't heal eventually. A few weeks' rest and she'll be good as new. I promise," he said, crossing his heart with his finger.

"She was beaten, has a concussion and a broken nose," Jeannette said with a tough of anger.

"Posh!" Gilbert said, rolling his eyes. "Honey, I've gotten worse than that during a beer bust at the Eagle!" He laughed a rich, deep guffaw that rolled over the room. But when Jeannette turned away, he squeezed her hand and continued. "She has her friends. That's a lot of love. One guy was here and literally sat in his bed for three weeks without a single visitor. Then he just died and someone came to put all his stuff into an orange bag."

Jeannette looked at him, eyes beginning to blur as a wave of fatigue overcame her. How long had she been without sleep? "That's a depressing story, Gilbert Sullivan."

"You're telling me! Orange clashes with EVERYTHING. It should be outlawed." He nodded to Jeannette and winked. "You look like you need rest. Here," he said, handing her one of his pillows, "sleep."

"Why do you do that?" she asked, unmoving.

"Sleep?" he questioned.

"No," Jeannette sighed, "talk to me like we're intimately involved?"

"I am?" Gilbert looked at her. "Wow. Really? Maybe it's some cosmic telepathy!"

"You have nice eyes," she continued, feeling herself grow lightheaded as fatigue struggled to gain a foothold over her.

"Window to the soul, they say," Gilbert said softly, stroking her arm.

"You shouldn't act like everyone is a nice person," she said. "You could get into trouble."

Gilbert chuckled. "These old bones are so brittle, I'm afraid of rupturing my pelvis when I fart. What more trouble could I get into?"

Jeannette looked away, glancing out the window into the clear azure sky. The puffy white clouds that floated over the bay seemed so close.

"She's my girlfriend," Jeannette said, nodding in Jenny's direction.

"I know," Gilbert whispered.

"That man here earlier? That goofy looking guy? That's her husband," Jeannette said, not moving her eyes from Jenny.

"THAT, I didn't know." Gilbert whistled.

"He said he wouldn't stand between us," she spat sarcastically.

"Extraordinary guy," Gilbert agreed congenially.

"He's still in love with her."

"And you?" Gilbert asked, perking up.

"Me, too."

Gilbert patted her arm and sighed a chortle. "Oh, what complicated webs we weave. There's enough love to go around, honey. No need to be stingy about it," Gilbert said softly, his eyes boring into her.

She looked at him and said in a slow, even, commanding voice, "I want her."

Gilbert laughed heartily. "You have her. Isn't that enough?"

Jeannette kicked off her shoes. What the hell was she doing? She was so tired she couldn't control her actions anymore; she was operating on automatic. "No. Yes. I don't know. Jenny's perfect. Can remember every word anyone says. It's obnoxious." She slid the length of the bed and came to rest her head in the crook of his arm. "Nathan said she 'harbored things.' Said one day she's gonna let down the defenses and her soul will open up and all her secrets will spill out."

"Wow!" Gilbert whistled. "That's fucking poetic for a straight boy. Does he have a brother?" Gilbert laughed.

But Jeannette didn't hear him. She breathed rhythmically now, her hands tucked under Gilbert, her head nuzzling his arm. He snuggled down into her, carefully rearranging the IV drip so it wouldn't interfere with her slumber. He, too, began to drift off, unusually earlier than his normal ten o'clock nap. Just before his eyes closed, he could have sworn he saw a woman enter the room across the hallway where Jeannette had been standing vigil moments before. He lost consciousness at that moment, a broad smile spreading across his face. He felt good for other people when they received visitors, especially beautiful people with fiery red hair.

*　*　*

Jenny looked up from inspecting her hand when she heard her name called. The harsh, intense light inside the stark white waiting room stung her eyes and she squinted. Where the hell was she, anyway?

"Jenny, dear, don't you hear me calling you?" the voice asked kindly. Jenny shaded her face with her hand, but after a moment surrendered to the fact that the light had no single source that could be blocked. She heard the sharp clicking of heels on tile and saw a silhouette of a woman stride towards her out of the light. Despite the fact that she couldn't see the woman's eyes, Jenny knew the woman's identity.

"Mrs. Hudson?" she asked cautiously.

"Well, dear, I declare!" Mrs. Hudson's ancient voice shuddered in surprise. "I am thrilled to death you remember me! Aren't you lovely?"

Jenny stared up at the petite woman in shock and confusion. What the hell was going on? "I'm sorry, Mrs. Hudson, but I thought you were dead."

"I suspected as much," she smiled at Jenny with a warm, withered face that maintained its youthful flush. Her long gray hair was pulled into a tight bun that sat atop her head in a mound of exquisitely arranged flower buds. Her wire-rimmed glasses perched on the end of her nose, giving them the appearance of clinging to her face for dear life. Jenny smiled at Mrs. Hudson. When she was a kid, the whole class had made bets on when the spectacles would fall off. Nobody won, of course, for Mrs. Hudson had

perfected the craft of snagging them at the last moment, saving them from a plummet to the floor by a hair's breath.

"I'm sorry for staring," Jenny began with a giggle, "but it's been a long time."

"I know, dear, I know. Time flies, doesn't it?" Mrs. Hudson sighed wearily with a slow shake of her head. "Yes, it does." The elderly woman stood silent for a moment, lost in thought. Then, with a curt nod, she locked eyes with Jenny and continued. "Since nobody else wanted this task, I am left to do the deed. I apologize I'm not more prepared," she said with a wink, "but I think we'll muddle through, eh?" Her dainty hand reached out and grasped Jenny's arm and gave it a quick squeeze. When she spoke, Mrs. Hudson's voice carried the gentle, yet firm timber Jenny remembered from her grade school years. "Come on, now, we must hurry. There's something I need to show you." She abruptly turned and strode off.

Jenny stood too quickly, causing her head to swoon as if she was buzzed. She couldn't remember feeling so woozy, especially before an audition. The audition! Jesus, she had forgotten all about the audition! Was she late? Maybe she should call the agency before they gave up on her. Why the hell was she hanging out here?

"Dear!" Mrs. Hudson called sharply to her. "Come along, now."

Jenny fought the urge to snap at the old lady, who had returned to her mysteriously quickly to grasp her elbow. She tried to pull her arm away, but the old woman's grip was extraordinarily strong. "The audition, Mrs. Hudson. I've got to get to the audition before—"

"Don't you fret, honey," Mrs. Hudson said, giving her a reassuring pat on the arm. "I'll take care of you."

As her words escaped her lips, Jenny felt a sense of elation. She suddenly felt like singing and breaking out in an impromptu dance number. Where was Dane when you needed him? Only he would appreciate an impromptu dance number. She smiled broadly. Mrs. Hudson would help her find the audition for sure! She was safe. There was no need to worry.

"Take my hand."

Jenny did and the teacher began walking at a breakneck pace through the huge white room.

As she walked, Jenny caught a whiff of the sweet nectarous perfume that surrounded the elderly woman. It took her back in time to when she was seven years old, attending Maplewood Elementary School. That year had been hard on her. She was the new kid in town, fresh from Iowa. The boys in class were cruel and vulgar, and every day, she could expect the taunts of 'lanky' and 'four eyes' to come hurling at her like knives. Once, in the middle of a math test, she felt a tap on her foot and looked down between her legs. On the floor lay a sheet of paper with a dead mouse on it, sliced from mouth to tail, guts exposed. Jenny screamed and ran from the room as a chorus of voices laughed uproariously.

She had locked herself into the toilet stall, choking on snot as sobs racked her body. Tears flowed down her face, soaking her threadbare dress. As if she didn't have enough to deal with from her crazy mother, now she had to endure the torture of strangers in a new place. She'd never survive—never. There was only one solution to this hell. She would run away. She would run far away from here, from the mean boys, from her insane mother…

From the chaos of her mind, hands emerged, grabbed her shoulders and pulled her into a strong embrace. The strong, soft arms held her tenderly and she felt a gentle rocking motion. When she looked up, she saw Mrs. Hudson's face full of compassion and heard her soft, soothing voice in her ear. As she tucked her tiny head into the woman's shoulder, she could smell her flowerey perfume and knew, somehow, that everything would be alright. At that moment, Jenny realized she loved this teacher more than anyone in the world and wanted to make her proud. Ever since that day in the girl's bathroom, Jenny had equated the scent of flowers with peace and safety.

How Mrs. Hudson got into that locked stall so many years ago, she never knew. But Jenny did know the woman was well over seventy years old when Jenny had graduated from high school. By now, the woman should be dead of old age. How was it possible Mrs. Hudson still lived? With a shrug, she cleared the depressing thoughts from her mind. What difference did it make? The woman was here now, and everything was going to be okay. Everything was always okay when Mrs. Hudson was around.

"Open your eyes, dear," Mrs. Hudson ordered gently. Jenny did as she was instructed and looked around. They stood in a huge stone temple filled with a glowing golden light. The tall, arched ceilings were decorated with colorful murals depicting images of biblical stories: Noah's flood, angels battling demons, the tree of life and other famous icons Jenny remembered from her days at Catholic school but couldn't recall their names. Between the two women stood a massive wooden podium, elaborately carved from a single block of wood. On top of the podium sat a thick, leather-bound book that glowed with a soft white light as if illuminated from beneath.

The cathedral looked vaguely familiar, yet she couldn't place it. "Mrs. Hudson, " Jenny began tentatively.

"No time, dear," Mrs. Hudson replied harshly. "Look."

Mrs. Hudson grasped Jenny's hand and turned towards the glowing tome. She redirected Jenny's gaze onto the book and, with her free hand, opened it. Suddenly, the book erupted in a blinding flash of white light. A piercing brilliance poured from the book's spine, flooding the ceiling of the temple. Jenny tried to look away, but found that despite its brightness, the light didn't sting her eyes at all. In fact, it felt warm and inviting, like the lure of a fireplace on a cold winter's night. She was overcome with an intense feeling of curiosity. Feeling the childlike thrill of exploration, she leaned closer to the pages. Her heart pounded as she anticipated what mysteries the book held.

The handwriting was tiny and thin, looking like the scribbling of someone quite elderly. Reading it was difficult, and Jenny had to squint to make out the words. The words began to shimmer and move of their own accord, rearranging themselves into black shapes, which slowly inched their way across the page, growing and changing into humanoid figures. Once they ceased moving, they lifted upwards, pulling themselves away from the pages until they stood atop the book, like miniature paper dolls come alive. Then the pages themselves came alive, separating from the book and folding back into themselves until they surrounded the black shadow figures, forming walls, furniture, and the décor of a lavish home. Soon, Jenny stood looking down onto a tiny set, like a giant director watching her minuscule cast on the stage from the catwalk above.

Below her, on the tiny stage atop the podium, two young women dashed frantically around the miniature room. Both were sporting brightly colored hoop skirts, corsets, and shawls. If she remembered her theater history class correctly, Jenny judged the scene to be taking place in the mid-1800s. One of the women, a slight girl with long chestnut hair, yielded a knife and stalked the second in a slow, menacing walk. The second miniature woman, a hefty young lady whose green hoop skirt looked shabby and threadbare, sported mousy brown hair that was tied back in a ponytail by a huge, hideous matching green bow.

Fascinated by the tiny drama, Jenny leaned over, bringing her face closer to the action. As if on cue, the tiny woman yielding the knife looked up towards her in a dramatic cry to heaven. How cute she was! Like a tiny china doll that needed to be swept up and kept safely tucked away on a shelf. Why was that face so familiar? In a flood of recognition, Jenny's blood froze as she leapt away from the book. Mrs. Hudson smiled gingerly back at her over the rims of the glasses and placed her hand on the back of Jenny's head, pushing it back down towards the pages of the book.

Jenny's face peered down at herself in the form of the woman with the knife. Hers was the face full of vengeful fury that stalked the second tiny figure in the green dress. The other woman, the hefty one, struck her as familiar as well, although the tiny figure kept her face turned away from Jenny. She was frantically searching for an escape from the knife-wielding woman chasing her. The tiny Jenny faked a dodge to the right, sending the pudgy one spinning directly into her arms. With a frenzied jab of her arm, the little Jenny brought the knife down with a quick thrust. But the pudgy girl sensed the move and spun around, breaking out of Jenny's grasp. In doing so, the second tiny figure turned her face upwards towards Jenny and Mrs. Hudson.

It was the face of the crazy woman from the bathroom.

Jenny gasped in horror. She yanked her hand out of Mrs. Hudson's grasp and turned towards the old woman, her eyes begging for an explanation. "I've seen HER! She's the one who—"

Mrs. Hudson smiled, pulled Jenny into a tight embrace and pointed to the book. "Keep watching, my dear," she crooned.

Jenny shook her head, refusing to face the minuscule drama unfolding beneath her. With a resigned sigh, Mrs. Hudson forced Jenny to face the dais and nodded towards the white light. Jenny pushed herself deeper into Mrs. Hudson's arms and reluctantly turned to the Book.

Although she could hear mumbling, Jenny found it impossible to comprehend the exact words the two miniature figures were saying. The stocky girl's cadence indicated that she was repeating a name—Lee? But her beseeching plea fell on deaf ears. The knife wielder, little Jenny, brought the knife up over her head and ran towards the pudgy one once more. The woman in green turned away from the knife and broke for the door. In a flash, tiny Jenny had caught up with her adversary and, as big Jenny stared down, horrified, plunged the knife deep into the woman in green. Blood poured from the wound. The pudgy girl's mouth opened in a cry of terror and pain, but no sound emerged. Again and again, little Jenny's knife disappeared into the green dress. More and more of the girl's blood soaked the dress, darkening it with crimson. Finally, tiny Jenny stopped stabbing the one in green and let the body fall at her feet into a lump on the carpet. A moment passed and tiny Jenny slowly moved away from the dead body and towards the room's door, where she pulled back the handle and motioned for an unseen person to enter.

A miniature Jake strolled through the door and into the arms of the tiny knife-wielding murderess. He swooped her up and kissed her passionately, his arms reaching around her and pulling her in a tight embrace. When the kiss ended, he looked into little Jenny's face and smiled triumphantly. Then, hand in hand, the two of them walked towards the corpse, now almost unrecognizable from the blood.

Jenny pulled herself away from the book, screaming in despair and confusion. "No!" she sobbed. "What the hell?"

"Dear," Mrs. Hudson said with a cool, calm voice, "you must know." Then her voice changed. "LOOK AT ME! JENNY!"

Jenny jumped slightly at the fierce, harsh command, but when she looked into the familiar hazel eyes, she went limp, stopped struggling and began to faint. In a flash, Mrs. Hudson grabbed her and gently laid her down upon the glowing floor of the temple. The light emerging for the book behind the old woman formed a halo behind her head, giving Mrs. Hudson the look of an angel. Jenny started to shake with sobs and Mrs. Hudson knelt on the floor next to her, holding her as tightly as she did in the girl's bathroom so many years ago at Maplewood Elementary School.

After a pause, Mrs. Hudson spoke with a cold, expressionless voice. "Nothing is perfect, dear, as much as we would like it to be. Nothing is without its own unique problems. Things happen, dear. Bad things. Terrible things. Things that aren't fair. No place is safe from accidents." She squeezed Jenny tightly, then turned to her and said harshly. "You must tell Dane what you've seen here."

"Dane? What does Dane have to do with it?" Jenny asked, confused.

"Everything."

"I don't understand," Jenny began.

"You don't have to," Mrs. Hudson interrupted in loving tone. "It's not your time to understand. Just be the messenger."

*   *   *

Cold engulfed her and Jenny shivered as the frigid air rushed across her naked arms. She threw her eyelids open and looked around in panic. Where was she? The room was pitch black. Out of the darkness, she saw a blinking green dot in the distance, but it held no clues. The dream with Mrs. Hudson came rushing back to her. She sat up, pain shooting into her brain. Mrs. Hudson? She was just here! In a flash, her eyes adjusted to the sudden change of light and the room around her seemed to brighten and come into focus. A hospital room. She was in a hospital room. The green blinking light was nothing more than one of the several monitors standing around her bed.

Jenny searched for the phone on the table next to her, but didn't immediately see it. Her left arm lay immobilized under an IV needle, so she used her right to lean uncomfortably across the bed to the nightstand. Suddenly, a small giggle erupted from dark and Jenny turned towards the noise.

Lily stood next to her bed, her face consumed by a demented smile. The large knife in her hand reflected the green glow coming from the monitoring machines. Before Jenny could scream, Lily lifted the knife high over her head and brought it down with tremendous force.

SATURDAY, JULY 8

7:45 AM

MRS. JEREMY WASN'T surprised when she looked at the clock and read 7:45 a.m. in large red numbers because she had just checked the time five minutes ago. She had been wide awake throughout the night drinking tea and pissing like a race horse.

She glanced down at the charts, graphs, and books scattered across the living room floor and shook her head in disbelief. She hadn't been able to sleep after Dane left, although she tried, but after an hour of tossing and turning, she admitted defeat and accepted that her body didn't want the rest. She doddered around the house picking up stray clothes off the floor, wishing to God Marshall was still alive and could offer his advice. They's always done great work together. But when the rug became visible again and the hamper overflowed with dirty laundry, she decided to get to work on Dane's problem before she gave in to her better judgment and did the laundry.First, she dug through the stack of papers in the den and found the one Jake had given to her when he and Dane had bought the brownstone. On it, Jake had scrawled both his and Dane's birthdays for her to embroider them onto a throw pillow for a housewarming gift. That was one of the few projects she had finished that month and she couldn't be prouder of the thing—a yellow pillow with pink triangles around the edges and two male symbols in the center. The names JAKE LUCAS and a birth date stitched into one corner and DANE BALDWIN and a birth date stitched into the opposite one.Then, she scrambled around the apartment pulling old manuscripts off the shelves. She wasn't sure which books she was searching for, but she trusted her instinct would alert her when she found it. Armed with her reference books and dates, she set to work plotting Dane's chart. She became so absorbed in the work that it was an hour and a half before she noticed the time again.

After completing the charts for the boys, she wished to hell she'd done it sooner. How had these two gotten together in the first place? Jake, an Aries and Dane, a Pisces, had so many contradicting planets the star chart looked like a child had spackled it with paint. Oh, many people supported an Aries/Pisces relationship, but she'd always felt it was too volatile. Dane, the Pisces, had an unusually heavy Scorpio influence, indicating a strong pull towards supernatural and spiritual endeavors. Mrs. Jeremy's gut told her it was no accident Dane had caught sight of another person's out-of-body-experience (for that's surely what it was, right Marshall?) that night in the hospital.Chuckling at the unbelievability of it all, she waddled to the stove and put on another pot of tea. In a few hours, Dane would be stumbling back into the apartment, she was sure of it, so she may as well settle in for a nice, lazy Saturday and wait for the boy to show up. She flipped on the TV and sat down in her favorite old chair while she waited for the water to boil. As soon as the TV flickered to life, the words MURDER DOWNTOWN spilled across the screen. Mrs. Jeremy leaned forward anxiously as the news anchor flipped to a slide of the deceased. Mrs. Jeremy sighed. Such a handsome man! Why couldn't the assholes kill the ugly men, for crying out loud? God knows there are enough of them around! She looked closer at the picture on her TV screen and felt as if she knew this guy...the man's eyes looked so familiar. She fumbled with the volume button so she could hear the story, but her stubby fingers wouldn't move over the controls fast enough. By the time the sound blared loudly across the apartment, the story was over and the newscasters had changed reports.

The tea kettle whistled and she got to her feet with a loud grunt. She toddled into the kitchen thinking about the last forty-eight hours: Dane's journey, his chart, dreams of the accident and the woman with the red hair. She stood pouring water over her Celestial Seasonings mint tea when her memory kicked in and she recalled whose picture it was she had just seen on TV. That was Ralph S.

Thompson, Jr! Of course she knew him! Everyone in San Francisco knew that man! She stopped and pondered the news report. Dead. And in a love nest, too. She didn't need to hear the rest of the TV report to know what good ol' Ralph was doing in that love nest. Not only did he have more money than God, but more pussy, too—being old didn't stop him from banging every woman he could get his hands on. But seriously, how could such a high profile man allow himself to be seen in a downtown hotel with woman other than his wife?Seen in a hotel with an unknown red-headed woman? She wondered if it happened to be the same hotel Kevin worked in with his boy-toy of the week. What was his name? Sam? Seth? It was a long shot, but didn't the TV say MURDER DOWNTOWN? And didn't Dane mention that Kevin saw a redheaded woman in a green dress? Long shot or not, she needed to ask the questions because now, more than ever, she needed some answers. She grabbed the phone and dialed.

*   *   *

"Yes, Mrs. Jeremy, the police HAVE asked me that question about a million times. I ONLY KNOW THE NAMES OF REGISTERED GUESTS!" Kevin answered the old bat forcefully. Good Lord! Didn't this woman ever accept "no" as an answer? He loved the old broad, but enough was enough."

"This is important, Kevin," she retorted sharply.

"I know it is. Hold on," he covered the phone and looked at Sean, who was standing at the foot of the bed.

"Aren't we going to shower?" Sean asked, a mischievous smile spreading across his face.

Oh! To be twenty-one again! Kevin thought. He nodded to the blond and covered the receiver with his hand. "I am NOT going to work smelling like rubbers and jism. Make me some coffee and wait in the shower. Naked." The boy grinned and trotted off down the hallway. He turned back to the phone. "What was I saying?"

"Kevin! You listen to me, you screaming black dyke you."

"That would be QUEEN, Mrs. Jeremy, and what the hell do you want from me?" he screamed. "I already told Jake that after that woman left–"

"Which woman?" she demanded.

"The woman the police are looking for. Hello?! Don't you watch TV? The police are looking for a red-haired woman last seen with that dead guy."

"Ralph Thompson, Jr."

"Whatever," Kevin sighed, bored with the conversation. "Yet ANOTHER straight white guy." The silence which greeted him was deafening. "Mrs. Jeremy? Honey? You didn't keel over with a heart attack, did you, honey?"

"No, you sarcastic little shit, I did NOT have a heart attack. Listen, I need her name."

"Now I KNOW you are NOT talking to me like that!" But before Kevin could continue, Mrs. Jeremy launched an explosive tirade of profanity. Kevin didn't bother to listen. He pulled the receiver from his ear and watched as naked Sean leaned into the doorframe and held out a steaming mug of coffee.

"You hear me, Kevin?" the woman screamed.

But she spoke in vain. Kevin heard nothing more of her tirade as he hung up and whipped the sheet from his body. "Come over here, boy! Daddy says you've been bad."

* * *

"I don't care what those silly researchers say with all their research and polls! When there is a full moon, all the nuts come out." The haughty voice on the other end of the phone said emphatically.

Mrs. Jeremy sighed. She'd known Penny for a lifetime and had to admit that she was one of the best registrars the hospital employed. Penny had worked at the hospital for years—some joked that she was on duty during the quake of 1906—and possessed an uncanny knack for remembering everything from patients' names to their addresses and ailments. If anyone could locate the identity of the mysterious red-haired woman whom Dane had seen astral traveling one year ago, it would be Penny. "Then get me a list of all the people admitted into the hospital that night."

"Are you kidding me?" Penny said exasperated. Have you even HEARD of the HIPAA regulations? That, my dear, is ABSOLUTELY confidential information."

"Screw the HIPAA regulations," Mrs. Jeremy shot back. Why the hell do people blindly follow stupid rules, anyway? What was she going to do with the names? Stalk them?

"Screw you," Penny shot back venomously.

"How about if I haul my butt down there and copy the names down myself?" Mrs. Jeremy tried to sound calm, but acting had never been her forte. Finally, she sighed in resignation and said, "You don't have to do anything but leave the computer signed in. You don't even have to be around."

Penny explained with the curt, short voice of a frustrated educator, "Dear, I'd love to help you, but I can't."

"Julio comes in about two o'clock to start his shift in the laundry, doesn't he?" Mrs. Jeremy asked, getting desperate.

"What does that have to do with anything?" Penny snapped angrily.

"He loves Butterfingers. I'll bring him a Butterfinger and he'll stand lookout. Just don't sign off when you take your lunch at two. Nobody's the wiser." She tried to sound smooth.

"Is this one of your hocus-pocus projects again?" Penny asked suspiciously. "If it is, I want NOTHING, and I mean NOTHING, to do with it."

"Penny, dear," Mrs. Jeremy said, running out of patience, "Just this once, pull the stick out of your ass." With a resounding "click," the phone went dead. Mrs. Jeremy looked at the receiver a moment before slamming it back into the cradle. Fine. If the uptight bitch won't help her with her research, then she'll do it herself. God-fucking-on-the-highest-damn, does she have to do everything herself? She could easily don her volunteer badge and pretend she was working a legitimate shift, but how would she get into the computer system? Maybe the paper trail still existed. How long did they keep hard copies? Where were they stored? In the archives? She had no idea, but sitting on her fat ass in this apartment wasn't getting the job done, so she'd better move if she meant to do anything worthwhile.

She heaved herself out of her easy chair and headed to the bedroom. After a few moments, she stopped and retraced her route back to the phone and hit the code for Dane on speed dial. Where was he, anyway? She was sure the boy would be over here by now, pummeling her with questions about the material she had sent home with him. Surely he had read it, hadn't he? At least some of it? Any of it? She stared at the receiver and ran the possibility through her mind that Dane had read the material and understood it so well he didn't need her explanation. She chuckled to herself. No way. This was Dane! He didn't go to the bathroom without another opinion! She waiting impatiently as the phone began to ring. She had no idea who this astral traveling woman was, nor how she was connected to Dane, but it didn't feel like a good connection. It would be better for both the boys if they stuck together until this puzzle could be sorted out. If Jake was planning on leaving for the East Coast in the near future, it was best if Dane could convince him to delay the trip as long as possible. At least as long as it took to track down the red-haired woman. She sighed as Dane's phone continued to ring.

*   *   *

"Phone's ringing!" Jake yelled from the bathroom.

"Let the machine get it!" Dane yelled back from under the pillow. He quickly turned down the volume on the machine so the caller's message wouldn't interrupt his conversation with Jake, which, Dane felt sure, would not be a pleasant one. He turned onto his stomach and buried his head deeper into the warm sheets. He'd spent the remainder of last night in a restless fit and it had left him exhausted and more confused than when he and Jake had crawled into bed after returning from the hospital at 3:30 that morning.

Jake emerged from the bathroom looking refreshed; his skin a bright pink and hair still damp. Jake glanced quickly at Dane and then, just as quickly, away again. Dane lay in bed watching Jake's skin palpitate as the tight muscles beneath it moved. Dane had always admired Jake's body, his well-proportioned healthy skin, just the right amount of hair and a perfect dick. But this morning all he wanted was for Jake to finish his packing and leave.

Jake reached into the dresser and threw some clothes into his duffle bag: a couple pairs of jeans, a couple shirts, jockey shorts and socks. Four pairs of underclothes. So, Dane deduced, he's going today. And it seemed that he would be gone for more than a weekend. Good. Maybe by the time he returned, they would both feel more clear-headed and ready to discuss the real issue at hand— their relationship. Dane felt relieved. It would be good to be alone for a while. Why hadn't he thought about the separation in this way before? It wasn't a bad thing at all; Jake leaving was going to be great for them both.

"I'll call you when I get there," Jake said abruptly, stepping into a pair of jeans.

"Okay," Dane muttered.

"I'll have Maggie fax me the papers I need and Craig–"

"The intern?" Dane interrupted.

"Craig can handle the rest via phone and email. I'll tell them I'm taking emergency leave, so I'd appreciate it if you didn't say anything to anyone about where I've been."

"Even Maggie?" Dane asked, stunned. Jake was as close to Maggie as he was to Jenny. Of all the people in the world, he thought surely Maggie would be in on Jake's plan for this little cross country jaunt.

"Even Maggie. I'll fill her in on the details when I return." Dane watched as Jake transferred some coins, his cologne, and his cheap Timex from the dresser into the duffle bag. Ace stalked into the room and headed directly for Jake. He nudged his master and whined. "It's okay, boy. Just for a few days. Daddy's got some work to do." Jake knelt down and took the dog's head in his hands. "Daddy Dane's going to take care of you." He hugged the dog firmly and returned to his packing.

"He knows something's up," Dane mused to himself, surprised to hear himself speaking out loud.

Jake nodded. "He wouldn't leave me alone all morning. He followed me into the shower." Jake picked up his briefcase and duffle bag and walked out of the bedroom.

"Wait," Dane said. "I'll grab Ace and walk you to the bus stop." Dane leapt out of bed and into his 501s. He pulled on his sweatshirt and grabbed his backpack.

"Ready?" Jake asked, hefting the duffle bag onto his shoulder.

"Yeah, I guess," Dane said, shouldering the backpack of books. Neither one moved. It was if some invisible gauntlet had been thrown, each daring the other to make the first move towards an amiable resolution. After a moment of total silence, Dane felt the tension within him build to a crescendo and he put the leash on Ace, wishing to hell Jake would reach out to hug or touch him, or make any gesture to signal to Dane that he, too was hurting. He felt obliged to be the one to make the first move, but not knowing whether it was from affection or habit paralyzed him. After this long with someone, you should want to hug someone farewell, right? He looked up and realized Jake was gone. He quickly snatched up his backpack and heaved the load onto his right shoulder, cursing Mrs. Jeremy and her heavy books.

On the front steps, Dane greeted the early morning mist with a shiver. At the bottom of the steep, brick stairs, Jake stood handing his duffle bag to the driver, who loaded it into the trunk. "How did you get a cab that fast?" he asked, hurrying down onto the sidewalk.

"Called one about an hour ago. I didn't feel like taking the train to the airport."

The driver slammed the trunk and strode to the driver's seat. Jake stood beside the taxi's rear door avoiding Dane's eyes. Neither said anything for a moment; they merely stood mutely and gazed at each other's outlines.

Finally, Jake ceased trying to dodge Dane's eyes and climbed into the back of the cab. "I'll call you."

"Yeah," Dane said, resigned.

"Dane," Jake said, looking up at him from inside the cab, "sometimes things don't work out for the best."

"No, I guess they don't." Dane said.

"You'll explain it to Jenny, I take it?"

He opened his mouth to say something, but changed his mind before any words came out. He simply closed his mouth, grinned sheepishly at Dane and slammed the door of the cab. Dane watched as Jake leaned in towards the driver and spoke a few words to the man. The cabbie nodded obediently. Dane stepped back onto the curb as the car pulled into the street and disappeared into the midday traffic. He glanced around him and noticed that not a single person occupied the street. He stood alone on one of the busiest streets of San Francisco.

Suddenly, he felt his heart race and his pulse quicken. He needed to be away from the condo. The last thing he wanted to do was return to the empty flat and listen to the sound of his own voice as he made the bed, which would be ripe with Jake's scent. He couldn't take that kind of remembrance, at least not yet. He needed to think of something else besides another failed relationship; needed to be a part of something other than the hollowness of an empty flat.

A cappuccino should do the trick. Like Jenny always said, there's nothing that a great cup of coffee can't cure. If ever there was a time to test the theory, now was that time. There's a new place on Ashbury he'd been meaning to try but had never gotten around to hit. It was a hike, but the morning mist was thinning and it was shaping up to be a beautiful day; besides, the exercise couldn't hurt. And he'll be able to grab a latte for Jenny. Hospital coffee always sucked.

*   *   *

Victoria Lemark awoke covered in sweat. She sat up in bed and scanned the room, trying desperately to remember where she was. She breathed deeply, forcing herself to remain calm. She had blacked out again, hadn't she? After every dark episode, she awoke with a throbbing headache, feeling all the world as if she'd been the victim of a violent beating. Her head pounded, and her body felt leaden and heavy. As the world swam into focus, she began to assess her surroundings: she was in a hotel room, that, judging by the thin sheets on the bed, the worn linoleum floor, and broken dresser, was a cheap flop house. Bright sunlight struggled into the room through threadbare curtains, casting a macabre pattern of muted white onto the floor. Victoria grabbed the corner of the sheet and wiped the sweat from her face. Her whole body was drenched in perspiration, and she needed a shower.

She swung her legs onto the floor, savoring the cool air on her naked body. Her muscles ached and her joints screamed for attention. Would this contemptible place have a bathtub? If so, would she risk catching a disease from it? She plodded across the floor, feeling the cold tile numbing the soles of her feet. What had she done this time?

She had gone to a hospital as Lily, she recalled that fact clearly. She remembered slinking into the alley and sneaking up the fire escape, her insides burning with anger, seething for revenge. She remembered prying open the window, thick with years of grime and neglect, then pacing on the landing of a locked stairwell, waiting for someone to come through the door from the hospital's hallway and, when they finally did, she remembered her sigh of relief. Yes! The memories were coming back to her now, filling her mind's eye with the events of last night. As the adrenaline surged through her, Victoria stopped in the middle of the floor, allowing the sensations to wash over her. Her body was nothing more than a puppet to be played by a stranger, helpless. Yet despite this psychic slavery, she could not deny she felt jubilant euphoria when Lily had taken control and plunged the knife into the sleeping girl, severing the head, and watched the blood gush onto the sheets. After all this time planning, plotting and almost losing her chance in the office building downtown, she had accomplished what she had set out to do. Her revenge was complete.

She closed her eyes and breathed deeply for three breaths. Over the past year, she had discovered this technique brought the obscure, elusive visions from out of the shadows into the realm of the visceral. Last night in her nocturnal journey, she'd gone back to the Book and read once more the words written on the pages of light. As with her previous visits to the temple, the Book brought the written words to life as she read them. The Book hypnotized her, rendering her helpless as the words lifted from the pages to swirl and flow in the stark light, morphing into three dimensional figures who staged a performance radiating a near tangible level of pathos teeming with color, energy, and beauty.

From the first time she saw this miracle, she had instinctively known it was her job to document these visions with extreme preciseness. Any mistake in the translation could prove lethal. If she weren't careful, it was possible that she would kill an innocent, although if it happened, then so be it. Luckily for her, the Book showed her which soul to take next.

When Victoria felt last night's vision firmly recreated in her mind's eye, she picked up her notebook and pen and walked to the bathroom. She stumbled on the suitcase lying open near the door and stepped over the array of weapons, which lay comically about the floor looking like props in a nasty murder mystery. The green dress, spotted with blood lay next to the knife—the murder weapon that had cleanly and neatly sliced off Jenny's head lay next to the mother-of-pearl knife she'd used on Ralph S. Thompson, Jr.

She lurched to the bathroom and sat heavily on the toilet. Her foot grazed something soft and she yanked it back with a start. It was only the hem of the dress hanging from the bathroom door.

I won't do this, Lily. Stop it. I'm not a murderer.

No, my dear, the voice responded, *you are not. You are the victim. Which is exactly why you need me.*

With that, Victoria felt the familiar punch of Lily's thoughts push past the front of her mind, grinding into her, feeling like an ice pick driven into hard snow.

When Lily Dayton had once again taken control of the body, opened the notebook, uncapped the pen and began to write.

The punishment of the last of the sinners is at hand. After completing my mission at the hospital, I returned to the temple, seeking guidance. This time, the ink waiting for me glowed red, as was the fountain pen I found lying next to the inkwell. I picked up the ink and the pen, and strode into the temple. Never before had I seen the golden temple shimmering with such power.

The Book sat on its podium, glowing more brightly than ever before, and, like the last visit, the pages were virgin. I set down my deeds:

Jennifer Ricks, known previously as Bethany Dayton: for her murderous act committed against Lily Dayton, AD 1795. The slaying of Jennifer Ricks' current incarnation was terminated.

Then I signed my name as I was then: Lily Dayton. I turned to leave, but the Book did not automatically close as I am accustomed to it doing. Last night, it spoke to me. It quaked and quivered upon the massive podium and, as I watched, the pages flipped of their own accord. Back they traveled in time, settling onto a page dated AD. 1795. Then the pages stopped. I looked into the book and there I saw written:

FATHER BASIL–GRETCHEN THE GYPSY–SONJA JEREMY.

This is the entity who had impeded my progress previously and the Book has warned me the entity will try once more. I will find this SONJA

JEREMY and ensure she cannot stop me from completing my quest. This woman, whoever she may be, will not stop me from the final revenge.

Lily closed the notebook, flushed the toilet and stepped into the shower. She languished under the water, soaking her aching muscles with the pounding of the stream. The cuts along her face and arms stung from the pressure of the stream, but she forced herself to stand perfectly still, allowing the clean water to wash the dirt from the abrasions. Her body had taken an unusual beating yesterday when she confronted Bethany in the restroom; she was unprepared for the resistance and was now paying the price for her shortsightedness. Today she would take no chances when she ventured from the dingy hotel. The hospital was sure to have found Jenny's decapitated head by now, and she had done nothing to cover her tracks.

She dried herself by using two of the thin towels and walked out of the bathroom. Then she withdrew the telephone book from the dilapidated bedside stand. She leaned against the headboard of the bed and folded the pillows behind her, providing her throbbing back muscles with added support, and placed the heavy book on her lap clicked on the TV. She flipped the phone book open to "J" and scanned the names, looking for a "SONJA" or merely an "S." But her search was interrupted by a late-breaking news broadcast. She looked to the screen just in time to see an artist's rendering of her own face. She scrutinized the sketch and grimaced in disgust. Her face was hideously ill-proportioned. She was not that fat! Who were these "witnesses" who'd seen her at the scene?

She sighed. No matter. She had known even before she began her quest that the authorities would track her down and apprehend her one day, but Lily was not concerned about that inevitability. The only thing she needed to be concerned with was finding soul number three before Father Basil, or rather Sonja Jeremy, found her. She took three deep breaths and felt much better about her circumstances. Humming to herself, she continued scanning the phone book. She stopped humming and smiled widely when she found the name she'd been looking for. Father Basil/Gretchen the Gypsy/Sonja Jeremy would pay. Yes, indeed she would. Pay dearly.

She copied down the address for Sonja Jeremy and put the phone book back into the worn table. Then, she hit the OFF button on the remote and returned to the bathroom, where she removed an old pair of scissors from her purse. She held her flaming red hair taut and began cropping her hair close to the scalp. After a few clips, she stood back to admire her work—not too bad. The close-cropped style was what she had hoped to achieve. It actually looked more like a hatchet job, but there was no controlling that. No, she would have to make do the best she could with what she had. For just as the news held no interest to her, neither did her desire to look like a woman. April and Lily were officially as dead as Victoria Lemark.

In her vision, the Book had told her she would never be a woman again. Her gender was to become male, and her name from now until her life ended would be Christian O'Keefe.

*   *   *

The walls are breaking down; the veil is lifting.

Dane shivered as a mysterious chill passed down his arms. He closed the book and looked up at the foot traffic on Ashbury, wondering how many people believed this kind of shit. He sipped the cappuccino, not really tasting the sweet liquid. Walls breaking down. Could truth be that simple, or was it just simple minds creating clichés?

He reached for his cell phone to check the time only to discover he didn't have it. Must have left it at the condo this morning. Great. How did people survive before iPhones? The Starbuck's clock read just after 10 o'clock. He still had a few hours before heading over to the hospital. Best to leave Nathan, Jenny and Jeannette to hash out whatever issues they had before popping onto the scene. He didn't need any more drama than he already had.

After watching Jake step into that cab and exit his life, maybe forever, he brought Ace to the coffee shop and sifted through the titles Mrs. Jeremy had forced upon him last night. Two hours later, he remained in the same wicker chair, downing his fourth cappuccino and staring at the array of pedestrians while Ace savored the attention from the tourists. Dane wasn't stupid; he understood what the books were saying, but the theories were a little far-fetched.

He didn't grasp all the nuances of the terms (soul retrieval, guides) or the fantastical concepts (karma, Akashic records), but was able to follow the gestalt of the message Mrs. Jeremy wanted him to glean from the massive amount of literature. The book that solidified all these outlandish ideas into a comprehensible manner was the thin, worn spiral notebook. It was Mrs. Jeremy's private journal, written in her flowing, yet somewhat jerky handwriting. In it, she had put down definitions of words, theories and hypotheses, along with practical applications of the more complex theories of psychic phenomena. From the look of it, the old woman was planning to write a self-help manual that was a combination of a Reader's Digest condensed novel and a spiritual treatise on metaphysical studies.

Dane looked down for the hundredth time at the oversized volume that lay in his lap and recalled last night's hypnotic journey in Mrs. Jeremy's living room. According to the material he'd just read, he had relived an astral projection called the "after life journey." Although parts of last night's vision were still murky, he definitely remembered the temple. But a temple is a place of worship. Worship what?

He closed the book and flipped through another, thicker book until he found the dog-eared page he wanted to re-read. He originally found it by accident when he spilled his second cappuccino and had let the book fall to the concrete rather than be stained by the spreading puddle of caffeine. When he bent down to recover it, the word written all in caps seemed to leap off the page and scream out at him. Along the margin of the dog-eared pages was Mrs. Jeremy's handwriting:

ANGAKOK—an Inuit term for a shaman—usually of the "third sex" or homosexual, *who holds* the power to access the sacred mysteries of life; one *who can travel* to other planes of existence to retrieve information to save innocents from harm. (Ask Marshall about this—it could be a crock of shit.)

Was that what Mrs. Jeremy thought of him? That he was special? Did she really give that much credence to his dreams, his mysterious uneasiness and his strange visions? Did she believe he was having some kind of psychic episode, rather than just cracking under the stress caused by the accident? Perhaps Mrs. Jeremy honestly believed all of his dreams were real in some other dimension, or place or time; or at least a different place other than the small coffee house on Ashbury watching the leather queens and dorky tourists. What she obviously wanted him to believe was that he, Dane Baldwin, ex-assistant editor and part-time social clown, had been endowed with the ability to access another realm of existence.

Dane slammed the book closed and gathered his belongings off the table, shoving them into the pack. He hastily threw some bills down on the table as a tip and then prodded Ace away from a particularly exuberant five year old. He grabbed the leash and the two of them set off towards home. The cool air felt fresh and soothing on his skin after all the hours sitting in an uncomfortable chair at the coffee house. He shoved his free hand into his pants pocket and picked up his pace, forcing Ace to forgo sniffing random spots along the sidewalk and follow closely at his heels.

The veil is lifting. What did that mean, exactly? That one day, he was an average, ordinary guy and the next, because of a freak accident, he could travel to another plane of reality? Bullshit. Total bullshit.

Yes, but it wasn't just an accident was it? A voice inside his head taunted him. You died. You were dead for four minutes.

He thought about the implications of being dead. He had heard stories all of his life about people's weird experiences in returning from the dead; why would his story be any different? If the idea was so outlandish, why did the Inuit believe it? Besides, as the books had stated, many Native American tribes believed that those shamans were people of unusual powers and abilities.

He didn't want this kind of weirdness in his life! Wasn't his life packed full of weirdness already? He didn't want to see some red-haired woman in his mind. He didn't want these frightening dreams. Besides, if he did become some kind of shaman, some kind of Angakok, why couldn't he remember what he saw during these journeys? But even as he thought this, he saw with vivid clarity the glowing book resting on a wooden pedestal.

He hurried across Page Street towards the condo. He would drop off Ace and then catch the bus down to the Castro. There had to be some kind of revival flick or other distraction showing at the theater—anything to take his mind off this mess. Maybe one of the old standbys was playing, maybe a Mickey and Judy film. Didn't he remember a Marilyn Monroe weekend? He jogged up Stanyon, his heart pounding and hopeful.

The walls are breaking down.

*   *   *

Mrs. Jeremy slammed down the phone as soon as she heard Dane's voice on the answering machine for what felt like the thousandth time. She grunted into her hands as she cradled her aching head. Where was Dane, anyway? Or Jake, Jenny or Jeannette, for that matter? When she couldn't reach the boys at home or on their cell phones, she called Jake's office on a whim and sat through the eternal phone tree options before finally giving up in frustration. Didn't all those ambulance-chasing lawyers have answering services these days? What the hell was going on around here?

Julio appeared briefly, shot a nervous glance to Penny and looked back at her with a questioning look. She shrugged back to the Latino.

"Leaving so soon?" Penny asked sarcastically, looking at her watch.

"Don't screw with me I'm in a bad mood," Mrs. Jeremy snapped, not moving.

"You shouldn't have come." Penny said laughingly. "I told you about HIPAA."

"I don't give a damn about HIPAA," Mrs. Jeremy shot back, dismissing Julio with a gesture. The poor boy shook his head, gathered his cleaning supplies and walked back towards the elevators. "You should have—"

"Should have nothing," Penny snorted. "I'm not going to get fired for you, Sonja, I told you that. Besides, I'm in enough trouble with these capitalistic assholes today. I swear! Is every motherfucker in the world rude?"

"Yeah," Mrs. Jeremy sighed, her mind searching for other options to get her hands on the admission information.

Penny looked at her in mock surprise. "Agreeing with me on something, eh? Look, Sonja," she said turning away from the computer, "why don't you just go before I get sacked?"

"Fine," Mrs. Jeremy said. "Still going to Tuesday night poker?"

"Yep. My turn for coffee. What kind do you want? And no, I am NOT buying tea," Penny added with force.

"Beans or pre-ground?" Mrs. Jeremy asked after a moment's hesitation.

"Beans," Penny said, turning back to her terminal.

"Something vanilla. Vanilla almond?" she said without conviction.

Penny nodded. "Can do. Prepare yourself for losing your last nickel!" Mrs. Jeremy laughed at her and flipped Penny the bird. She grabbed her purse and turned toward the exit.

As she stood in front of the elevator doors, her eyes spied the directory on the wall. In large white letters, the words THIRD FLOOR–PATIENT ROOMS leaped out at her. Could it have only been a year since that hellish night? The memories of Dane lying flat on the gurney, tubes extending from his nose and mouth flooded back to her. The twisting pain of horror, grief, and despair threatened to overtake her once more when she heard voices behind her.

"Yeah," a man said loudly, "those Slam Dunks are horrible. I'd avoid 'em."

Mrs. Jeremy spun around. Did he just say Slam Dunk? She had never heard that term until a year ago, when she sat in a hot, cramped waiting room awaiting news of Dane's condition. Didn't the EMT who responded to the call use that word to describe Dane's accident? She spotted two men in uniforms headed towards the exit.

"Never been on one yet," the second voice responded, sounding weak and unsure.

"Lucky for you," the first replied, "they can be dicey—particularly if the biker isn't wearing a helmet. Have more of 'em here than in Nebraska."

"Excuse me!" she screamed after them.

They spun around to meet her as she waddled towards them.

Excuse me!" She didn't remember what that night's attending EMT looked like, only that one of them carried an insanely huge Slurpie from the 7-11. As neither of these men had a huge plastic cup, she wasn't sure if they were involved in Dane's care or not. Didn't the EMT last year mention being from Kansas, Nebraska or one of those useless states? It was worth a try.

"Yes?" the blue-eyed blond responded. He had the tired, haggard look of one who had worked too many hours on too little sleep.

"Last year, my friend was in a motorcycle accident down on Judah, near the train turn around," Mrs. Jeremy said quickly. "I think you helped him. You called his accident a Slam Dunk call."

The blond thought for a moment and shook his head. "I'm sorry, but we have so many of those," his voice faded out.

Mrs. Jeremy thought quickly. What could jog his memory? She looked him over and noticed his mismatched socks. Typical straight boy fashion violation, she thought. "He was brought in with an attractive woman. A redhead."

His eyes lit up. "Oh! Yeah!" he laughed and nodded as the pleasant memory came back to him. "I remember now. Beautiful woman. Red dress. You were here with a few other people waiting when your friend..." his voice petered out again.

"Died," Mrs. Jeremy answered for him. "Yeah. That's him. I'm Sonja Jeremy, by the way," she said, sticking out her hand.

"Rodney. This is my new partner, Bob." Rodney said, pumping her hand.

Mrs. Jeremy nodded to Bob, keeping her hand glued to Rodney's. "I want to thank you for your help," she said, trying to sound as awestruck as possible. Straight men love awestruck women. Sure enough, the man shrugged and nodded. "He's fine now. A bit fucked up and still out of work, but okay." The blond smiled broadly.

"Look," she began, not knowing where to go from here. "I'm wondering, by any chance...you don't remember anything about that woman, do you?"

The man stared at her with a stunned expression. Damn! He was probably as anal-retentive about that damn HIPAA thing as Penny! Shit. "I want to contact her and, you know, see how she's doing."

He nodded approvingly. "Very neighborly of you!" he said, eyes twinkling. "Good luck finding her, though. We got her info off of her driver's license, but couldn't verify her address, next of kin, nothing."

"Really?" Mrs. Jeremy said, heart racing with excitement. "Poor girl! Her family must have been worried sick!" She lowered her eyes and shook her head. Could she force herself to shed a tear?

"Yeah, guess so," Rodney agreed. "The license said she was from L.A. Figured she was here on vacation, but her landlord said she'd moved without giving notice and he hadn't heard from her since. Nobody in the city had ever heard of her."

"Sad, isn't it?" Mrs. Jeremy said with a nod. "You don't by chance remember her name, do you? I so want to contact the poor darling. It's been a year, you know." She brushed her eyes, as if the thought of it brought a tear. As least she could fake the sorrow. "I might be able to find her. I'm old, you know, and us old people have our ways!" She laughed a false giggle that Rodney seemed to think was cute.

"Sure do," he nodded. "Same as my ex-wife's: Victoria. Last name was same as my first job: Lemark's. It's a quick mart in my home town."

Mrs. Jeremy reached in her purse looking for a pen and paper. Victoria Lemark. Why did that name sound familiar? She jotted down the name. Victoria Lemark. What was it about that name? It danced at the edge of memory, taunting her, defying her to remember. She stared at the paper in her hands: VICTORIA LEMARK.

Suddenly, she remembered where she knew that name from. She had seen it before written in large, bold print. Her blood chilled and goosebumps broke out on her neck. Her chest tightened and she couldn't breathe.

"Rodney," she said, although her breath came out a raspy whisper. "What's your last name?"

"Thompson," he replied, adding quickly. "But don't hold that against me. I'm nothing like my dad."

"Ralph Thompson. Of Thompson construction."

"You've heard of us, then."

Mrs. Jeremy nodded.

"When you see that guy, tell him I'm sorry about what happened to his friend. You've heard, right? You work here, right?"

"I've been...occupied all morning. Haven't watched the news. What friend?"

Rodney exchanged a quick glance with Rob. "The...incident with the patient. The...attack"

Attack? Mrs. Jeremy's mind raced. The notes from home, Dane's recent journey into the Unknown. "Was it a young woman? The same young woman who was here in the hospital with him last year?"

Rodney nodded. "She was a cute woman, too. Nice. Friendly. Brought me donuts and even sent a thank you note after the accident. Jenny."

Mrs. Jeremy felt as if she had been struck in the stomach.

"Mrs. Jeremy?" Rodney's voice asked, panicked. "Mrs. Jeremy?"

The world spun and tipped as her legs collapsed from under her. Her purse dropped to the floor, sending its contents rolling across the white tile as the dark consumed her.

*   *   *

The taxi was almost to the airport when Jake slammed his cell phone closed with an angry grunt. Long ago he'd gotten in the habit of calling the airlines before arriving at the airport, a trick he'd learned from his ex-boss in Montana. Although most of the time, the call was a waste of time, the ritual proved to be a wise habit, as more than once he'd saved himself the trouble of arriving early through the harsh winter weather only to discover his flight had been delayed or cancelled. Luckily for him, today was one of those times when the call wasn't a waste of time.

He leaned over to the driver and shouted at him over the voices of the radio talk show. "Excuse me. The flight's been cancelled, so we can turn around."

The driver stared at him in the rearview mirror with an expression of total boredom. "Cancelled?" Jake nodded and shrugged. With a sigh and a roll of his eyes, the cabbie maneuvered into the right hand lane. "Where to then? Back home?"

Jake pondered this for a minute. Where would he go? He didn't want to go back to the condo. Dane would start talking about their relationship again, and he didn't want to continue that discussion. He had planned on using the time in Maine to figure out how to accurately convey his feelings to Dane and if he saw the man now, he was sure whatever tumbled out of his mouth would be misconstrued. Although Dane's habit of misconstruing Jake's comments was frustrating, at least it was predictable. Dane had many character flaws, but inconsistency was not one of them. But the airline's customer service representative didn't have any further information regarding the flight's rescheduled departure; more than likely it would be late this evening, giving him several hours to kill. He couldn't sit in a cab all day. And Dane really didn't need to know he was still in town, did he? What purpose would that serve? Regardless of his choice, he needed to do something quickly if he didn't want the cab fare to run higher than his salary. There was only one option, and that would be the office.

"No," he said to the driver. "Downtown, please. I guess I'm going back to work."

He seethed with irritation as the taxi turned back towards the city and its traffic congestion. Well, at least he could get some work done before leaving. He just hoped he didn't run into Dane between now and the time the flight left. He doubted he would, what were the odds of meeting anyone he knew downtown on a Saturday?

*   *   *

Nathan stared helplessly as Jeannette finished stuffing the rest of Jenny's belongings into the large pillowcase he had brought from home. He had almost picked up the overnight bag he bought for her on their honeymoon, but changed his mind when his eyes lit upon the matching pillowcases Jenny purchased in Spain. She had always loved those pillowcases. His fond memory of the trip made him turn away from Jeannette; he couldn't stand to see Jenny's things shoved into the bag as if their disappearance would erase her spirit. He blinked back tears as he stared out the window, watching the fog crawling across the city, pulling an ethereal blanket over the landscape. The sun, which shone brightly earlier in the day, had disappeared suddenly—sometime between the telephone call from the police and his arrival at the hospital.

He had known something was wrong the minute he heard the gruff voice on the telephone introducing himself as a police officer.

Only cops with bad news sounded this way. The timber of the voice too flat and emotionless to be a sick joke, yet hesitant enough to cause Jeremy to suspect it was one. The situation went from bad to worse when he asked the officer why he needed to report to the hospital immediately.

"There's been an incident," was the deadpan reply.

He immediately called Jeannette, who hung up on him before the entire story was out of his mouth. She stayed on the line only long enough to hear him say. "The police called me from the hospital." He'd immediately heard a soft click and found himself speaking to empty air. By the time either of them arrived at the hospital room, Jenny's body was gone, as were most of the crime scene investigators. They waited while the yellow CAUTION tape was removed, and then were approached by two plainclothes detectives holding notepads loaded with questions. Two hours later, they were free to remove the remainder of Jenny's possessions.

"I want to be free," he mumbled under his breath, watching small circles of condensation spread across the glass.

"What?" Jeannette asked, not looking at him. She sounded exhausted.

"A line from 'Don't Let the Sun Go Down on Me'. John Lennon, right? Just came into my mind," he said, trying to keep his voice light. "Losing everything is like the sun going down on me."

"Congratulations," Jeannette muttered. "You're wrong again. Sir Elton John." She looked around at the empty hospital room and sighed. "That's all."

Nathan turned toward her, watching as she surveyed the room. He noticed how her eyes moved quickly, yet thoroughly as if she was a robot scanning the area for data. He admired her bravery in the face of adversity, her thoroughness in the midst of chaos and her ability to function during an emotional crisis. She wasn't much to look at, but if the world ever came to an end, he wanted to be on this woman's team. As if reading his mind, she turned to him and met his eyes.

"I said that's it," she sounded downright hostile.

"I heard you the first time." He turned back to the window just as a pigeon flew past, headed to where ever it was that pigeons hung out. Behind him, he heard her opening the closet door. "What are you looking for?"

"Jenny had some of my pictures in her coat pocket. I want them back," she growled as she rummaged through the tattered coat.

"You don't have to be so defensive, Jay," he retorted, hurt.

"I asked you not to call me that, and I know what you were asking. Don't worry, I'll be out of here soon enough," Jeannette shoved the pictures into her pocket and replaced the coat. "I'm just taking what's mine."

He shook his head in resignation. "I don't care. Take whatever you want," he began, but she cut him off.

"I tolerated you when she was alive. I don't have to do that now," Jeannette glared at him.

Nathan sank into the overstuffed chair next to the hospital bed. Something grazed against the back of his hand and he turned to face the vase of daisies Dane had sent. "She loved daisies," he said softly. He pushed himself further into the chair and stared at the yellow flowers, wishing to hell Jenny would storm into the room and yell at the two of them to stop fighting. He wanted to see her one last time. He wanted to say he loved her and wanted her to be happy. Why do people always talk about everything except what they really feel? "I'm sorry, Jeannette."

"About what?" Jeannette snapped, grabbing the stuffed pillow case and heading for the door. "About hanging on to her when you should have let her go? She stopped and stood staring at him in silence for a moment. She shrugged and shook her head. "Whatever." She turned and headed out the door, but Nathan's voice halted her.

"Jenny never hated anyone," Nathan said, "but you hate everything. I don't get it." He shook his head. "I just don't get it. Why are you so fucking angry?" He stared at her.

Her mouth fell open slightly, as if the brazenness of his question shocked her. "I'm leaving."

"No," he said getting up, suddenly pissed off at her for being such a bitch, at Jenny for dying, but mostly at himself for wanting Jeannette's approval before she'd exited his life forever. "I'll go. I think you need her memories more than I do." He picked up his Stetson and headed out into the hallway. As he passed over the threshold, he stopped and turned back.

"I loved her, Jay," he said simply, his voice suddenly steady and strong. "I know she didn't love me like I wanted her to, but I still needed to fight for her."

"As if you were able." Jeannette sneered.

"I've got to sign some papers in administration," he said to her back, keeping his voice steady and calm. "If you ever want to talk, or you need anything—"

"I don't need you. I don't need anyone!" she screamed, spinning around to confront him, not caring if she woke the whole damn building. Nathan nodded.

"It would have been nice if you needed her. I did."

* * *

Jeannette opened her mouth to respond, but he was gone before she had a chance to reply. She ran into the hallway and saw Nathan whip around the corner into the vestibule with the elevators. Who the hell did he think he was? She stepped towards him, the burning nugget of anger burning within her, twisting her gut. She opened her mouth, ready to scream after him to go fuck himself when she heard a voice from the room on the opposite side of the hallway.

"He's gone, sweet peach. Too bad! He's a cutie! Can I get his number?" The voice cooed seductively.

Jeannette willed herself to calm the fire burning within her. What the hell was he doing here anyway? Hadn't Jenny made it clear to him that he was not a part of her life anymore? How many times did the moron need to hear it before he finally let go? She was with Jenny now. She should have received the phone call from the police.

"Helllllooooo?" The voice sang from the other room. Forcing herself to pull her gaze away from Nathan, she stepped towards the doorway and leaned on the doorjamb of the room containing the weak, yet musical voice.

"He's straight, remember?" she warned, as if confiding in him that Nathan was a satanic biblical prophecy.

"Shit, that's right," he sighed, "you can't have everything, I suppose. Are you coming in, or is the party out there?" the man asked, holding out his arm to her.

She shouldn't go in. She knew that. She should run towards Dane, or Kevin or another of Jenny's circle. But that's the real issue, isn't it? During their entire relationship, Jeannette had tried to fit into Jenny's world, Jenny's friend, Jenny's circle. Where was hers? Where was her own inner sanctum of support and love? She knew the answer, of course. She didn't have one. That had been the problem with her and Jenny all along–Jenny needed a partner and Jeannette had only been a tagalong, bringing nothing new to the table. No new adventures. No new people. She had suspended her own life in the hopes that Jenny's life would cover them both. But in truth, it had only served to tear them apart.

As soon as she entered the room, she was overwhelmed by a physical onslaught of smells: antiseptic, roses, feces, and musky aftershave. Her legs buckled. The pillowcase fell to the floor, sending Jenny's belongings over the sterile tiles as she reached for the bed, landing half on and half off of the thin mattress, her knees colliding on the hard floor. She felt Gilbert's hands on his shoulders, caressing her more strongly than she thought such a fragile body capable of doing. Jenny had been the only one who could ever hold her with such determination. The tears stung as they erupted out of her, and she found herself melting into his hands.

How often had others wanted something from her? When she was young, it was the teenage boys wanting sex. When she gave up men, it was the young queers along Castro who wanted a drinking buddy. Her boss wanted her time, people begged for her money and even Jeremy wanted her understanding. But Gilbert? He thrived on the energy of people, becoming invigorated and excited about the prospect of connecting to the human race. As if this place of healing had imprisoned him in a cocoon of people who tended to him, yet lacked the element of caring for him. He was the living proof that humans needed each other.

Gilbert handed her a box of tissues. He stroked her buzzed hair and began humming to her with a strong, soulful melody. He seemed to try his best to pull her to him, but his weakened arms could only pull her an inch or two, nothing more.

*   *   *

Mrs. Jeremy arrived home much later than she wanted. The damned nurses made such a fuss over her fainting in the hallway that she was afraid she'd have to sneak away before the bitches released her. Now, thanks to the Nazi nurses, she was stuck on the bus crammed full of tourists headed to Fisherman's Wharf for the afternoon. Thank the fuck her stop was next.

At the red light, a group of leather bikers stepped off the curb and into the street. Something about their swagger struck her as comical and she let out a small giggle. The giggle grew into hysterical laughter that soon caused her chest and stomach muscles to scream in pain. The other passengers turned to her, fear etched in their eyes. Fuck 'em! They had no idea how ridiculous she had looked lying on the floor of the hallway like some poor beached whale wondering what the fuck happened to high tide. She grabbed a tissue from her purse, dried her eyes and blew her nose. Well, at least she'd gotten her blood pressure and other vitals checked while at the hospital.

The jerk of the bus halted her reverie. Her stop loomed just ahead and she prepared to hoist herself out of the seat. The husky black driver with the short beard and huge basket—just a peek at the pecker, that's all I want—Mrs. Jeremy thought, helped her down the steps and onto the sidewalk.

Walking up the small hill to the apartment building, Mrs. Jeremy reveled in the sounds and smells of the street: egg rolls, sauerkraut, fish, and laughter. These were the familiar sounds of home that had caused Marshall to love this area of town so much. Over their years in the city, he taught himself a smattering of Chinese and enjoyed translating the curse words he overheard on their nightly walks. Sometimes, after understanding part of a conversation, they would walk arm in arm as she invented the characters and situation that set the tone for the cursing.

Victoria Lemark. The name burned in her mind's eye as clearly as it was yesterday. Marshall's elongated, loopy "O" and "E" with the overly large "I" that she knew so well. The name appeared several times on the pages of his notebook, sometimes as part of his journal entries, sometimes alone in the margins, all of them accompanied oily smudged fingerprints caused, no doubt, by his addiction to vinegar and salt potato chips.

She shivered as she pulled her sweater around her shoulders. She must find Dane and Jake immediately. The three of them had much to discuss about Victoria Lemark.

*   *   *

From the vantage point half in, half out of the alley across the street, Christian O'Keefe watched the plump woman pull her sweater tightly about her shoulders and turn up the steps of the apartment building. As soon as she entered the building, Christian pulled on his gloves and pulled his hat down over his eyes. Finally! He'd prepared himself to stand here all afternoon waiting for the old bat to return! The positive aspect of the wait was that he had had plenty of time to formulate a plan on how to gain entrance into the building. Looking both ways for cars, Christian crossed the street to the fire escape. Yes, he could easily scale the dilapidated fence that barred the alleyway and gain access into the old lady's apartment via the window.

But a hunch told Christian it wouldn't be necessary to go through such elaborate means to get to the old woman. True to his suspicions, when he grabbed the exterior door's handle, it opened easily. Thank God for lazy repair men. In front of him stood the massive stairway and to his right, a single ancient elevator. He stood in the small, tiled foyer unmoving, staring at the numbers above the lift. Which floor did the old woman live on? Christian heard muffled curses and shuffling echoing down the stairway. Had Mrs. Jeremy really taken the stairs? As lithe as an acrobat, Christian bound up the stairs, keeping full attention focused on the sounds of Mrs. Jeremy directly above.

Christian climbed faster than Sonja Jeremy, and almost gave himself away when he rounded the second floor landing and found himself a few feet from the old woman, who stood in front of the door searching her purse for the keys. Christian squelched a gasp of surprise and backed down the stairs, out of sight. It wasn't until he heard the door's latch open, the door close and the final click of the lock that he allowed himself to breath freely.

How could she have been so careless? Part of the mission was the element of surprise. To fill the victim with the same fear and surprise they had forced onto others in their previous lives. If Mrs. Jeremy had seen Christian, he would have been robbed of that element of fear.

Christian reached into his suit coat and pulled out a thin, black cigarette case. Opening it, he withdrew his lock picking tools. Blessed Ralph Thompson, Jr. His life as a petty thief was known to so few people that he reveled in teaching April a few tricks before his demise. The ancient deadbolt easily succumbed to her will after just a few seconds. Christian cracked open the door and peeked inside.

The door opened into a small foyer. Christian could only see the closet door immediately to the left, as a sharp bend in the hallway blocked the view of the rest of the flat. He inched the door open, stepped into the foyer and closed the door.

Mrs. Jeremy opened the cabinet door for the Mrs. Fields cookies when the phone rang. She answered it and listened as Jeannette's voice filtered through the receiver. Then she began to cry.

*   *   *

Jake contemplated digging his cell phone out of his briefcase but decided against it. What more was there to say? And who would he say this nothing to? Dane? Jenny? Jeannette? Fuck it. Better to let the silence of the afternoon flood over him for a bit. Quiet was always the best time to think.

*   *   *

Mrs. Jeremy sat on her favorite stool, smelling her favorite incense as panic spread through her body. Her pits stuck together as if glued. She had to pee. Dane's going to die, she thought to herself. The thoughts came to her like without invitation, flooding her mind with gruesome images.

She clutched the phone to her heavy bosom. Jeannette, the poor girl, was crying and could barely speak. Did Mrs. Jeremy know where Dane was? When Mrs. Jeremy was able to decipher her sobbing, heaving voice, she heaved herself into the nearest seat and began to tremble.

Jenny. That poor, sweet girl! Beheaded! And in the hospital no less! As bad as that was, what scared Mrs. Jeremy more was the fact that with Jake safely out of town, she and Dane would be next on the hit list for that crazy bitch. She was safely barricaded in her apartment, but Dane?

"Please, Marshall, keep him safe. Send him to me.

A board creaked from somewhere within the apartment.

She thought she heard something, but had been so deep in thought about Jenny's murder she could have been mistaken. Oh, God, how did Dane not know about Jenny? Had nobody called him? Was he still not looking at his cell phone? Their group was a thick as thieves! None of this made sense.

"Hello?" she called again. Silence. Mrs. Jeremy moved slowly and deliberately across the room. As she stood in front of the stove, she heard another creak from the living room. She was not alone.

Acting on instinct, she opened the drawer beneath her left hand. From inside, she withdrew a large meat cleaver. Clutching the weapon, she inched her way through the archway of the kitchen towards the foyer, keeping her back to the wall. How many times had Marshall told her to protect her back? He had driven her insane with the advice through the years. Thank you, Marshall.

The living room was empty. She scanned the area: one closed window led to the fire escape, and the room held no tables to hide under, no furniture one could use as a shield. This room was safe.

A loud knock broke the silence. She froze, suddenly aware that she had to piss like a race horse. What now? Answer the door? Run to the phone and call 911?

"Mrs. Jeremy?" an inquisitive voice floated in from the hallway.

"Dane?" Mrs. Jeremy said back, hoping her voice didn't convey the fear she was feeling.

"Are you alright?" his voice sounded worried.

She breathed a sigh of relief and slid sideways along the wall to the front door. Without removing her back from the wall, she leaned over to spin the deadbolt.

The door wasn't locked. With a single motion, she reached out and yanked the door open. Dane stood in the hallway, a look of concern on his face.

"Mrs. Jeremy?" his eyes stared at the meat cleaver in her hand. She placed a finger to her lips and motioned for him to enter.

"Hi," she said, struggling to make her voice sound cold, flat and impersonal, sure that Dane would pick up on the uncharacteristic monotone and play along with her. In the living room, she snatched a pad of paper from the coffee table and hurriedly jotted a note.

"What brings you over?" she asked while shoving the pad into his face.

WE ARE NOT ALONE. CHECK APARTMENT.

Dane nodded his understanding and began scanning the area with his eyes. "Oh, fine," he responded, trying to remember if Mrs. Jeremy had just asked him a question. He mouthed CALL POLICE. "And you?" he asked trying to sound calm.

Mrs. Jeremy shook her head furiously, mouthing NO! Dane shrugged. Mrs. Jeremy jerked her head in the direction of the bedroom and Dane followed her, walking backwards down the short hallway.

"How was your day?" she asked, raising the knife defensively in front of her. Suddenly the loose board in the foyer squeaked, and then was followed by the sound of someone descending the stairs and the dull thud of the heavy exterior door being slammed. Mrs. Jeremy looked at Dane and shouted, "THE FRONT DOOR!" giving him a shove. From somewhere beneath them, the loud barking of a dog punctuated the sounds of the activity below.

Dane dashed out of the apartment and down the stairs. Mrs. Jeremy ran to the kitchen window that overlooked the street, knowing that neither of them would find any trace of the intruder. Sure enough, Dane returned a moment later shaking his head. "Did you look around for missing stuff? Did you call the police?"

"No. This wasn't a burglary. It was her." The barking continued, grating on her last nerve. "Will someone shut that fucking dog up?"

"That's Ace. Her who?" Dane asked securing the front door before joining her in the kitchen.

"Ace?" she asked.

Dane nodded at her.

"You brought the dog?"

"Yeah," he said defensively, "I was taking him back to the condo when, I don't know, I just felt like I should come visit you."

"Well, my boy," she laughed more out of relief than hysteria, "I am fucking glad you did. Go get the poor beast."

Dane didn't respond, instead looking at her blankly while saying, "Who's 'her?'"

"Dane, boy, go get Ace, then come here and sit down. I've got some bad news."

Dane remained frozen in place. "Tell me. Mrs. Jeremy, you're scaring me."

As she turned the knob of the burner with a shaking hand, she said quietly, "I know who killed Ralph Thompson. It was the same person who you saw the night you..." she hesitated before continuing, "...died in the hospital. It was the same woman who was just in this apartment uninvited. But before I say anything, I need you to get that dog before I go down there and strangle him."

While Dane retrieved Ace, Mrs. Jeremy mulled over the various ways she would have to tell him that Jenny had been murdered. Not knowing what else to do, she searched for the Mrs. Fields cookies and began to cry.

*   *   *

Christian bolted down the steps of the building, barely avoiding the leaping, howling animal chained to the railing of the exterior stairs. He turned to the right and dashed down the small hill towards Market Street. The world around him twisted and swayed, disorienting him so badly that he ricocheted off streetlights, buildings and signposts. He slammed into pedestrians knocking grocery bags from their hands, shoving them into other tourists.

His chest caved in around his lungs and he struggled to pull air into his lungs. Without realizing where he was, he found himself skidding to a halt against a newspaper machine and bent over it, panting for air. As the world slowed its spinning, Christian wiped the sweat from his brow and spun in circles, looking past the throng of people milling around the city's streets without seeing them. There is nothing to be won by cursing the past, only walking into the uncertain future, isn't that what Gretchen had always said? Ironic, then, that the advice should be turned back against the gypsy a hundred years later. Christian began to walk, sorting out options as he weaved among the crowd.

Damn the witch! Christian wished he had known about the Gypsy long ago! He could have killed the old woman first! This time around, however, Christian would gain the upper hand, as Gretchen was now trapped in the body of an ailing fat woman. No longer strong and young, the gypsy would be unable to fight back when it came time to kill her.

What frustrated Christian was that the two entities were together: Gretchen the Gypsy and…him. Why? Christian had assumed that he had done what Victoria Lemark had done—read the Book and understood its power. But if that was true, what was the need to seek counsel? Was it feasible that for the past year, he had not journeyed to the Book at all? He had not delved into the wonder of the temple?

Christian turned this idea over in his mind. If he hadn't done any of the work she had done, then he would have no idea who Christian was, would he? But if this were true, it wouldn't take long before the Gypsy led him to the Book and began uncovering the secrets locked within the sacred pages and the power that went along with that knowledge.

But that would take time, wouldn't it? Yes, it would. It took Victoria several weeks after her first visit to the Book to step aside and let April through. How long would it take him? Weeks? Days? Even with Gretchen the Gypsy helping him, he wouldn't be ready to confront Christian until long after the final revenge was complete. And by the time Gretchen and he were ready to begin searching, they would be looking for Victoria, not Christian.

Christian smiled and looked up into the crowd. Yes. This was not so bad after all. He had a day, perhaps two, to locate and slay the final victim.

Christian stopped suddenly. The Book. Gretchen would surely show Him how to access the Book. This would mean he would be in the other realm soon, journeying through the land towards the temple. He would be journeying alone.

Christian smiled. He had a fantastic idea of how to dispose of him and, quite possibly, Gretchen the Gypsy as well.

*　*　*

"I've got to get there!"

"It won't do any good, son—"

"Fuck you! She needs me...she...I thought she...if she got the role, she had gone out...got drunk...she . . ."

"She's gone, dear," Mrs. Jeremy repeated. "They've already removed...her. She's gone." Dane sank to the floor, sobbing loudly. Ace whined and creeped over to the boy, and lay at his side.

Dane had been like this since he returned to the apartment. She fought back the tears herself. No sense having both of them sobbing messes. There was the matter of Victoria Lemark to attend to. She knew what had to happen. But with him like this, how would that be possible? She sat in the oversized chair and watched the boy cry. Crying always made things a bit better, isn't that what her husband used to say?

Plus, she needed time to plan the next move.

*　*　*

Christian took long strides down Market Street towards the bay, keeping his head down, staring at the pavement. If, as he suspected, the boy and the Gypsy were conspiring, Christian must reach the Book first. If he were clever and quick, the death blow could be struck before anyone suspected anything was wrong. But Christian needed nourishment. When had he last eaten? Yesterday? The day before? This body had changed so drastically since its time as Victoria Lemark that the closer he got to her attaining her goal, the less hunger he felt. It was as if the very act of visiting the Book nourished the body so fully that eating was unnecessary. But a body is still a three dimensional creation and must be kept operating. With luck, the dingy burrito stand around the corner was still open.

Christian looked up to check the intersection for traffic when he spotted the handsome man that he had sensed so frequently these past months was directly ahead. Why was this man here? The hour was much too late for a common businessman, was it not? Perhaps the man was looking for someone? Or the Gypsy? Christian froze mid-stride and watched as the man strode to the building on the corner, fumbled as he slid his magnetic card through the electronic reader and stepped through the glass doors. Christian gazed up at the tall Edwardian building and smiled. Of course! This is why she had felt his presence so often during his stay in San Francisco! April had come to this corner daily as she tracked down, seduced, and then plotted the death of Ralph S. Thompson, Jr! If this sodomite visited this corner as well, then the mysterious feeling of being watched had just been explained. How convenient! First, Christian would kill this one, then the gypsy and, finally, fate would come full circle as he returned to the street where he killed the first traitor on her list in order to kill the last.

Christian began singing "Onward, Christian Soldiers" as he strode gallantly past the green Holiday Inn sign and followed Jake.

*   *   *

Mrs. Jeremy peeked around the corner to make sure the boy was preparing himself. He was. Satisfied, she stationed herself into the straight-backed kitchen chair to watch as he breathed along with the CD, the rhythmic rising of his chest in time with the beating drum. Dane inhaled deeply of the incense mixture she'd concocted. It took her almost an hour to calm him down enough to convince him this Christian/Victoria/April person was a threat that must be dealt with before grieving Jenny. Dane took one last deep breath, pushed himself deeper into the overstuffed chair and sat very still. She'd known him much longer than the few years since they met in San Francisco— much longer. She was about to find out exactly how long.

She sank two squares of sugar into her tea and sat back to watch; distant enough to be unobtrusive, yet close enough to see every nuance in his face. The phone sat unplugged, the lights extinguished and the windows shielded from the outside noise. It was time for Dane's journey into the void.

She fondled the notebook sitting in front of her. The cover sported large, block lettering. THE THINK TANK. Marshall's handwriting permeated it, listing ideas, thoughts, poems and commentaries on everything from reincarnation to cinnamon-raisin oatmeal cookies. Towards the back of the notebook was a detailed account of Marshall's own journey through the void and the subsequent visit to the Book of the Temple—the Akashic Records.

Within this book lay many secrets Marshall had never published, lectured about nor spoke of with anyone save his wife. On the red-lined pages of the book, several names were listed, among them: VICTORIA LEMARK=APRIL (may?) LILY/(cross reference J (ennifer??) MALE–CHRIST or CHRISTIAN (cross reference R. CORNORIE)

DANE (?) (Daniel, dan)/JACK (jake?)=R(something) CORNORIE SONJA=GYPSY/PRIEST BASIL

Thanks to Marshall's work, it was simple to guide Dane through the steps he'd have to take to prepare for the journey and how to find his way through the other side. Dane groaned. She shifted slightly, checked to make sure Ace was soundly sleeping at her feet and pressed RECORD on the tape recorder. She then sat back to wait.

*   *   *

Dane felt himself become weightless and an odd sensation spread through him, as if his whole body had fallen asleep and succumbed to a pervasive tingle; while not altogether frightening, it did startle him. His first instinct was to open his eyes, but his eyelids felt heavy and unmovable. He felt a deep, throbbing vibration tickle the top of his head and leak along his scalp, down his face, through his neck, shoulders and back. As the warm oscillation rolled through his pelvis, a jolt of pleasure spread into his crotch and he moaned. By the time the quivering reached his feet, he was so stoned he'd lost his last shed of muscle control and felt his leaded filled head fall to one side. From somewhere far away, he sensed someone calling his name and felt a slight lurch as his consciousness untangled itself from his body.

The blackness around him began to brighten. He swung his focus towards the source of the light and, without opening his eyes, found himself looking down upon the city. He floated high over the flat roofed buildings, gazing not onto plaster and stone, but rivers of blue, red, lavender, peach, and maroon.   Throbbing, pulsating ribbons of multicolored luminescence streamed through the buildings beneath him as the energy of the city weaved the people, animals, trees and grass into a glowing web of light. The figures far below held little resemblance to actual people. They had mutated into translucent ovals encased in liquid color prisons. The birds that flew past him shimmered with a florescent gold as they glided on the violet wind, soaring out over a glowing green ocean. Even the vehicles, bikes, and buses emitted their own hues as if every iota of matter pulsated with its own unique tint.

Dane looked towards the heavens, expecting to see the sun encased in another hallucinatory hue, but instead found the orb eclipsed by a dark shadow. He stared at the shadow and after a moment realized what it was that he was looking at. A sphere of thick, inky blackness hovered in the air so close to him that he could almost touch it. Dane felt chilled by the sight of a lifeless hole cut out of the fabric of pounding color, an abyss of nothingness. With a firm determination, he swam towards the sphere.

In a rush of understanding, an old forgotten memory flooded back into his mind and he knew what the void represented. Just as everything alive swam in vibratory colors, the void was the space between spaces. The void was neither living nor dead; neither of this Earth nor separate from it. The void was, is and always shall be. He swam closer to it, feeling both its dense chill and the heat of excitement.

Just as he had seen during his last journey, the glowing silver leash sprouted out of him, only this time it lost its definition, melting into the kaleidoscopic swirl of energy that pulsated all around him. Dane hovered on the edge of the void and faced the inky blackness. With one last glance behind him, he smiled down onto the city below and then abruptly turned to swim into the sphere.

Blackness swallowed him. He looked behind him and saw the city had disappeared behind a wall of nothingness. For a brief, cold moment he floated in the darkness, panic flowing through him. What if he couldn't return? What if the void was nothing more than a hoax, calling him towards death? Slowly, he became aware of a dim light emanating from out of the dark. The soft silver glow of his leash remained fastened to him; intact and visible against the dark backdrop. Hadn't Mrs. Jeremy said something about this? He remembered vaguely how she warned him that he might become lost, and if he did so, to pay attention to the silver thread of his life force. He would trust her, no matter how wacko she sounded; she hadn't led him astray thus far. He felt a gentle calmness come over him just as a gust of frigid wind blew across his face, biting his skin and stinging the tips of his ears. Gooseflesh broke along his arms and he forced himself to clamp his jaws tightly as his body instinctively started to shiver.

He heard a noise. It came from far away; a distant, low wailing like a lost animal pining for home. It grew louder and more painful to his ears, and soon the wailing became a single note of a high pitched soprano cutting through the night. Dane pressed his palms against his ears, trying to block out the sounds as the music changed pitch and scale. He could feel it reverberate through his bones and soon the note became a shrieking onslaught of noise, ripping at him, threatening to tear him apart.

Dane sensed the flash of light rather than actually seeing it. In an instant, his chilled flesh warmed as though a fleece blanket was being wrapped around his shoulders. He opened his eyes. He lay on a beautifully manicured lawn that extended as far as he could see. The gently rolling hills in the distance had a uniform, painted appearance. A rich green slope lay beneath him, ending several yards downhill at a blue stream sparkling in the sun.

I've been here before, Dane thought. Where is it? He knew the place, of course he did! Although he couldn't recall when he'd visited, he knew the twists of the paths through the woods and the turn of the brook as it wound into the fields. What was this place called again?

HOME HOME HOME HOME HOME a voice repeated in his head. He suddenly felt the urge to see more.

* * *

Jake fumbled with the card key at the entrance to his office building. Damn the firm! Why couldn't they have taken space further up Market in that newly renovated building with the smoky glass and granite entryway? That building had twenty-four hour security so they didn't have to fumble with these fucking magnetic cards. Jake sighed. He knew it was no use cursing the firm. He was just grumpy. After the taxi pulled away, Jake realized that in his preoccupation over Dane, he had tipped the cabbie a twenty instead of a five. Now he would have to take a break from the office and run down to the ATM or go across the street to the Holiday Inn restaurant, which took plastic.

He should go home and save the money. But why? Dane thought he was safely on the plane to Maine. If he ran into Dane, it would be impossible to get out of the condo without talking to the guy, which would turn into another fight and, possibly, another missed flight. No, better to let everything ride as it is until he knew more about his travel plans.

Besides, it felt deliciously naughty being in the city when nobody knew he was in town.

As he opened the lobby door and shouldered his huge duffle bag, he felt an eerie sense of being watched. He spun around, half expecting a mugger to descend upon him, only to be surprised by the empty street. He shrugged it off to nerves. It wasn't everyday he broke up with his partner. But still, he thought, the quickening of his heart, the pounding of the blood. He felt just like he had when he'd seen that mysterious red-haired woman.

*   *   *

Dane stared at the naked woman, mesmerized by her soft, china doll features, the flowing auburn hair, the orange construction hard hat sitting atop her head and the powder blue butterfly wings sprouting from her back. She couldn't have been more than ten or eleven inches high, but the miniature tool belt fastened around her waist gave her an air of superiority. The tiny winged nymph giggled softly, tickling Dane's ears with the sound of wind chimes as her cobalt blue eyes took him in. Her bountiful breasts stood firm, round and pink, each nipple a perfect circle surrounded by fine chestnut hair. Her teeth, brilliantly white, peeked at him from behind rich, thick lips as she smiled coyly.

Suddenly, a second miniature naked woman swooped down on Dane and hovered inches from his face. She glared at him as she shook her head in bitter disapproval before turning her back on him and fluttering to the power blue creature. With a fierce jerk of her hand, she clutched the wrist of the miniature construction worker and pulled her away from Dane. Dane watched the two of them fly away, becoming smaller and smaller, until they were nothing but dots in the distance.

Dane began to walk again. After several minutes, he spied a huge boulder sitting in the middle of the grassy hillside. He altered his course and headed towards it, feeling that a good rest was well-deserved. As he approached the boulder, however, the rock shimmered and began quiver. It sprang to life, its round, rough texture rippling like waves on a pond as it grew. The surface of the rock shot skyward in a thin needle-like point as the rounded edges expanded outward, burying the lush lawn beneath its new shape. By the time Dane stepped backwards several steps, it had morphed into a spiral staircase of smooth white marble. The wide, narrow stairs sported several landings, each one larger than the one beneath. The final landing high above Dane's head disappeared into the chamber of a magnificent crystalline structure gleaming in the sun.

Dane walked to the base of the imposing staircase tentatively. A visceral wave of fearful awe washed over him as he craned his head to behold the splendor of the shining marble. The stairway led into what? A temple? "Temple" seemed too trite a word to describe the building high above, but "shrine" or "altar" gave the feeling of a hierarchical religion.

Suddenly, a dam broke within his psyche. Bits of the nocturnal dreams which had haunted him for the past year flashed through his mind. He had seen this structure before. He had visited it often but had never remembered it after waking. He stared at the crystalline edifice with a new awareness of what it was.

He knew he had to go inside.

To Dane's left, a massive cloud of deep purple materialized of out the air. As he watched, the grassy pastures beneath the mist collapsed into themselves and whirled until they transformed into plum-colored water, which grew into a lake undulating with gentle waves that erupted from the lake's center and lapped at his feet. Within seconds, Dane found himself standing on the grassy shore, staring into an enormous purple lake. Looking down into the transparent pool, he saw hundreds of rainbow trout clustered beneath the surface of the water. Dane marveled at the luster of their color, the scales reflecting the yellow sunlight and translucent tails that brushed the water with grace. Their eyes glowed with a pinkish radiance, as if an inner light flowed out of them into the water. Dane realized with a jolt that the fish were staring directly at him.

From several yards away, a loud splash resounded and Dane spun to see amethyst-colored water spurting up from the center of the lake. From within the widening circle of ripples, a huge blue dolphin jumped from the water into the air. Along its side, a stripe of auburn luminance radiated softly. In a flash, the creature was upon Dane, its short snout inches from Dane's face.

In that instant, Dane's perspective shifted. No longer standing on the grassy shore, he now found himself looking into Mrs. Jeremy's apartment as if he was peeking through a hole in a door. The old lady sat at the rickety table, Ace curled at her feet, watching an unconscious version of himself. A tape recorder sat next to her and she scribbled furiously in a notebook, chancing an occasional glance towards his sleeping body.

The dolphin nudged him gently and Dane focused back into the present. He pulled away from the floating cetacean, regaining his balance and gathering his thoughts. What the hell was that all about? With another gentle nudge, the dolphin urged Dane towards the marble stairs. As Dane shuffled along, the dolphin swam next to him, shoulder to fin, guiding him up the great marble steps toward the glowing shrine. The building's staircase vibrated so strongly that its gentle cadence tickled Dane's feet and legs, filling him with a giddy headiness. On and on he climbed, one foot after the other as the marble steps passed beneath his feet. As he ascended, the sky changed color from the crystal clearness of a fine summer's day to a light green tint, then to a lavender haze and, finally, stark white so bright that Dane was forced to squint as he surveyed the expanse of grassy fields far below.

Dane pulled his focus from the landscape below and, to his amazement, found himself standing before two huge wooden doors made from thick planks of wood anchored by huge slabs of shining metal, reminiscent of the medieval period. When his fingers made contact with the door, it didn't feel like wood at all, but like glass.

The doors lit up to reveal hundreds of squares embedded beneath the surface of the wood. Like an enormous wall of televisions within an electronics store, the screens flashed with events from his life. Dane stared, dumbfounded, as the macabre video montages broadcast scenes he had forgotten existed: his mother with her hair piled high in a heavily coifed beehive; a replay of his ninth birthday party when he'd gotten his first brand new bike; attending his high school prom. Man! Was he really that much of a geek?

He felt a jab on his arm and turned to face the dolphin, whose nose prodded him impatiently. From within his mind, he heard a soft, soothing voice saying:

COME, ANGAKOK. WE MUST GO.

That voice! He was sure he had heard it somewhere before. He racked his mind, trying to remember where he had heard that soothing, gentle voice. With an eerie chill, he remembered. This was the voice that had spoken to him in the hospital the night he died.

Dane turned from the hypnotic eyes of his companion and back to the images of himself on the screens. There! He had totally forgotten the family camping trips to Yosemite! He really had lived a blessed life.

ANGAKOK!

He pried himself from the wall of images and addressed the dolphin. ME?

YOU MUST REMEMBER, ANGAKOK.

From one of the flickering images playing across the door to the shrine, he heard the squeal of tires, a woman's scream, and then a dull thud. He turned towards the moving pictures and his blood froze. He looked onto the scene of the accident that took his life one year ago: the crumpled motorcycle, his limp, unconscious body and in the foreground, a red Mercedes with a laughing blonde behind the wheel sucking on a cigarette. She looked at nobody in particular when she yelled, "DOES ANYONE HERE KNOW THESE TWO PEOPLE? WHO ARE THEY?"

In answer, the dolphin guided its dorsal fin to Dane's hand, and Dane wrapped his fingers around its warm rubbery appendage. With a violent jerk, the dolphin shot forward, passing through the giant doors, through the flashing images of Dane's past and into the structure. As he passed over the threshold, the dolphin stopped, shook Dane free and swam away. Dane looked around the chamber and stood aghast, feeling overwhelmed by the shrine.

When he graduated from college, his gift to himself had been a month-long backpacking trip through Europe, a gift he had planned for years as he scrimped and saved from his meager earnings at the bookstore. His original plan was to see as much of the continent as possible, taking in the scenery by sticking to the back roads. But on his first day, during a random visit to an old, innocuous looking cathedral in Venice, he stepped through the ancient stone vestibule looked to the ceiling. Staring down on him was an intricately detailed mural of the crucifixion. The painting struck a chord within him, and he cried at the idea of such striking beauty surviving in this harsh world of wars, famine, and corruption. The amount of love and commitment that had gone into creating the piece of art seemed incomprehensible to him. He himself barely had the patience to hang onto a single boyfriend for longer than a year. How could any one person invest so much of their time, effort, or soul into a single endeavor? He instantly changed his plans, opting instead for a tour of old churches, a decision he never regretted. Upon his return home, he felt satiated and content in the knowledge that he had seen some of the most splendid architectural achievements ever made.

Until now. The structure in which he stood was grander, larger, and more extravagant than anything he'd seen in Europe. The arched roof stood hundreds of yards above him, supported by thousands of gleaming white stone pillars. The stones that comprised the shrine were immense, each one several feet long and a yard high. The mortar between them was almost invisible, giving the building the appearance that it had been carved from a single, mountain-sized rock. The whole building glowed with a stark white illumination that came from nowhere, yet everywhere. No furniture of any kind occupied the single, huge room, save one lonely wooden pedestal that stood in the center of the floor. It was a massive, domineering piece of handiwork, carved from a single tree stump. Eloquently detailed with ornate designs and symbols, it struck Dane as more of an altar than a podium.

The top of the wooden lectern glowed with a soft, silver light that beckoned to Dane with emotional telepathy. Overcome with an unstoppable desire to touch the light, Dane inched towards the podium, straining to see through the silvery glow and catch a glimpse of what called to him.

A book. Large, thick and ancient, the tome sat unopened upon the wooden frame, its leather cover cracked and frayed with age. It looked perversely out of place amongst the glorious surroundings, a blemish upon the face of the divine. The leather cover bore no title, emblem, nor picture. Its plain, fractured surface gave no hint as to what lay within. Dane circled the podium, working up the courage to open the book.

The moment his hand touched the leathery surface, his brain seared with pain—a sharp, stabbing sensation ran through his temples making his eyes water and the world around him to swim into a blur. Instantly, his mind filled with pictures—the Earth from afar, his dead grandparents, his sister's wedding in the snowy haze of January, flashes of his childhood home, all of his life's forgotten yet poignant moments flooded his mind's *eye. A rapid infusion of knowledge filled him, and his mind reeled with the onslaught of data. He suddenly knew pi to the infinite decimal. He could quote the Old Testament. He computed the sun's circumference using geometry. Algebraic theorems now made sense to him.*

He instantly became aware of his own lifetimes before this one, ages dead and gone, energy patterns that lived light years away on the stars he admired as a young boy. The Book forced every scrap of data imprinted on its ageless pages into Dane, showing him the people, places and things that were and continue to be. In a flash, his perspective of life on the planet Earth shifted and the fierce intensity of the information pouring into him threatened to explode his aching brain.

He wanted the pain to stop. He tried to yank his hands away from the tome, but they'd been fused to the Book, his fingers melding into its cover. Without warning, he felt himself being pulled down into the light. The Book had him in its grasp and yanked him in. Like soft, wet sand, he felt the energy of the Book creep up his body, feeling the warm tingling sensation spread over his skin as he sunk into its binding and slipped between its pages.

*   *   *

Summertime.

In the distance, Dane heard birdsong. Through the hayloft's open stock door, he marveled at the brilliance of the sky as the soft glow of the sun shed its dying rays through the horizon. A reddish hue streamed through the cracks of the wooden slats of the barn's roof, illuminating the bits of straw and dust that danced in the air. Dane stood on a pile of dried hay and the pungent scent of manure stung his nostrils. Around him, insects flew and dived through the last remnants of the day. To his left, a pile of animal furs lay stacked two feet high—cured and ready for the marketplace. Horses neighed and a cow cried out in defiance. The barn was readying for sleep.

Off to the left, outside of the structure, Dane heard men whistling a tune over the loud clop of horse's hooves. Directly in front of him, on the floor of the barn, stood a man who looked to be about thirty-five. The man's loose fitting clothing, which looked to Dane like clothing from a movie on the Revolutionary War, were stained and torn. The man's ruddy face bore the deep lines and scaly skin of one who spent too much time under the summer sun. His sun-bleached hair hung tangled and filthy about his shoulders.

As Dane studied him, the face of the haggard man began to droop, its features stretching and thinning as the chin grew longer and more peaked. To Dane's horror, it then began to twist upon itself, turning upward again in a slow, oozing motion. Then the flesh solidified as it formed a new face— a face with fresher, softer features. Dane recognized this new face, but from where? He was positive he had seen this man before, in some long ago dream. Dane's mind raced, flipping through the still frames of history, trying to remember who now stood beneath him.

Then, in a sudden flash of insight, he remembered where he had seen this man before: on television. While he sat in his worn leather chair awaiting Jake's return, he had flipped through the channels and caught a news report of a wealthy socialite, found dead in a downtown penthouse. Dane realized that the haggard farmer in front of him was Ralph S. Thompson, Jr.

But Dane also felt he was watching someone else, someone who shared Ralph's face and body, someone who he knew better than Ralph. Daddy. Yes! That's it! Instinctively, Dane knew that although the facial features belonged to Ralph, the figure in the barn was his father.

Dane felt an inexplicable burst of affection course through his veins. He loved his dad, this man who stood before him, who shared a face with a dead man. Once this memory returned to him, an entire lifetime followed. Often, when things on the farm slowed, Daddy would take his youngest son, Dane, fling him onto a pony and ride around the perimeter of the property. Dane enjoyed these rides, for he felt safe with Daddy, as if nothing in the world would harm him as long as this man stood at his side. Often, when he and Daddy stopped for lunch, he would dismount, tie up the pony and pretend they were trappers who had left home to go in search of pelts and gold. He had been a small boy, but his size never compromised his exuberant passion for helping around the farm and for this, Daddy was full of praise and support. He fantasized that someday, he would leave the farm, find fame and fortune, and then return as a man, ready to usher in a new generation of farmers on the family's land.

Feeling like he was eight years old again, Dane stooped to jump down from the hayloft, ready to run to this man, wanting to hug him. He was ready to be welcomed back home after such a long absence. But as Dane stepped out of the shadows towards the edge of the loft, Dane noticed a second figure standing to Daddy's right and he froze.

The red-haired woman from his dreams stood, cowering away from Daddy.

But just as the face of Daddy stretched and morphed into another set of features, so did the image of the redheaded woman. While Dane stared at her, her face shifted and changed, changing itself from the familiar to the unknown. When the features settled, the woman had turned into a young, pale-skinned girl with a lean, long face and deep set eyes. No longer did she sport the red mane. It, too, had changed to a deep brown tangle of filthy hair. Tears streamed down her face, leaving lines of clean skin slicing through the dirt and her red, puffy eyes made her look like a freakishly evil ghoul.

The urge to run to his father faded. He no longer felt the exuberant rush of love that he had felt just moments before. The warm tingle of love had been replaced by the cold sensation of fear. What was the woman doing here? He glanced around the barn. They were alone. Confused, Dane took a step towards the loft's ladder, but after the first step, the shining blue dolphin zipped down from the rafters and across his path, cutting him off from his egress.

"What?" Dane demanded. He didn't understand how these two people had anything to do with him. He had never met either of them.

NOT IN YOUR CURRENT LIFE, the dolphin told him, its sleek body sliding up to his side. Then, with a gentle nudge, it forced Dane to turn back towards the scene before him.

Daddy slapped the crying woman fiercely,. She hit the wooden floor of the barn with a dull thud. With a terrified whimper, the woman crawled backwards, pulling her broken body across the wooden floor. With a smirk of pleasure, Daddy strode towards her, his face red, his nostrils flaring with every intake of breath. He easily overtook the sobbing woman and descended on her, balling his hand into a fist and striking her again and again with growing ferocity. At first the woman held her arms in front of her face in a vain attempt to ward off the attack, but after several punches, she ceased her weak attempts at self-defense and fell to the floor of the barn, opening herself to his attacks. Watching the figure cower and whimper on the dirty straw touched a sympathetic part of Dane—he felt sadness for her, empathy almost. What was going on? Why was he watching this?

The figure of Daddy grinned madly and reached into his jacket pocket. Dane was unable to see what Daddy had until the man had pulled the object from his pocket and the glow of the lantern reflected off its surface–a knife. Dane knew that knife. From the recesses of his mind, Dane remembered seeing that mother-of-pearl knife a hundred times, for it was Daddy's favorite. The older man kept it with him, using it to skin a deer, gut a fish, or cut a rope. With a loud grunt, Daddy threw himself upon the weeping figure and shoved the knife deep into her chest. Again and again the knife cut into the girl until, finally satiated, the figure of Daddy stood panting heavily, sweat dripping down his face. He backed away from the corpse, glaring at it with disdain.

"Well, boy," Daddy said to an unseen entity, "try and wed your dear April Stokes now." His voice rang sharp and cruel through the barn. Daddy stared at her for a moment, watching the blood ooze from the lifeless body and then turned abruptly towards the door.

"She had five years remaining on her contract, boy, five years. What good was she to be soiled and with child?" Daddy turned and kicked viciously at a spot to the left of the door and Dane heard a muffled groan as Daddy's boot hit flesh. "Go bed another wench.."

Daddy kicked once more at the unseen body and another muffled groan filled the air. He wiped the blood from the mother-of-pearl knife and put it back into his coat. Grabbing the lantern from the wall, he turned and walked away from the scene. As he turned, the lantern's pool of soft light illuminated the dark corner and Dane saw clearly the face of the person receiving Daddy's anger.

Jake. Only in this scene, Jake was reed thin and sported long blond hair which was tied neatly at the nape of his neck with a blue ribbon. He looked young, perhaps only nineteen or twenty.

"Ralph!" a woman's voice screamed from outside the barn. "Ralph, do you remain in the barn? What has happened to you?" The voice drew closer as it spoke, and Dane could hear the soft padding of feet on the grass outside. Daddy dashed to the door and threw himself against it just as the door cracked open.

"No, Mary," Ralph/Daddy said, "Saul is washing himself. You remain outside. I shall come out in a moment." With one last glare of disgust to the crumpled, sobbing Jake/Saul, Daddy/Ralph opened the door and exited. As he did so, Dane caught sight of the woman standing on the other side of the doorframe. A trim, handsome woman with thick black hair stood clutching a shawl around her boney shoulders. Just as the door swung shut, her face transmuted into a figure Dane knew very well — she became Jeannette.

Alone with the whimpering Jake/Saul Dane felt more alone than he ever remembered feeling in his life. Should he leave? Should he watch? What was the purpose? Like Ebenezer Scrooge waiting for the ghost of Christmas Future, he looked around for the dolphin and saw it in the air near the roof of the barn. It looked playful and innocent, as if it had no knowledge of the carnage below.

Dane heard the squeaking of the barn door. He spun, expecting Daddy/Ralph but to his surprise, three short figures entered, wearing threadbare riding cloaks and hoods. The leader of the trio limped prominently. The limping one went immediately to the bleeding Jake/Saul, while the other two dashed to the dead woman.

"April is dead," one of the figures said.

"I know," the limping one said, with an odd sense of sadness, "and with her, the baby she carried. Well…that is that, then. The boy is not dead, however," the leader replied, pulling the hood down, revealing the worn, wrinkled face of an olive-skinned woman. "Quickly, or he will die. Take him to the cart. Quietly! Master William may be watching." As she coughed violently, her face melted and shifted, becoming Mrs. Jeremy.

One of the men tending to the dead April stood suddenly and looked around the barn. He threw his hood back, revealing Sean's face. He sniffed the air. "We're not alone," Sean whispered ominously.

"I know," the version of Mrs. Jeremy responded. "I feel it, too. Go!"

Dane watched Sean and his disguised partner as they hefted the dead April onto their backs. As they staggered towards the door, Dane caught a glimpse of the third figure's face—Kevin. He watched as the two carried the corpse over the floor of the barn and out into the night.

"Sharikia," the weak voice of the boy on the floor croaked, "you must not aid me. The master–"

Mrs. Jeremy's face answered him. "I do what I must. It is not my duty to question the spirits, Saul." She untied the boy and reached down to him. "We must be off. Come!" With a grunt, the boy rose to his feet, placing most of his weight on the small woman who helped him struggle towards the door. As the two approached it, the boy reached out for the handle and in that moment of stillness between the door standing closed and being opened, the wizened woman turned towards the hayloft and looked directly into Dane's eyes.

"Ah! I see," she whispered.

"What? Do you see another vision?" the Jake boy asked in a small voice.

The woman hesitated. "No," she said softly, not taking her eyes off of Dane. "I see only that which must be."

"My future? The departing soul of my unborn child?" he asked hopefully.

"Time is an illusion—past, present, future are mere words," she said, touching the door. Then she nodded at Dane and said in a whispered tone, "I see you." Then, without another word, she spun and the two disappeared through the barn door and into the darkness.

Dane felt pressure on his shoulder and jumped wildly, almost crying out in surprise. The blue dolphin's smiling nose floated inches from his face. It seemed to nod, then turned and shot straight up through the boards of the ceiling. With a sigh, Dane jumped into the air, the power of his legs propelling him into the rafters, and then, with a kick of his foot, through the roof and beyond.

*   *   *

Autumn.

The kaleidoscopic colors of the trees contrasted starkly with the deep blue of the bay beyond the garden window, painting the landscape with a brilliant palette of hues. From the vantage point on the hill, Dane could see the city sprawled out beneath him, vast, inviting and warm. Despite the fact that the Transamerica building was gone and the Golden Gate Bridge had yet to be invented, Dane knew he had returned to his city. During his years of service at the gallery, he had seen a large number of historic photographs of the city, most of them quite good. But standing from his vantage point gazing down onto the streets below, he realized none of them did justice to the City by the Bay. Judging from the clothing of the pedestrians on the narrow streets below, he guessed himself to be in the 19th century.

Dane turned from the huge window framed by a set of what used to be deep green velvet curtains that had now faded and lost their luster. A small group of people lounged on the worn and tattered couches and chairs. The room reminded Dane of a museum; the walls of the square room were covered in oil paintings of flower-filled vases, elegant horse drawn carriages and bowls of colorful fruit. Loaded with walnut tables and heavy furniture, it bore an air of wealth and fashion. The teacups which sat in front of each guest were small and delicate. The haunting sounds of a piano concerto played softly and the sound of it instantly calmed Dane's anxiety. Turning towards the music, Dane could see that dozens of rose petals lay atop the piano, surrounding a huge vase full of the flowers.

After having witnessed the murder in the barn, Dane was prepared for the twisting alterations of people's faces and stood waiting for the shift to take place. Like pupils adjusting from darkness to light, the features of each of the people quivered and shifted, finally settling into the familiar faces Dane had expected. He craned his head around the flowers, anxious to see who sat at the piano. The body, that of a young girl—probably another offspring of the house—was topped by the face of Jeremy, Jenny's ex-husband. Dane had never taken the time to get to know Jeremy very well, and now, after realizing his deep connection to the man, wished he had.

Seated in the chair nearest to Dane sat an impeccably dressed, impossibly old man wearing an expensive wool suit. Leaning against the chair, near the old man's deformed leg, was a walking stick carved from mahogony. The man's wrinkled hands flowed through the air, as if he himself conducted the music. The hands, although large and hairy, looked soft and pampered. His head lay against the back of the chair and his eyes remained firmly closed as a huge smile spread across his face. The face belonged to Jeannette.

Across from Jeannette's male form sat an elaborately dressed woman; chestnut hair was pinned back with fresh flowers, and a thick golden chain around her neck held a large golden cross. Her dress clung to her portly frame, giving her body the look of a stuffed sausage. Her face, too, gleamed with joy as she gazed lovingly at the piano. The face of Kevin shone from under rouged cheeks. With a wave of her arm, a dark-skinned man strode to her, hands submerged within white cotton gloves grasping a china teapot. He refilled the cup silently, then turned and returned to his perch a few feet away, then turned to look in the direction of Dane. With a surprised gasp, Dane realized the face belonged to Sean and carried the same faraway look and glazed eyes that annoyed Dane so much in the present. The man wrinkled his nose as if smelling something nasty, then made a hand gesture of dismissal and turned his back on the spot where Dane stood.

A male body with the face of Mrs. Jeremy, dressed in the black crisp uniform of a preacher, sat at the far side of the room at a huge table, hands folded, looking calm and cheerful. If he had stood, the man's frame would *have been over six feet tall, with broad shoulders, large stomach that hung over his belt and an elongated face that ended in a pointed, malformed chin. Across from this male Mrs. Jeremy sat, the era's version of Dane. Judging by the hard, lean body of this alter ego, Dane guessed this incarnation of himself to be about twenty-five years old. The two sat leaning towards one another, exchanging quick, furtive comments in a hushed tone.*

"Pastor Basil, I don't understand," the young Dane said, an identifiable Southern accent permeating his speech.

The holy man chuckled. "You will, Matthew, you will."

Almost without realizing it, Dane's mind flooded with memories of this life. The pastor, Pastor Basil, had always struck the young Matthew as bizarre—he enjoyed dominating conversations as well as others' lives too much for Matthew's taste. As a child growing up in South Carolina, Matthew feared the old man, even from the far rows of the pews. Many a Sunday he had sat on the hard wooden seats, obsessed with the holy man's movements, vocal power and mannerisms, yet repulsed by the figure as well. The young Matthew had always felt an unexplainable force radiating from the pastor, invisibly wrenching control from the congregation as it sat listening to his sermon. Regardless of the fact that he had matured into a young man of great wealth, leaving his ties to the South behind him, the pastor still scared him. Matthew leaned over to ask the Pastor another question, but the large man spoke first.

"Matthew," he said with intensity, "there is more to life than meets the eye. Take heed you do not live life with reckless abandon, but with mindful abandon." Matthew shook his head in confusion. What did that mean? As if answering the silent question, the Pastor continued. "Your sister—"

"Lily or Bethany?" Matthew asked.

"Lily," the holy man responded at once. "Fear her actions, not her—for she will be led astray."

Matthew thought about this a moment. "By the forces of the devil? By the devil?"

"By the taste of revenge," the Pastor responded. "The die has been cast. The story is about to unfold. Watch and remember the events of this day, my son."

Matthew turned away from the old man to ponder this sudden burst of cryptic communication. Revenge? For what? Matthew turned towards the piano, lost in thought, hoping the wretched young girl playing the concerto would finish soon and be gone. He understood this girl to be his parents' choice of a bride for him, but she was much, much too young for him. Besides, he didn't fancy her. He couldn't wait for the Christmas season so he could take the interview with one of the largest investment firms in the city, a secret he refused to divulge to anyone, including the nosey Pastor Basil.

Suddenly, a loud crash broke through the concerto and for a moment the music stopped.

"Never you mind," the portly female figure of Kevin responded. "It is just Lily and Bethany again. They do have tempers, don't they?" With a gentle gesture, she urged the piano player to continue and, after a moment, the music once again spread through the room.

Dane watched himself as young Matthew looked towards the ceiling and sighed. Dane followed the gaze and instantly felt himself lift from the floor of the sitting room and rise through the ceiling, emerging into the room above. He stood in the corner of another large room, one whose walls were filled with tall windows through which the last remnants of the sun could be seen as the sky shifted from blue to crimson. Richly colored portraits lined the remaining two walls, while huge plush area rugs concealed wooden planks. Dane instinctively knew that this room belonged to Matthew's sisters, who now stood face to face with eyes bulging and faces red, screaming at each other.

"I've seen you look at him, Bethany!" The hefty, plain looking woman in green yelled.

"You are a liar, Lily!" the thinner, prettier one yelled back.

It came as no surprise that the thinner, more beautiful woman, Bethany, took the face of Jenny; somehow he had suspected it would. But when the face of the other sister, Lily, solidified, he once again gasped in shock—it was the redhead from his dream. His mind worked feverishly to piece together the clues. Why did she keep appearing? What did she do? What didn't she do? Did Mrs. Jeremy make some mistake, sending him on a drug-induced trip?

"I see you! That means you think about him. You think bad, impure thoughts!" Lily spat angrily.

"I see you stand naked in front of the windows!" Jenny/Bethany shot back. "Does that mean you wish for all the city to lust after you?"

"That's a terrible thing to say!" The red-haired one said, sounding honestly hurt. "I like the feel of the wind on my body, that's all."

"On your nakedness, you mean," Bethany said smugly.

"The wind is from God, too, you know!"

"I never dreamed my own sister would become my enemy!" Bethany said, sounding hurt. "I would never, never behave in such a fashion! I can't believe you think so ill of me as to—" She didn't finish and instead threw herself onto the large canopy bed and lay face down, crying into the pillow.

Lily paused, watching her sister for a moment before walking slowly towards her and joining her on the bed. She gently stroked Bethany's hair. "I didn't mean it, Bethany." She sighed and pulled herself onto the bed with her sister. "I just love him so much."

"I know you do, Lily!" Bethany responded, tears flowing from her eyes. Dane knew that the tears were conjured. He didn't know how he knew; perhaps his years of being friends with Jenny in the 20th century helped him read her moods. Regardless, he knew Bethany was lying to Lily. Whatever the reason for his knowing, the end result was the same; Jenny—Bethany—was going through a lot of trouble to convince her sister, Lily, that she didn't like some guy. Clearly a premeditated deception. But why?

"You never cease to have a parade of suitors," Lily said quietly, "while I've only ever had Paul."

Bethany looked at Lily. "He does seem to like you an awful lot." Lily nodded, a smile spreading across her face. "And once the two of you are married, I am free to marry, too. That's why I'm happy for you."

"Because he loves me, or that you'll be free to marry?" Lily asked, a hint of laughter in her voice.

"Both," Bethany said with a giggle. "It isn't fair I can't marry as long as you remain without a husband!" Lily nodded in agreement. "I hate father sometimes. He is so old fashioned!"

"You mustn't say that!" Lily responded. "He has faith in his convictions!"

"Still, as long as you remain here without a man, I am . . ." her voice trailed off. Lily brushed her hair once again.

"Silly of me to be jealous of you and Paul!" Lily said with a giggle. "You couldn't hurt a fly! You are sweet, smart, beautiful, and kind. You have always been the good one." She leaped from the bed and ran to the large wooden desk in the corner of the room. She grabbed at something and returned to the four poster bed with equal vigor. "Here," Lily said, holding it out to Bethany.

"What is it?" She asked, sitting up.

"My letter opener," Lily responded with a smile. *"While I am visiting Aunt Ruth, I will write every day. I want you to use my letter opener when you receive my post. That way, we can still be connected even though we are worlds away!"*

"Oh, Lily! Thank you! What a lovely idea!" Bethany screamed, throwing her arms around her sister's neck. *"I hate using that old knife to open letters. The handle is so big and bulky."*

"But it is beautiful." Lily whispered. *"I love mother-of-pearl."*

"Yes," Bethany agreed, *"But to open letters?"*

"True," Lily laughed and paused a moment to soothe her sister's hair. *"Just remember—after Paul puts me onto the train this evening, you shan't hear from me for several days. Nobody shall."*

"Alright, I'll remember," Bethany smiled. *"I am so jealous that you are to be gone so long. Why can't I go with you to Aunt Ruth's?"*

"Who will stay here and make Paul his favorite pecan pie?" Lily asked. *"Remember—every Sunday after church, both he and the Pastor like their pecan pie."*

Lily nodded. The two women looked at each other lovingly and embraced, rocking on the bed. Dane watched Bethany's face closely. He was sure he saw a smirk spread across her lips. Dane knew this expression, as he knew Jenny's caustic humor from years of enduring it himself. This was her *"fuck you"* look.

Without warning, Dane felt the house shudder. After all these years in California, he knew an earthquake when he felt one. Instinctively, he scanned the room for a doorway to stand in and took several steps towards the bedroom before remembering he wasn't actually in any danger. He froze mid stride. Across the room, pictures flew off walls, tables toppled and vases tumbled off shelves and smashed onto the floor. The world around him went black and for a moment he sensed his body spinning wildly out of control.

*   *   *

As suddenly as it started, the sensation ceased and he found himself looking down onto a tiny room filled with miniature people. Beneath him, the toy-sized people stood on a small stage that was an exact reproduction of the sitting room he had just visited. It rocked wildly, sending furnishings *sliding across the floor. The sound of glass shattering split the air. In the corner where the piano sat laden with rose petals and the immense vase of roses, the huge instrument danced as if alive. However, in this scene, the only two people present in the room were Bethany and Lily, both frantic, eyes wide with fear.*

The tiny dollhouse below him was reminiscent of the time he accompanied Jenny to a rehearsal when she was cast in a slapstick comedy in Oakland. Jenny called it a "speed through" and explained it was actors' terminology for something called "pick up rehearsal." As he watched from the back of the empty theater, the actors of the farce ran through their movements on stage at a breakneck pace, spewing their lines so quickly he missed most of what they were saying. Dane laughed, not from the play's innate humor, but from the comical way the live performance felt, like watching a movie on fast forward. Doors flew open and shut, actors jumped up and down like people on crack and before he had a chance to digest the material, the actors were taking their curtain call. Within an hour, he and Jenny were on their way to dinner.

Now, for the second time, he was watching a live drama set on fast forward. Almost faster than he could follow, he watched as the two girls began screaming again. Did they ever stop, he mused. But his grin faded the minute he saw the sharp weapon in Bethany's hand. He felt goose bumps break out along his arms as he saw Lily, her green dress gathered in her hands, rush to the sitting room door, grabbing wildly at anything to steady herself from falling. While Lily dashed around the room panic-stricken, Bethany froze, oddly calm. From within the folds of her dress, she pulled a large knife with a mother-of-pearl handle, which she flashed ominously in Lily's direction. Unknown to the frightened Lily, Bethany came at her from behind. In a blinding flash of speed, Bethany sent the knife plunging into Lily's back. He groaned in sympathy as Bethany stuck her sister again and again, shoving the knife deep into the green velvet dress as the room around them tore apart, walls crumbling and plaster falling. Then, as Lily crumpled to the floor, the sitting room doors burst open and a handsome young man entered.

He knew that this man was the mysterious Paul the girls spoke of earlier and the cause behind their sibling rivalry. But when he spied his betrothed laying on the floor bleeding, rather than bemoan the death, Paul laughed sinisterly, strode to Bethany and kissed her passionately. From far below, Dane heard the faint voice of Paul saying, "I love you, Bethany Dayton."

"And I, you, my dear." Bethany replied sweetly.

When the tiny actor on the miniature stage beneath him looked up, Dane saw himself staring into the face of Jake. He recoiled backwards. Jake? His Jake? He felt a sharp jab in his back and spun around wildly. The blue dolphin floated in the darkness, its eternal smile forged on its snout. He looked into its eyes.

REMEMBER ANGAKOK.

He nodded. Twice he had witnessed the red-haired woman from his dreams be murdered. Both times, the murderers were people he knew, or at least in the case of Ralph S. Thompson, someone he'd heard of. Were these murders somehow connected to the present time? Neither Jenny nor Jake mentioned knowing this red-haired woman, did they? He felt sure that Jenny would have mentioned it, as he had recounted the dreams several times to her and each time she acted as if they were products of his imagination. If she knew–

REMEMBER ANGAKOK.

Dane glared at the dolphin. He had always thought they were carefree, curious, delightful creatures. Now found them totally annoying. He looked at its face and felt that for once, the snout didn't look like a smile, but a smirk. Remember what? Was he, as Mrs. Jeremy suggested, recalling some form of past life, or was he experiencing some hallucinatory dream triggered by his years of drinking and drug use in his twenties? The sensation of dreaming permeated these visions, so who could tell the difference? Was there a difference? He didn't know Ralph S. Thompson at all, not even a chance meeting. What did he possibly have in common with Jenny, anyway?

They had both been attacked.

Dane's blood ran cold. He struggled to remember the news report about Ralph Thompson. The man was found dead in a hotel room, wasn't he? Yes. The police were searching for a woman with whom he was last seen. Did the report say what she looked like? Dane tried to replay the TV report in his mind, but he couldn't focus. Damn! If this was the red-haired woman from his dreams, Ralph had sure as hell seen her, perhaps been murdered by her, and Jenny was…what? How could the two incidents be related? But the facts were impossible to deny. The past life Ralph and Jenny had both killed the redhead, while the present Ralph and Jenny had been attacked by her. Surely the coincidence couldn't stop here, could it?

He looked up into the eyes of the dolphin. "Show me more."

*   *   *

The tiny stage disappeared and Dane found himself standing in a large, cavernous room. An enormous quilted rug lay on the cracked wooden floor, covering the planks from the fireplace to the entry door on the opposite wall. The room was sparsely decorated with tasteful and expensive looking bric-a-brac that seemed to have no theme. Before him, huge bay windows overlooked a thick, green forest, cut by a narrow dirt road leading from the house in which he stood into the forest's dark interior. Standing along three of the four walls of the room, a band of shabbily dressed people stood silent, their dirt stained faces looking grim. They exchanged fervent glances and shifted their weight from foot to foot as if remaining still was a chore. The center of their attention, however, was a large, round table that dominated the room.

Dane had become accustomed to inheriting an entire lifetime of memories whenever the scenery changed. This time, however, he received no intuitive knowledge, no flash of information. Dane only knew for sure that the year was 1899. He studied the solemn, frowning people scattered throughout the room and tried to figure out who they were. Judging by their mismatched clothing and eating utensils hanging from their belts, they were nomads. Thieves? Outlaws? Settlers? He spotted both Kevin and Sean's faces amongst the sea of riff-raff, but he didn't recognize anyone else. Again, like the visions before this, Sean looked directly at Dane, and Dane felt a chill crawl along his spine. Why did the boy give him the creeps? And why did he, of all of the people he knew, seem to find him no matter where he stood?

Dane turned to the table and studied the people sitting around it. Immediately to his left sat a short, squat man of about twenty-five years. On his head, a threadbare hat sat trying to hide the oily mess of hair beneath it. He looked at the face once it stopped fluctuating and wasn't surprised to see Jake staring at him through the dirt and grime. He grinned at the irony. Jake wouldn't be caught dead in public without a shower and fresh clothes today. Sitting opposite of Jake was an ordinary man of medium height and stout frame, dressed in ill-fitting, dirty clothes. His thinning hair ran to his shoulders and stayed tied into a ponytail with a strand of leather—another version of himself. Great! So male pattern baldness gets to follow me forever, he thought grimly.

Between them sat a small wisp of a woman dressed in flowing robes of dark colors. Several necklaces hung from her scrawny neck, earrings dangled from her lobes, and rings bedecked her fingers. She held a deck of cards between her hands and her head was thrown backwards as if in ecstasy. She moaned and rolled her shoulders dramatically. Her face was Mrs. Jeremy's.

The ponytailed man with Dane's face leaned over to the Jake figure and whispered, "Is she alright, Master?"

"Shhhh! Michael, you must not speak!" the man with Jake's face snapped. "Gretchen the Gypsy is a powerful force. Do not anger her. You must let her do her magic without question."

Dane nodded as he watched the exchange. So, his name was Michael. Gretchen the Gypsy was Mrs. Jeremy. Did she always play the part of a mystic?

"You, Michael, you were there!" Gretchen yelled. "Did Robert cheat?" she asked, pointing her gnarled finger at the man with Jake's face.

"No, I think not," Michael stammered, shooting a glance to Robert.

"Then you say to me that Christian Kelly is more skilled than I, Robert Davenport?" Robert leaned across the table menacingly and glared at Michael. Dane, watching form the sidelines, felt queasy. He didn't like arguing with Jake in this lifetime, why the hell would he want to watch himself argue in a past lifetime?

"No, Master," Michael responded fearfully. "I say only that luck cannot follow us every day of our lives, sir."

"I see," Robert answered. "I'll remind you, Michael, that you are in my employ and living in my house."

"Yes, sir, and for that I am grateful," Michael whispered, looking away. "I am eternally thankful you find me fit as a valet. Nevertheless, my answer remains the same."

Gretchen held her hands in the air, quieting the two men. "The cards...not look good still...time is bad. BAD!" she screamed, startling those watching. "You say sorry and go home."

Her words dripped with an odd accent, one that Dane had never heard before. He noticed her nervous fiddling with the cards and the deft way in which she fondled them.

"I'm telling you, you old bat," Robert said, standing, "the lying dog cheated me in this battle of skill! I will not be made to look the fool—even before you dirty gypsies!" He slammed his hand upon the table.

Angakok   177

Gretchen's eyes popped open and she glared at him while holding up her hand to stave off the spectators, who had moved in Robert's direction. Robert turned to the posse and glared at them with disdain. "All of you! Go back to whatever hole you crawled out of! Michael!" He spat, without turning, "my horse!"

Gretchen sighed and shook her head. "What is foretold…will of the gods. Do nothing." With that, the old woman gathered her cards and stuffed them into a large woven bag. She then turned to Michael, "I done teach to you now. I helped you, yes?"

Michael nodded. "Thank you. You…were good to me"

She sniffed and gathered her skirts around her. Before stepping from the table, she turned to Michael and stared at him intensely. "Remember, boy," she said ominously. "Remember what you see today. Important, what you see today. We meet again. Remember." Without another word, Gretchen motioned to the band of gypsies and exited the room. One by one the party left, making sure to walk backwards out the door, keeping their eyes focused on Robert. When the gypsies were gone, Robert motioned to Michael to follow and the two left the room.

Dane instantly felt himself shifting in place, like an elevator lifting. Dane braced himself for the scene change as the world around him blurred into a mass of melting color. When his vision cleared, Dane found himself in a clearing in the woods, standing next to Michael and another young man, this one barely eighteen, with long legs and arms, dressed in a simple shirt and breeches. He watched the face of the boy and, once the shifting had settled, was relieved to see it held the face of Jenny.

"Kurt," Michael whispered to the young lad, "Gretchen the Gypsy said bad blood breeds bad times."

Kurt guffawed. "You spend too much time with that old bat. Remember what she said about my master?"

Michael nodded sheepishly. "Yes. And he would have killed me if I delivered that message. The woman was betrothed to another."

Kurt scoffed and turned his attention to the clearing in the woods where two men were boxing. "Oh! Christian got in a good punch! Careful or your master will need you to drag him home once again on this night."

Dane followed Kurt's finger. A few feet in front of him, Robert, stripped from the waist up, bounced on the balls of his feet, fists clenched in front of him. He boxed with another lean, young man with flaming red hair, also stripped to the waist. Dane wasn't surprised to see the face belonged to Lily. The two men fought viciously, like rabid dogs turned upon each other. It became apparent, however, that Christian was by far the better boxer. For every punch Robert landed, Christian landed three. Robert's left eye puffed out to three times its size and blood cascaded down his cheek. Robert thrust towards Christian, but the redhead was too quick for him and dodged to his right, throwing Robert off balance and sending him falling into the dirt.

Christian sidestepped over to the fallen Robert when suddenly he began to flail. His arms spun madly in the air and his right leg buckled under him. He collapsed to the ground, clutching his right ankle. "God be damned!" he said through clenched teeth. "A rabbit hole!"

Robert rolled onto his back and looked up at Christian clutching his foot. "Ah! Too bad my friend."

"Robert, help me up." Christian said, holding out his right hand.

"This is a battle of honor, Christian Kelly!" Robert spat back at the man, rising to his feet. "You expect me to come to the aid of one who has dishonored me?"

"Robert, I told you no dishonor was meant. If you so choose—" Christian said calmly.

"I SO CHOOSE!" Robert spat, leaping onto Christian like a ravenous animal.

"Robert! No!" Christian screamed as Robert landed on him. Christian held up his arms in defense and yanked at his foot, desperate to free it from its prison. But the actions were in vain, as Robert grasped Christian's head between his massive hands and twisted.

The snap of Christian's neck reverberated through the woods. Dane joined both Michael and Kurt as they turned their eyes away from the murder.

"Michael! My horse!" Robert's voice rang through the darkness, shrill with panic.

Dane turned towards the young valet and watched as Michael turned away from the scene to do the bidding of his employer. Dane shot a glance to Robert, who stood gazing down upon Christian's lifeless body. Could this barbaric man be the same one that he currently lived with? Dane shook his head in disgust.

He saw the blue dolphin approach from behind Robert, its annoying smirk plastered on its stubby snout. He knew what the fucking dolphin would say—REMEMBER. Dane rolled his eyes. He is remembering, isn't he? Every incarnation there was a murder. The victim remained the same.

The red-haired woman who died that day in San Francisco. The same day he died. She was murdered by someone who impacted his life: Ralph Thompson…Jake. Yes, he saw the pattern. He knew why he had been shown these visions. He never wanted to see A Christmas Carol *again.*

He turned towards Robert and watched the dolphin getting closer through the clearing. As it moved, the forest around him began to lose texture and substance and was soon fading away, the outlines of the trees and people becoming one with the blackness of the night.

Suddenly the blue dolphin shifted direction and shot straight upwards into the sky and out of sight.

"Hey!" Dane shouted after it. "Where are you going?"

"NO!" a woman's voice bellowed from out of the darkness. "NO!"

Dane spun, seeking out the source of the voice. What the hell was going on? Without warning, the remaining bits of forest began to shift and twirl. As the dizzying revolutions engulfed him, Dane felt queasy and felt as if he would throw up. The world collapsed around him in a flash. After a second of weightlessness, he felt himself plummeting downward, toward a bright white light. Dane felt himself colliding against something hard and found himself lying on stone. He sat up, letting the world around him settle before opening his eyes.

He stared into the face of Christian Kelly.

"I could have killed you long before now," Christian sneered. Feeling dazed and drained, Dane got to his knees. Christian Kelly? What was going on? Christian strode towards him, saying in a flat, dull voice, "I offered you a chance to join me, Dane. I had hoped you would rethink your bad decision, but it seems you haven't."

Dane? Did he just call me by name? Why did this guy look like Christian Kelly but sound like a woman? "I don't know what you're talking about." Dane croaked. His throat felt like sandpaper.

"We can do this the traditional way, then." Christian said. He motioned towards Dane and Dane felt himself flying backwards, crashing into the wall of the shrine with a violent thud. With another gesture towards him, Dane felt his guts squeeze and a sharp pain radiate through his bowels. Dane clutched his stomach and rolled forward, gasping for breath. What the hell was going on? He heard footsteps approach, a soft click of heels on stone. When he sensed someone above him, he opened his eyes and looked at Christian.

But the man's face shifted and changed. Just like the previous visions, the features altered themselves until they settled into a new pattern and then solidified. The face was no longer Christian Kelly, but the red-haired woman from his dreams.

Dane said. "I know you."

Christian/Lily/April laughed heartily. "You think so?"

Dane nodded. "I remember."

"Dane!" A voice shouted from far away. "Dane! You come back this instant!"

Christian looked around, frantically. "You're too late, Gypsy!" He screamed to the sky. With another gesture, Dane felt his brain pulsate and a pressure erupt behind his eyes so strong, he felt as if his eyeballs would shoot out of his head.

"DANE! IT'S ME, SONJA JEREMY! COME HOME! NOW!"

Dane struggled to hear the voice. Who was it again? He recognized it from somewhere. But it sounded so far away and the pain of his head! His head seared like it was in a vise!

"You should have followed my suggestion last time," Christian said.

Dane rolled on the stone clutching his head. The yelling! Shut the fuck up! What last time was this crazy hermaphrodite talking about? He rolled over and looked up, expecting to see the crazy red-headed man/woman/Christian/Lily person but instead he saw the walls of the shrine glow intensely. As he lay clutching his temples, the pictures on the shrine's walls began to move. In a sudden burst of color, the walls came alive with a flurry of images that flashed before him.

The red Mercedes. The motorcycle. The dark sky over San Francisco. Dane floating above the hospital, a long cord reaching from his navel to the third floor. A second cord next to him. The void. The shrine. A red-haired woman sitting with him at the foot of the pedestal while the Book glowed brightly. Her saying, "My name is Victoria. Victoria Lemark." Calendar pages flew past. Jenny's voice boomed out "You weren't just in coma, you were like—only half there, know what I mean?"...Victoria reading from the Book "Come with me, Dane. We have power now."...Dane running, running, running...Victoria following, chasing him down...the Book has powers, Dane...power...revenge...Don't you want revenge?...Together we can be unstoppable.

SATURDAY, JULY 8

2:16 PM

"DANE, YOU FUCKING SON OF A BITCH. COME BACK RIGHT NOW!" *the familiar voice screamed at him. Who was that?*

"IT'S ME! SONJA JEREMY!" the voice screamed from all around him. He felt a punch on the shoulder and a giant hand shaking him. He forced himself to speak, swimming against the pain.

"Mrs. Jeremy! Help!" he bellowed.

Dane felt a strong tug and suddenly his body was falling backwards through the stone floor of the shrine. He fell, plummeting downwards until he came to rest with a jerk. He opened his eyes and stared into Mrs. Jeremy's concerned face.

"Welcome home, boy," she said. "Want some tea?"

* * *

Christian convulsed as the spirit sank back into this body. The ritual of returning from the Book never varied and never became easier, only faster. Since he had made this journey so often, he needed only a short time before he was able to function normally again. Once grounded, Christian sat up, wiped the sweat from his forehead and concentrated on focusing his eyes on the world around him. He quivered slightly as the cool night air played over his naked skin, which was covered in a fine mist of perspiration.

Damn! Dane escaped! This time she felt so sure he would be the victor. After all, he had been taken by surprise. He coughed and cursed Gretchen the Gypsy while he wiped the bloody spittle from his lips. The old whore had once again chosen to side with that boy against him, did she? So be it. Christian had expected as much, which was why Christian had planned on killing the old bat earlier. If he hadn't arrived at such an inopportune moment, the fat woman would be dead by now. Keeping with tradition, the two of them seemed locked into another lifetime of cooperation and mutual support. Next time, he would have to kill both Sonja Jeremy and Dane at the same time. That shouldn't be too hard.

The journey was not a total loss, however. True, Dane had escaped her, but Christian now had much more information. First, proof that Dane had never consciously returned to the Book. After Victoria's first visit, when she and Dane had met in the shrine after their accident, Victoria returned to this lifetime with full memory of the Book, and with each subsequent visit, returned more powerful and less confused. He, on the other hand, knew nothing of the Book's purpose, power, or possible uses. This ignorance could prove to be his downfall.

Second, information about this "friend." Until today, Christian had no idea the hotel was in close proximity to the Robert entity. Foolish not to realize it, as Christian clearly remembered feeling the familiar tingle of connection whenever one of the entities from the past was in close proximity. But he had been so absorbed in the plan to kill Ralph S. Thompson to notice.

Christian stood, wrapping himself with the threadbare sheet from the lumpy bed. He went to the window and closed it, cutting off the chilly bay breeze. Looking into the afternoon sun, he noticed that the full moon was already visible. How appropriate that tonight of all nights, while the moon shone bright and full like it had the night Victoria first heard the Book call to her, that she would die. Christian coughed again and realized that this time, the lungs brought up a great deal more blood than ever before.

*   *   *

"The walls are breaking down," Dane repeated to her as if he had never said the words before. "The walls are breaking down."

"Dane, if you don't stop saying that, I'm going to smack the shit out of you," Mrs. Jeremy sighed, grabbing another cookie and breaking it in half for Ace, who sat looking at her expectantly.

"But it's so appropriate!" Dane nearly screamed, as he had rarely felt so excited. "Get it? Yeah, yeah, sure, breaking down, meaning the barrier between me and the Book, but also breaking down the mystery of who this woman is."

"Slow down boy, before you give yourself a coronary."

"It's breaking her down, too!" he said hurriedly. Then, to Mrs. Jeremy's confused look continued. "I think she's dying. I think the visits are killing her."

"Doubt it," Mrs. Jeremy said between bites of her Oreo, "the shrine doesn't detract from your health. It's probably making her stronger. If anything, it's the misuse of power that's killing her. It always does. Guaranteed. Besides, look at you. You've been making visits and you're fine."

Dane eyed her inquisitively. "I've never been back."

"Oh, Dane, please!" Mrs. Jeremy laughed and tossed the remainder of the cookie to Ace. "What the fuck do you think those crazy dreams are?"

He stared at her in disbelief.

With a sigh, she continued. "Remember your physical therapist? She said you were coming along so well that it looked like a fucking miracle? Hello! Welcome to the miracle network." She reached for another cookie.

"That's not the same thing. And stop giving Ace so many cookies."

"Not scientifically, no, but Dane, Jesus! You were dead."

"I know. People keep reminding me."

"AND," she said, raising her voice, "within weeks you were fine. You tell me how that's possible." She put down the tea cup and moved to him. She laid her hand on his head and he jerked in pain as she kneaded the sore spot on his head. "And how, pray tell, did you get that lump?"

Dane looked sheepishly at her and shrugged. "I don't know. I wish I had the answers."

"Careful what you wish for. You'll get it," she wagged a finger at him. "I'll tell you how you got that lump. There's a crackpot fucking theory that says anything that happens to your spirit body while on a journey can affect your physical body. Odds are that I'm wrong and it's not a crackpot theory. Maybe it's true. If not, then maybe the connection between you two is so strong, it can manifest in the physical realm."

"Well," Dane said slumping into the chair, "that sucks. I can get hurt here, I can get hurt there."

"Boo-fucking-hoo! Boy, listen to me because I'm old." She leaned over until her eyes were inches from his. "There is no such thing as 'safe.' It's a concept the fucking insurance companies concocted so they could make people feel 'unsafe' and sell them products to feel 'safe' again. Nobody's ever fucking 'safe' from anything!" She pointed a crooked finger at him. "There's so much about the other side we don't know," her voice faded out.

"I don't know," he replied after a second, "blue dolphins? Shrines of light? Purple water? I never dropped acid but it seems like a bad trip."

"Well, I DID drop acid and this is a butt load better than a bad trip." She laughed uproariously, stopping only when she saw the concern on his face.

"Do you know how many people would give their left tit—or nut—to have experienced a journey like that?" She placed her hand on his knee and squeezed.

He smiled weakly at her.

"You've got a direct connection to the other side, boy. True, you had to die to get it, but it happens that way sometimes. These things happen to people who have cheated death, or suffered blows to the head…the veil between here and there has lifted for you. The curtain is open and now you're seeing a wonderful production of history!"

"Group karma," she nodded, jotting down notes in her book. "Theory. People incarnate together at the same time, rotating between the roles of parent, child, blah blah fucking blah."

He laughed loudly as she finished jotting a note.

She then turned to him and said harshly. "Laugh if you want, but this red-haired woman is playing the role of the villain this time, and we need to know everything about her.

*   *   *

Jeannette slammed down the phone, sending the nurses into another tizzy.

"Sorry," she said, although she wasn't sorry at all. Where was everyone? Jake hadn't answered, Dane was incommunicado and Mrs. Jeremy had left the hospital before her volunteer shift was over. What the hell was going on?

*   *   *

Jake looked at the phone on his desk for the hundredth time that day. The urge to call Dane was so overwhelming that Jake felt like an addict looking for his next fix. What bothered him was he didn't know if the urge to connect with Dane was because he missed the guy, or habit. Shouldn't he know the reason behind his needing to speak to him? After all this time together, shouldn't he want to talk to his partner, or do all couples reach a point in their relationship that habit replaces desire? Is that normal or codependent?

Jake pushed himself away from his desk and stood up. Damn this indecision! He was not the indecisive type and this kind of mind fucking was too disconcerting. He didn't like feeling dependent on anyone—Dane included.

What he needed was a break. Maybe he should go visit Jenny in the hospital. Jeannette had tried to call him several times, but talking to her was one thing he was not going to do. Not yet. Jenny was originally Dane's friend and visiting her without Dane while he and Dane were on the verge of breaking up seemed . . . somehow a betrayal. He should go see her, though. Tell her his side of the story before he left. Maybe it would–

No. It would only end badly. Best he let Dane contact her first. Let the two of them have their time together before he brought the attention to himself. He looked at the clock and was surprised to see that a whole day had elapsed while he had been drowning in the documents pertaining to the land sale. He grabbed his jacket, made sure his card key was firmly attached to his belt and headed out of his office. When the airlines called him back earlier today, they had offered him two choices of replacement seats: either two o'clock or the midnight red-eye. Since the early afternoon flight had a three-hour layover in Denver, he opted for the direct, nonstop at midnight. The good news was that it gained him an extra day in the office to catch up on paperwork. The bad news was this it gained him an extra day in the office to catch up on some paperwork. But, he had made his decision and he planned to make the most of the situation.

He pushed the button for the elevator but decided to take the stairs instead. He'd been sitting all day and wanted the opportunity to stretch his legs. As he pulled the stairway door open, he said a silent thank you for the chance to be in the office alone. Although a bit surprising that none of the attorneys, interns, or secretaries showed up even for a few hours on a Saturday, it was a welcome surprise, as he relished the time alone. He hit the first floor and opened the door to the lobby. His eyes instantly went to the Holiday Inn across the street and he made the split second decision to stop by the bar and grab a burger.

As he opened the side door to the hotel, he got that eerie sensation of being watched again and looked around him. He stood, door in hand for several minutes, but after satisfying himself that nobody was watching him, he stepped into the building and headed down the hallway towards the bar.

*   *   *

Christian stood on the corner of Market waiting for the traffic to clear when he looked up and caught sight of Robert. He seemed to be daydreaming, paying no attention to the traffic or the people around him as he hurried across the street and into the hotel. Christian smiled. This was indeed a stroke of luck. Kill the low hanging fruit first. Conserve energy.

She checked for traffic and heading for the side entrance. After April and Lily had been spotted in the vicinity of the hotel, it would be wise to avoid confronting any more people than necessary. Perhaps all he would do is wait by the exit for Robert to appear, thus negating the need to enter at all. Yes, this is what she would do.

She coughed violently into her hand as she headed for the door.

* * *

Jake listened as the phone rang. Where was he? Dane had no plans today. Maybe out with Ace? Jake waited for the beep of the machine and spoke quickly. "Hi. It's me. I'm not in Maine yet. It's a long story and I'll tell you about it later. But I know how much you worry. So don't. I'm fine. Bye." He hung up wishing he had said "I love you" or something.

* * *

Christian pressed his back against the hallway leading from the lobby of the hotel to the restaurant waiting for the entity known as Robert.

The man hung up the phone and turned away, headed down the hallway and straight for him. He spun around, facing one of the many posters advertising the hotel's amenities and pretended to read the propaganda. Christian felt Robert's energy approaching. Just as he was upon her, Christian felt him change direction. As soon as Robert walked out of range of his senses, he turned to investigate the cause of his course re-direction. The restaurant. Christian thought for a moment he may follow, perhaps calmly sit at his table and toy with him a bit before snapping his neck.

The fantasy felt good, but she knew it would be more fun to wait. Until the entity was alone in his office. Then Robert would feel the pain and fear he inflicted so many years ago return.

* * *

They had polished off an entire pot of tea and two more bags of cookies, ginger snaps and Nilla Wafers, as Dane finished his tale. When he ended the long story of his journey, he waited for Mrs. Jeremy to finish jotting her notes into the journal and gulped down the last of his tea. Mrs. Jeremy closed the book, thought hard for a moment and then looked him in the eye.

"I think you're right. She's going to go after Jake." The old woman said flatly.

He was afraid she would agree with him. "But it's so ..." he gasped, looking for the right word.

"Logical?" She asked. He rolled his eyes and began to protest, but she shouted over him, "Dane! Will you fucking THINK for a MINUTE!" She paused to make sure she had his attention. "You said yourself she was killed by the man you thought was Ralph S. Thompson Jr; then a woman who looked like Jenny, then Jake. That's the reason your spirit guide showed you those particular incarnations." She leaned over and gently grasped his hands in hers.

"I don't know" Dane muttered. "This whole thing sounds so..."

"What?" Mrs. Jeremy said harshly, thrusting her finger into his face. "Outlandish? There is more to heaven and earth than are dreamt of in your philosophy, Dane. Plenty of civilizations believe we've lived before. What's so odd about it, eh?" She smiled broadly and cupped his face in her hands. "Is the idea we've lived before any more outlandish than the idea of dying and living on white puffy clouds for all eternity? Or some fiery pit of hell that tortures us for past sins? Open your mind, boy."

"Fine. I'll open my mind." Dane said, leaning forward in his chair. "Say it's this group karma thing is happening. Why Ralph S. Thompson Jr?"

Mrs. Jeremy laughed and waddled to a large oak bookshelf against the far wall of the apartment. "I don't know why, dear, but he is, as you saw, affecting both you and the redhead now as he did then, isn't he?" She said, pulling from the bottom of a stack of books.

"You saw him commit murder when you were the young boy in the barn, which affected you at that time, and you did nothing. Understandingly so," she added quickly, seeing the hurt expression on his face. "But the opportunity to do something this time is presenting itself. A second chance to make the right choice." She tugged once, twice, three times before the newspaper would give up its place and allow itself to be jerked from under the stack of books. "I saw this article a couple days ago and found it significant. Ralph's wife doesn't accept his murder as a random act. She's the one pushing the police to question that girl he was seen with the night he died." She took the crumpled newspaper over to Dane, who waited impatiently.

Dane took the paper, looked at the headline and accompanying picture and reeled as if struck. The picture of Ralph S. Thompson was the same one he had seen several times on TV over the last couple of days. Only this time, Ralph's eyes stared at him through the years. It was the same face he had seen in his vision: the man punching a helpless servant. He nodded soberly and handed the paper back to Mrs. Jeremy. He suddenly felt sick to his stomach. The overwhelming smell of Mrs. Jeremy's tea lingered in the air. He needed to be free of here, of this room with its memories and possibilities and worst of all, its pressing sense of responsibility. He suddenly felt like his life was a runaway train that had taken its passenger into the Twilight Zone.

"No, we're not exempt from her hit list, either," a voice filtered into his consciousness. "That's what you're thinking, right?" Mrs. Jeremy's voice continued. "She's after revenge. She wants those people who killed her in previous lives. We're not on the top of the list, boy, but we are on it. Oh, yes, we certainly are."

She fumbled through a stack of books, finding a small black one near the bottom of the pile. She opened it and thrust it into his hands. Dane looked onto its red-lined pages and examined the list of connections that had been made by Mrs. Jeremy's late husband.

"I suspect you see exactly what Marshall meant," Mrs. Jeremy said softly.

Dane closed his eyes, but violent images haunted him, growing stronger and more vibrant in the fertile imagination of his mind: the harsh, cruel man smacking his fists into the servant over and over again; the sisters quarreling in the house and the dress growing dark with blood from the stab wound; the clearing in the woods. Is this how she would kill Jake? Was she going to grab his skull, twist his head and snap his neck like Robert had done to Christian?

"I've got to go," Dane muttered. "Ace has to get home."

"Dane!" She shouted angrily. "Dane, snap out of it. We've got to–"

"TO DO WHAT?" Dane shouted at her, leaping from the chair. "Go to the police? Tell them, 'Hey! I just saw my past lives and know a murder is about to happen'? How about this one: we'll call everyone we know and tell them to be on the lookout because this nut just killed my best friend?"

"Jake is in danger," she said calmly.

"We are all in danger," he shot back, not listening to her. "You said so yourself. There's no such thing as 'safe'"

Mrs. Jeremy stared at him, her face flushed and puffy, and the veins in her neck throbbing with each pump of her heart. She walked to him and took him by the shoulders. "Jake will believe you, Dane. He knows. We ALL know. Deep down, we all know because our souls remember."

He pushed her away and stormed past her, heading for the leash which hung on the chair.

"Dane, listen to me, please. As children, we all remember. Back before we're fed that bullshit of our culture: Kids. Family. Job. Before all of that, we remember. Jake will remember. Just tell him. Not the police, not yet. Just Jake. Tell Jake."

"I can't," Dane said softly, his hand closing around Ace's leash. "He left this morning."

"I know that!" She laughed. "Call him in Maine."

"I don't know where he's at." He turned back to her and looked into her confused expression. "I told you things weren't . . ." he stopped, trying to phrase the words. "I don't know when or if he's coming back."

"Oh, my God," she sighed. "Well, this does present a dilemma."

"You think?" Dane stood motionless, as a terrible thought raced into his mind. "Do you think she'll be able to find him before . . .?" Mrs. Jeremy's silence answered for her and he nodded in understanding. "What was that Book?"

"It is the basis of all knowledge," she explained. "And the redhead knows how to use it. But," she paused, placing both hands on his shoulders again, "you have access to it, too."

Dane nodded and snapped the leash onto Ace's collar. "I'll try his office. The firm usually has people there on Saturdays. Someone has to know where he is. What time is it?" he glanced at his watch. "Damn. They might have all gone by now, they usually only go in for a couple hours in the morning."

"Cover all the bases. I'm afraid this old body can't do the footwork, but by God I can still push the fucking buttons on a phone. I'll call the boys, and Jeannette." She turned and waddled towards the phone.

"Listen," she said intently, "when you're out of your body, your body is vulnerable. You need someone to protect it while your spirit is away from this plane. You almost got fucked–well, not fucked, but close–over there last time."

"I feel like I'm in a really bad B-movie," he said, dazed.

"Life's a bitch. Go. Good luck." She followed him to the door and the moment he was outside, she locked it. Then lodged a chair in front of it.

*   *   *

Dane and Ace hit the corner of the bus stop and stood for a moment. If he started walking now, he could make the law firm within twenty or twenty-five minutes.

But if he waited for the bus, it may be twenty minutes before the next one came along. Besides, he looked like crap—wrinkled shirt, his remaining hair unkempt and red, bloated skin as if he had just woken up. Shit! He just wanted to know what to do. What would they say to Jake as he questioned them about hunting him down? But what was the price if Mrs. Jeremy was right? Was he willing to bet Jake's life? Damn that man! Why the hell couldn't he stay and work things out before jetting off for the East Coast? But, no, Jake was too stubborn—always doing what he wanted, never allowing for variance of any kind, and expecting his way to be the only way.

Maybe he should head home for his cell phone. But Jake's office was much closer than the condo. And, like himself, Jake probably didn't think of his cell phone during times of stress. Both he and Jake were too similar to be truly unique. Each wanted the other to relinquish power in the relationship like they were debating points in a political debate. The troubles they were having seemed so ridiculous now, so childish and stupid. Their problems were issues of pride, not values. All Jake wanted to do was help in the only way he knew how—to cure the cause of Dane's ills and overlook the symptoms. All Dane wanted to do was address the symptoms because the cause was too painful. Well, now he had the chance to stop behaving so childishly and he wasn't about to let it slip by.

Deciding he'd rather look foolish than risk harm to Jake, he turned and walked briskly towards Jake's office, Ace taking the lead. The dog seemed particularly agitated today.

*   *   *

Jake listened as the phone rang, shoving the change from the burger into his pocket. But when he heard the machine come onto the line, he hung up. He'd already left one message and leaving anymore seemed pathetically codependent. He grabbed the takeout box and headed out of the restaurant.

"Sir!" the voice bellowed after him.

Jake turned back towards the perky young lady and looked to her blankly.

She held up a small bag. "Your extra horseradish sauce." She laughed. "Can't eat those fries without it, can you?"

Jake smiled and headed back to the smiling hostess and grabbed the bag from her.

He had made it down the hall and within feet of the exit when he suddenly felt a strong pain shoot through his stomach. With one hand against the wall of the hallway, he doubled over and breathed deeply. What the heck? Gooseflesh broke out along his arms and he felt suddenly chilled. Something was wrong. Stomach flu? Had he eaten something this morning to give him indigestion? As quickly as the pain hit, it subsided and Jake straightened himself and walked briskly though the door. Even though he couldn't explain it, he felt the need to be back in his office right away.

*   *   *

Mid-stride, Dane's stomach flipped, sending a shooting pain through his stomach. He gasped for air in short, painful gulps. After a moment, the pain subsided and Dane forced himself to stand upright. The flesh on his arms still stung from the sudden uprising of the goose bumps, but that was the only sign of his odd feeling of impending doom. Ace sniffed his feet noisily and suddenly began to bark.

"What, boy?" Dane asked, beginning to walk again. Ace barked twice more, then stopped, turned, and took the lead once more as he and Dane headed up the small grade towards Jake's office. Dane shook his head. Strange behavior with the dog today, he thought. That was Ace's bark that meant a stranger was near.

*　*　*

They were driving quickly over the Golden Gate Bridge, Sean staring blankly at the stereo as Bronski Beat belted out "Tell Me Why." Kevin, oblivious to the music, daydreamed and drove onward, lost in his own thoughts. Sean shifted in his seat uncomfortably. The guilt sat in his stomach, eating at him from the inside. He had gotten a call from Jeannette earlier. Frantic, she alternated between sobs and screams as she pummeled him with questions, "Where was Dane?" "Did Kevin get a call about Jenny?" He didn't know what to do. He always shrank from confrontation and her passion seemed to physically oppress him. Later, when Jake called, he knew he should have mentioned it, but . . . he didn't. He couldn't explain why. Only that the group of friends were so close, so intimate that his revelation seemed like a betrayal to their intimacy. Jenny had been murdered and he was the only one who knew. When Jake called he should have referred him to Jeannette. But he didn't.

He always avoided confrontation. Always took the easy way out. Always played the innocent one, shirking responsibility and he had survived because of it. Someone always appeared to take care of him. But now he felt as if something inside him had changed. Perhaps it was time to play things differently. But could he? Should he? Should he be the one to say something? Shouldn't that be Kevin? Or Jeannette? He couldn't shake this piercing burn in the pit of his gut that told him something was not right. Kevin, bless him, had helped him feel much better when he told Sean about the problems Dane and Jake were having and how they might break up. Not that he wanted the two men to split, but that bit of information made Sean feel less guilty, as somehow he could help the two stay together just by wishing it to be so.

Sean's mind spun and whirled, working double time trying to figure out the cause of his restlessness. Bits and pieces of the strange, ethereal dream had flashed across his mind after awaking, making it impossible to fall back asleep, and he lay staring at the ceiling for most of the night. He tried to blot the visions out by closing his eyes, but that seemed to make the shards of memory stronger, urged on by the power of the darkness behind his eyelids. It wasn't an average, run-of-the-mill dream where he woke up with a raging hard on. Something unsettling was lingering; it was a feeling of familiarity mingled with fear.

Much like a dog that refuses to relinquish control of a toy, Sean's mind was tenacious. This tenaciousness usually worked against him, but in the battle to retrieve the pieces of last night's dreams, his tenaciousness worked in his favor. The work of tugging fragments of the fading night visions back into his consciousness was taxing work, as Sean had never been good at thinking logically. He managed to get whatever he wanted by his good looks alone. But there was an urgency about his restless sleep last night that practically screamed for release and damn if he wasn't going to give it the space to run.

Sean's father was conceived, born, grew up, and worked in a small town in northern Indiana where the towering steel mills spewed black smoke into the sky. At night, nagged by a wife he didn't want and a piece of shit kid he'd accidentally made one night at a drive-in, he figured drinking excessively was a good escape from the monotony. During those bouts of drunkenness, Sean would hide in his room, playing quietly as his father bellowed at the TV. Most of the time, the silence worked and he would drift off into sleep without seeing the old man. Other times, when he failed in his attempt to be quiet, he cowered in the corner of the room looking into the huge man with the leather strap as he felt the sting of it against his skin. Those nights, Sean would have difficulty falling asleep, which was fine with him, as the open wounds leaked blood onto his sheets, which would need to be stripped off the bed before his father woke for work.

It was during these quiet play sessions, while struggling to hide from his father, that Sean had his first visitation. He'd lie in bed, imagining a bruised and battered peasant was pleading for his help. He always helped people in his daydreams, and this was no exception. He handed the poor peasant a scrap of bread and reached out to console the poor soul with a washcloth soaked in tree bark. He held the wretched man's head in his lap, stoked the soft hair and spoke of happier times.

Sean began to remember his dream and felt chilled.

*   *   *

He opened his eyes, looked around and realized he no longer lay on his bed, but outside. He froze for a moment, unable to remember leaving his room, much less leaving his house. But, nonetheless, here he was, sitting on the cold ground as the crickets chirped around him. The night was dark and in front of him, two figures struggled wildly. One man was on the ground, while a second stood over him, glaring into the eyes of the fallen one. The standing figure twisted the neck of the man on the ground. Sean quickly lifted a thick stick high over his head and brought it down onto the murderous man's head. The crash of the wood sent a dull thud into the night air, and the figure toppled over into the grass. Once again, Sean saved the day, as he had so many times in previous daydreams. He reached down to help the wounded one to his feet, but the sound of his bedroom door being thrown open brought him back to the cramped room where his father stood holding the slim piece of leather with the metal belt buckle. As he cowered away from his old man, Sean felt something in his hands. Tree bark lined his palms.

He pushed the memory from his mind. History was in the past and best to leave it there, isn't that what his grandmother said? He had survived and escaped Indiana, hadn't he? The last laugh was his. But his daydreams of heroics didn't stop when he left the Midwest. Making matters worse, nocturnal journeys, like the one last night, frequently haunted him, hunting him down while he slept, and no matter how much he wished they would go away, they never did. In last night's dream, he remembered standing in a cold, empty field. He walked and walked and came upon a forest where he heard the sounds of a fight. He hustled through the underbrush, finally coming into a clearing where he saw three men. One stood looking down onto a still figure lying on the grass; the second stood with his back to Sean and the third stared directly at him. Sean looked to the immobile figure on the ground and his blood ran cold.

*   *   *

That's when he woke up, covered in sweat and thrashing. He hadn't been able to sleep a wink after that because the picture of the prone figure lying on the dark grass haunted him. He knew the men in the dream, in that far away manner which we simply know people in a dream. He wished he could figure out who they were! It was driving him crazy. It was like knowing the answers on *Jeopardy* but being unable to phrase them in a question. He didn't know why it was important, but Sean felt as if remembering the names of these men were very important.

"Dane and Jake..." Kevin's voice filtered into his thoughts. The babble continued, but all Sean could hear was "Dane and Jake, Dane and Jake, DaneandJakeDaneandJakeDaneand . . ."

"STOP THE CAR!" Sean shrieked.

Kevin spun towards the boy with eyes wide.

"Dane's in trouble!" Sean said quickly through a mouth that was suddenly dry and filled with cotton. "They're trying to kill him. Go back. Go back now." He grabbed for the wheel and the car spun madly to the right.

An irate driver behind them laid on the horn and the shrill blaring screamed across the bridge as the Toyota's brakes squealed.

"Sean! Sean! What are you doing?" Kevin screamed, trying to push the crazed lunatic away from the steering column.

"No!" Sean yelled, tugging at the wheel.

"You're going to get us killed." Kevin yelled, hoping to hell they'd make it to Sausalito before the car careened into the bay.

But Sean couldn't stop himself. Like a wall collapsing, Sean suddenly saw that which had been hidden; he saw the faces and heard the names that had eluded him for ten years. The men in his dream were the same ones who were in his vision years ago as a child in Indiana—they were Dane and Jake. And one of them was going to die.

*   *   *

"I've seen you here before," the redhead quipped.

Jake stood grinning, his foot propping open the glass door to the lobby of the law offices. He looked away long enough to replace the card key into his pocket, but when he looked back, he saw that the redhead hadn't moved. The mirrored sunglasses reflected his own image, making Jake a bit uncomfortable, as he preferred to look into the eyes of the person to whom he spoke. The redhead appeared a few moments ago, seemingly out of the shadows, as he turned his back to slide the cardkey through the reader. One minute, Jake stood alone on the sidewalk with his lunch balanced on the crook of his arm, the next he stood addressing a trim figure with the shoddy haircut and mirrored sunglasses.

"Really?" Jake asked, trying to sound calm. "Do you work downtown?"

"In a manner of speaking."

The two stood facing each other and a strange quiet descended around them. Jake took in the lad and sized him up quickly. Jake never had been attracted to younger men; he much preferred someone his own age. In addition, this guy was rather effeminate in mannerisms and androgynous in appearance, so much so that Jake saw no evidence of beard stubble. All told, there was nothing about this lad that would attract Jake. He preferred beefier men with five o'clock shadows and brazen machismo. But despite all the reasons why he shouldn't be attracted to him, Jake felt an odd magnetism towards the young man. He assumed the redhead was most likely transgendered, but that was not what bothered him. He found himself transfixed by the stranger and unable to tear himself away.

What bothered him was the loss of control.

Without speaking, the stranger grabbed the door and held it open.

Jake nodded politely and entered. "I don't think there's anybody left in the building," Jake said trying to sound collected. "I was the only one here all day, I believe. Odd, yes, but true nonetheless. Who are you here to see?"

"I came to see you." The man responded in a voice so soft that Jake almost missed it.

"Me?" Jake asked, stopping short. "I'm sorry, have we met?"

The redhead smiled and nodded. "Oh, yes. Yes, we have."

Jake stared into the reflection of himself in the sunglasses. Why couldn't they come off? He wanted to see those eyes behind the glasses. He needed to see those eyes. "I'm sorry, Mr. ...?"

"Christian. My name is Christian." Christian did not offer his hand.

"Christian?" Jake mused. "I'm not placing the name."

But he never finished his thought. With a deft move, Christian reached up and snatched the glasses off his face and glared at Jake intently. The eyes bore into Jake, dissecting him, tunneling through his mind and purging him of all thought. The eyes seemed to twinkle and glow. Jake stood frozen in place, unable to speak or move. He suddenly felt light-headed and queasy. What the hell was happening?

"You'll place the name. Soon." Christian said. "I am not one to be forgotten easily." Christian stepped towards Jake, bringing himself within a few inches of the startled man. "You knew me once before, as well. Long before. Remember?"

Jake saw Christian's face moving towards him, cutting the distance between the two, but Jake was unable to respond. As if his body suffered a strange catatonia, he merely stood and watched as Christian brought their lips together. He felt the warmth of their tongues exploring each other's mouths before he realized what was happening. Suddenly Jake's body shifted into auto-pilot. He reached out with his free hand and pulled Christian close, wrapping his arm about the thin, boney shoulders and shoved his tongue into the waiting mouth. What the hell was he doing?

Christian's mouth felt soft and velvety, devoid of the rough coarseness with which Jake was familiar. But it didn't matter right now. Christian's touch sent jolts of electricity through him, sending his heart racing and his cock stirring. Why did this feel so right? What was this boy doing to him? Every fiber of his body awoke and the very touch of his clothing excited him. Jake felt his erection pressing against his pants uncomfortably and shifted position in order to press the bulge against Christian's frail leg. Why was he doing this? He didn't want to kiss this guy! He was way out of line. Or was he?

He was...what? Married? To whom? That whiney piece of crap who, after one measly accident spent the next year in near coma? He wasn't in a relationship; he was in prison, forced to cohabitate with a guy he barely knew. Dane wasn't like Christian. Dane couldn't excite him like Christian did. Dane couldn't make his balls ache the minute his tongue played along Jake's lips and Dane certainly couldn't–

Breasts. Somehow Jake's other hand had dropped the takeout burger and found its way to Christian's chest and instead of feeling muscled pectorals, he found himself kneading breasts. He broke away from Christian and stepped back, slipping in the French fries that now lay scattered about the lobby. He pinwheeled his arms to no avail and, after a brief moment, found himself crashing down onto the cool tile. His head bounced off the hard floor, sending spots of white in front of his eyes and the world spinning. He shook his head to clear his vision, but it only caused him to feel more nauseated. He looked up into Christian's face and beheld the demonic smile glaring down at him. The eyes he moments ago felt drawn into now seemed vicious and dark.

The eyes! Now he remembered! Those were the eyes of the woman in green—the one he locked eyes with as she entered the hotel across the street. The one who the police were searching for.

"I know you," he whispered, crawling backwards, suddenly terrified.

"That," Christian said, reaching into his coat, "was for Lily. Remember her? You were betrothed, once, long ago." Christian stepped over Jake, planting one foot on either side of him. "The one you betrayed? The one you, along with your whore, Bethany, murdered the night she was to leave town?" Christian sat down on Jake's chest, knees pressing against his arms, pinning them to the floor. "She wasn't missed for weeks, you know. She was scheduled to be out of town—a perfect cover for her disappearance. She died loving you. Loving you to the end."

Christian bent over and planted her lips on Jake's mouth, parting his lips with a probing, desperate tongue. Then, suddenly, Christian sat upright once again.

"But today I come to you, not as Lily Dayton, but as Christian O'Keefe. Ah! I see you do not remember him, either, do you?"

Jake stared up at the contorted face, red with anger and shook his head. "Let me remind you." Whipping a gloved hand from the inside of the coat, Christian produced a small metal rod and held it over Jake's head. "I believe it was my foot which was smashed first."

Without turning, Christian brought the bar high overhead and thrust it downward with a grunt against Jake's foot.

Jake heard the crunching of his bone and screamed in pain. He looked through clenched eyes as Christian bent towards his face.

"But what you really did was snap Christian's neck." A smile broke out along Christian's face as the two stared into each other's eyes.

Jake never felt the blow on his head, only saw Christian's hand lift the metal bar high into the air and the glimmer of the setting sun on the metal. Then all went black.

*   *   *

Christian raised his weapon again when the sound of a barking dog broke through the silence and Christian spun towards the lobby door. A wild, frantic animal clawed at the glass, trying to burrow its way into the building. Damn! Christian had every intention of making this kill count. Robert hadn't nearly suffered enough. No matter. The end could easily come upstairs in the vacant office. After all, Jake was certain to have a key to his own office in his pocket.

All Christian had to do was find it.

*   *   *

"What is it, boy?" Dane cursed under his breath. About a block ago, Ace had gone crazy barking, straining at the leash and spinning in circles. Dane had no idea what was wrong, but when the dog yanked the lead from his hand about fifty yards ago, he did nothing to entice the dog back. Ace ran straight for Jake's building and began howling, scratching and growling at the lobby door. Dane sighed. Ace didn't do this kind of thing often, and when he did, it was usually due to a reflection of a squirrel in the glass.

Nevertheless, Dane meandered up to the building's main lobby doors with a sense of foreboding. It was approaching sunset on a Saturday, and the odds were slim that anyone remained inside. True, Connie often worked a full shift on Saturdays, along with the partners of the firm, but judging by the lack of lights in the offices upstairs, they had left as well. Dane sighed and shook his head. If the office was empty, then he'd have to settle himself with waiting for Jake's phone call. The good side to that bad news was that with Jake safely back East, he was in no immediate danger.

"Ace, boy, back!" he snapped at the dog, much harsher than he meant to do. He grabbed the leash and pulled it taut, yanking Ace away from the door. Thankfully, he hadn't left permanent marks on the glass, so nobody would be the wiser. Still, it was awfully strange for the dog to act that way. Dane peered into the deserted lobby and felt his heart sink. With the exception of the remnants of somebody's lunch on the empty tile floor, there was no evidence of inhabitants.

"Ace! Stop it! They're only French fries. If you're hungry we'll get you something when we get home."

He paced for a moment, wondering what he should do. He could go back to Mrs. Jeremy's, but why? He knew he should go home. He was exhausted and Ace hadn't eaten yet, but somehow he couldn't bring himself to face the empty condo knowing Jake could be in danger.

"Ace, come on!" he said exasperated. The dog refused to budge. He stormed back to the animal and, grabbing it by his collar, tugged Ace backwards. As he wrestled with the beast, his eyes flickered into the lobby and came to rest on the lunch mess splayed on the tile. Amongst the lettuce leaves, scattered fries and lump of onion, Dane saw something that made his blood run cold: several foil packets labeled in black letters. HORSERADISH SAUCE. He froze. On their first date, Dane learned of Jake's horseradish habit when they went to Burger Meister and, while Dane squeezed ketchup onto his plate, Jake opened the jar of horseradish and began heaping it onto the fried potatoes.

Dane's mind whirled. Who else in the office ate horseradish sauce with fries? Did he know of any? Ace tugged at the leash as he pawed the bottom of the door. Come on, Dane! Get with the program! Horseradish sauce. Ace going nuts. What more do you want? Jake's in there. Suddenly, Dane knew the voice inside of him spoke the truth. He knew with complete certainty that Jake was inside the building. And something was wrong.

*   *   *

With one final heave, Christian lifted Jake's heavy frame through the door of the office and plopped it onto the plush carpet. The man was heavy, there was no denying it. But the effort was well worth it. What better place to dispose of the man than here in his place of employment? Christian unbuckled the belt and pulled the leather strap from around Jake's waist. Should he wake up before Christian completed the task, there was no reason to have the man unrestrained. Working quickly, Christian bound Jake's hands together and then used the shoelaces from Jake's own shoes to tie his ankles.

Once he was securely tied, Christian loosened the neck of his shirt, sat cross-legged on the floor of the office and closed his eyes. He envisioned the Book before him and felt the gentle tickle of the temple's energies as he reached out to it with his mind.

*   *   *

"Where is Dane?" Kevin screamed into the phone.

"How do I know, you little shit?" Mrs. Jeremy screamed back.

"We need to get hold of him," Kevin yelled into the phone as Sean tried to yank the cell from his hand. "Sean is losing his mind. He thinks that something's wrong."

Mrs. Jeremy thought about this for a minute. Could the idiot kid be connected? Well, like Marshall always said, it's impossible to spot a powerful person when the power they control is invisible. "He's probably on his way home. I need to call him, but I don't have his cell number." She continued, only to be cut off by Kevin speaking to Sean.

"Sean, please, daddy's on the phone," he said, his voice strained.

She ignored the comment and continued. "He was hoping to find out Jake's flight information. Dane's in trouble."

Kevin cut her off with a sarcastic sigh. "There is no flight, woman! The flight was cancelled. He's probably not leaving until the midnight flight."

Mrs. Jeremy felt chilled. Jake was in town? If that was true, then Dane wouldn't be in immediate danger. If the pattern held, the redhead would go after Jake first. She checked her watch. Plenty of time for the crazy ass bitch to find Jake. "Kevin," she said calmly, "We must find Jake. Do you hear me? We must find him."

"Well, Sean here's forcing me to drive back to the city, thank you very much, to find Dane," Kevin shot back angrily.

"Tell that little faggot," she snapped, "that if we find Jake, we'll find Dane. And Kevin. Jenny's dead."

Silence.

"Did you hear me?"

"Oh, my god." Kevin said flatly.

"I know. The poor girl." Mrs. Jeremy felt her eyes water again.

"Oh, my god." Kevin said quietly. "Sean said…Sean told me…a couple minutes ago he said he saw a dream. Mrs. Jeremy, I…"

She didn't let him ramble. "Go find them. Hurry!"

She hung up the phone before Kevin could reply. She laughed despite herself. What a great idea! Avenging yourself a couple hundred years later! Marshall, while anti-violence would love the romance of it. Just the idea of going into the Void.

Of course. The Void.

She slammed the phone back and shuffled to the chair where Dane had sat moments ago. If the boy could do it under her direction, then she could certainly do it herself, couldn't she? If the crazy ass bitch could use mystical energies, so could she. In fact, she could do it better. She was older and more experienced. And had been married to Marshall.

* * *

Dane slipped the card key back into his wallet. He let the door slide shut, thankful that Jake had urged him to carry a key for emergency purposes. He was quite sure this is not what Jake thought of when he said an "emergency," but he was glad despite that. Ace had quieted the moment they crossed into the building and now zigzagged across the floor, nose grinding into the tile looking for a scent. After a moment, the dog picked up his head and bolted to the elevator where he scratched at the metal doors and whined.

Dane dashed to the panel and hit the UP button with such force, his thumb felt numb afterwards. He glanced to the floor indicator and saw a glowing white "5." After another minute, the number didn't change and Dane suspected the elevator was either locked on the fifth floor or someone had shut it down. Could that be done without the alarm going off?

"Come on, boy," he said, urging the dog towards the stairway. They bounded up the stairs two at a time. Ace reached the fifth floor first and stood on the landing panting as Dane trotted up behind him. Trying to keep his breathing under control, Dane pressed his ear to the door. Nothing. He grasped the door handle and twisted, tugging the door only after the latch had fully retracted. He crouched down and started into the hallway.

Several dim lights illuminated the posh reception area of the fifth floor. Dane knew that to his left lay the principals' offices, the restrooms and meeting kiosks, while to his right lay Jake's office. A soft glow pressed from under Jake's door. Ace trotted past Dane and up to his master's office door in a flash. Dane followed, grasping the door knob firmly. He pushed slightly and the door swung open. He could feel Ace pressing against him, but Dane fended the dog off, kicking him softly backwards, forcing him into the hallway. If there was one thing he didn't need, it was Ace getting hurt as well. He slipped into the office as quietly as he could.

He first spotted Jake's shoes—the horrible light green Adidas he had begged Jake to throw away—sticking out from behind the desk. But before Dane could make a move toward his prone lover, an invisible force from behind shoved Dane into the middle of the room and slammed the door shut behind him. Trapped outside in the hall, Ace barked loudly and the heavy wooden door shook with his furious scratching. Dane looked up from the floor into the glowing, pulsating light on the other side of the office. There, sitting cross-legged on the floor was a redheaded figure whom he had seen just hours before on his journey to the temple: Christian O'Keefe. Radiating from the boy's body was a golden light which pulsated in perfect rhythm of his heart. A thin silver beam of light shot out of his head and disappeared into the ceiling above.

Dane could feel an electrical charge crackling through the air, sending his arm and neck hairs onto their ends. He had felt this just hours before. In Mrs. Jeremy's living room visiting the Book. Before he could process any further, a strong wind swirled around Dane, sending his sparse hair dancing. Stray papers fluttered around the room as an unseen hand flung them away. The room brightened a bit more and Dane could see the form of Christian shuddering in the brilliant glow. What the fuck was going on?

A voice penetrated his mind. HERE MONSTER.

Dane could see the frozen body of Christian, yet he could feel the pulsating waves of energy coming from the form. An invisible hand touched his head and he felt a burning, searing pain scald his temples and forehead as something squeezed his brains.

"NO!" he heard himself cry. From far off, a shrill laughter pierced the air, but Dane heard it through his eyes, hands and every pore of his body.

YOU HAVE RETURNED. YOU SHOULD HAVE LEFT ME TO KILL HIM. YOU COULD BE SPARED. ASK FOR MERCY, AND YOU SHALL HAVE IT.

"Get out of my head!" Dane screamed, willing the pain to stop. With a huge mental shove, he pushed against the force grabbing his mind. The pain subsided. He lay on the carpet, panting. "Leave him alone."

NO.

A kick to his stomach sent Dane writhing in pain against the far wall. Another whirl of wind and Dane flew into the air, spun and came crashing down onto the carpet, his head slamming into the floor with such force, Dane saw spots.

Dane squeezed his eyes shut, then forced them open, hoping to clear his vision. A pressure closed around his throat and Dane struggled to inhale, but his deflated lungs only burned as the need for air screamed through his chest. He clutched at his neck, clawing against invisible fingers, to no avail. He felt himself weaken. He felt an odd queasiness, much like when he entered the Void earlier and an odd tingle in the pit of his stomach. He suddenly felt tired. Very tired.

*   *   *

His eyelids dropped and his body went limp as he slid through darkness, rocketing into the blackness. He felt a wind cut through his jacket. He loved this ride. A roller coaster. It was high speed and high powered.

"Dane," a voice shot out of the dark, lively, sweet, warm and inviting. "Come on, man! We don't have much time."

"Jesus, Mary and the Donkey!" a rough voice bellowed. "Wake the FUCK UP!"

Dane's eyes shot open. There, standing over him, looking fresh and vibrant, stood Jenny smiling at him. Behind her, stood Mrs. Jeremy.

"Jenny...Mrs. Jeremy...what — "

"You've got to go back. Go to the Book." Jenny said as she kneeled beside him. He looked at her, helpless as the blackness closed around him again.

"The Book, you airhead!" Jenny laughed. "Go."

"Its power," Mrs. Jeremy crooned, "is for us all. Go on, now."

Dane saw the temple all around him. Inexplicably, he lay on its stone floor, its bright light illuminating every corner of the structure as if the air itself were aflame. Cascading from his torso and continuing down his body into the air, glittered the thin silver thread. Next to him stood the wooden pedestal and, lying open on it, the Book. He reached up, willing his arm to touch the glowing pages.

"It's beautiful, Dane," Jenny cooed. "You've done it before. Remember?" He looked to her and rolled his eyes. "That's SO like you! Come on, a LITTLE more."

Dane groped at the pedestal, his fingers digging into the smooth wood, desperately trying to find a fingerhold in the carvings that would help him stand. He groaned and he gathered his legs beneath him and tried to raise himself up. In the distance, thunder filtered through his head, hollow and throbbing. He managed to get to his knees before running out of energy. He clung to the dais and closed his eyes. If he could only rest for a second . . .

"You SHIT! Get your ass moving!" Mrs. Jeremy bellowed at him.

The shock of the scream startled Dane, causing him to jump slightly. Dane opened his eyes and saw that he was standing at the podium, his hands firmly placed on the open Book of Life. All around him, the walls sprang to life with moving pictures from his life, playing out scenes as quickly as his mind could grasp them. He felt weightless, yet alive. He felt energized. He felt strong.

A laugh cut through the air. He knew that laugh. It was a laugh he had been hearing for a year now, taunting him from the darkness of sleep, scaring him so badly that he backed away from slumber and took refuge in the beat-up old chair by the windows overlooking the park. He stepped away from the dais, spinning around madly searching for the source of the laugh that had stolen a year of his life.

He found it standing feet away. The face of Victoria/April/Lily/Christian smirked at him. He glared back. His chest hurt and, looking down, noticed the silver cord growing dim, becoming translucent in the gleaming light of the shrine. Frantically he recoiled the thread into himself and followed it towards its source, his own body lying limply in the corner of Jake's office.

"Not too late, boy," Mrs. Jeremy urged. "It's still alive. Hurry."

With a sudden burst of insight, he knew what to do.

Placing one hand on the Book and another on his prone body on the floor, he focused on his unconscious body and pushed with his mind. He felt his body jerk with pain as he crossed time, space and dimensions, through the Void, down through the air and into the physical reality. Like crawling through a small cave, he could feel the sides of his skin scraping his soul as he entered his own thoughts.

*   *   *

His mind ripped. The searing pain of the fissure seemed to explode from the inside as his brain pushed against his skull. As he crawled into his own flesh, the veil covering his psyche slowly peeled away from his consciousness and the last shred of the shield separating him from the two existences flew away.

He saw it all—the temple, the Book, the office, the sky and the stars. It was colorful, bright and warm, surrounded by a pulsating energy like a rainbow after the storm. Light waves replaced hard wood and soft carpet. Energy patterns lit the room in a glorious spectrum of color.

Standing in the middle of it all was the redhead. Without thinking, Dane lashed out with his mind. A streak of red and gold spewed forth from a mass of light that used to be his hand and struck the figure before him. A wall of agony slammed into the glowing woman and she stumbled backwards. Without breaking his attack, Dane lashed out with his mind again, focusing on driving the woman back, away from Jake. Sparks crackled across Christian's surface and a lump of bronze colored fluid plopped into the floor as the blood from her physical body leaked onto the floor. The colored patterns of the room shimmered and Dane heard a loud crash in the distance.

A woman screamed. Dane felt the pain rip through his arm. From the dim glow of the single lamp atop Jake's desk, Dane looked down to see the body of Christian Kelly fall to the floor. As he stared at the limp form, Dane saw it shift and change. As he watched, the shining face with perfect skin broke and split as the psychic blows manifested onto the physical form. The face cracked along the jaw line and blood poured from the open gash onto the carpet. The nose, shattered, squashed, spurting blood onto the lips and chin.

Tears stung Dane's eyes. Had he done this? Is this what hate looks like? Pain? Revenge? He had no idea despair had a face.

"Dane! Look out!" Jenny voice screamed through the air.

Suddenly, Christian's eyes flew open. She screamed a loud, piercing war cry and lifted her arm. Dane spun and saw the pistol in Christian's hand and despite the blood and exposed meat, Christian Kelly fired. The bullet dug into Dane's injured shoulder and he crumpled onto the carpet, rolling into the base of the desk. He heard Christian behind him, stumbling madly. Dane tried to lift his head, but he felt dizzy and confused. The room swayed and buckled violently.

With a loud crash, the door burst open. Dane heard Ace's angry snarls right before a scream rang out and a tremendous crash resounded through the room. Dane heard voices mumbling in a tone so low he couldn't distinguish words. Soft hands enclosed his head and tender arms wrapped around his shoulders as more voices appeared. Suddenly, faces came into view and he found himself staring into the wide, horror filled eyes of Kevin and Sean. In slow motion, the two looked at him, and Kevin's mouth forming the words: call an ambulance. Dane closed his eyes as the darkness passed over him.

*   *   *

"Twice in one year," the voice said from the darkness. "What's his name?"

"Dane Baldwin," Sean's voice.

"Dane. Dane. Right. I remember him. I'm Rodney. Come on back to me, Dane. Follow my voice." The voice rang out smooth and calm, like liquid velvet.

Dane struggled against the clutches of sleep and pried his eyes open. He stared up into a rugged, handsome face holding a small pen light.

"Good, Dane," Rodney said. "I want you to follow the light, okay? Just follow it with your eyes."

"Rodney. I think it's a girl," another voice said over Rodney's shoulder.

"Woman. Yeah?" Rodney asked, peering into Dane's face.

"I think she's dead," the voice hesitated.

"Again?," Rodney whispered, placing a blood pressure cuff around Dane's arm. "What about the other guy?"

"Fine. Nasty bump on his head and a broken foot, but he'll be okay."

"Concussion?" Rodney asked with a voice which was calm yet authoritative.

"Don't think so," the unseen voice said. "We'll check it out, though."

"You know," Rodney said lightly, staring at Dane. "We've got to stop meeting like this."

"Who are you?" Dane squeaked.

"The guy who saved your life a year ago." Rodney laughed. "You can either thank me or kill me later, okay? For now let's see what's wrong with you."

Dane reached out and grabbed Rodney's arm. He stared into his face and whispered, "Thank you."

Rodney winked. "Don't move. A backboard is on its way."

*   *   *

"Knock knock," the voice asked. Gilbert pulled his focus away from the fading yellow daisies and looked to the doorway. Jeannette stood holding a huge bouquet of roses. "Permission to come aboard?"

"Permission granted. But warning!" Gilbert grunted. "I'm in an anti-lesbian mood."

"Oh. I'll take these back," she said, turning.

"Don't you dare! I'm anti-lesbians, not roses. Sit," he insisted.

Jeannette smiled and strode to the vase full of yellow daisies. She tossed the dead stems into the trash and began to fill the vase with water.

"What brings you here?" he asked

"A friend. Admitted last night," she said, placing the roses in the vase and replacing it on the table.

"Bad?" Gilbert asked cautiously.

"Don't think so. He…was in a fight. He'll be okay, they say." She debated mentioning the metaphysical conversation Mrs. Jeremy had just put her through, or the retelling of Dane's remembrance of the strange journey he had taken. She opted to edit out those portions of the tale. The two sat in silence for a moment, neither giving, nor asking for conversation.

"Why, my testosterone-impaired friend, is that?" Gilbert asked, gesturing to the chair.

"What?" Jeannette responded, sinking into the stiff backed recliner next to him.

He sighed and rolled his eyes. "Why," he said, looking at her with great indignation. "Why do you do it? Sit here with me when you should be out doing something young, vibrant, and dyke-ish? What do you need from me?"

Jeannette dropped her gaze to the floor. "I don't need anything," she began tentatively.

Gilbert rolled his eyes. "Oh. One of those," he said with great emphasis. "Stoic. Determined. Solitary." He scowled at her. "I'm a man. Aren't your dyke friends going to give you hell?"

"What's gender between friends?" She dropped her gaze.

He nodded politely and smiled. "Do you think people come back again?"

"I'm currently debating the idea. Why?" she asked.

"Nobody's brought me flowers the entire time I've been here," he said simply. She pointed to the trash and began to speak, but he silenced her. "Stole them. Off the flower cart. I know. Hell is my home. Deal with it."

"Talk my ear off next time around?" Jeannette answered for him.

"I'll bring you flowers," he said falling back onto his pillow.

"Come on," Jeannette said, "Let me introduce you to some pretty spectacular people." She pulled the wheelchair from the corner of the room.

"How do you know they'll want to meet me, my dear?"
"Because I suspect you already have."

*   *   *

"What the hell did I tell you? Why the fuck do you think I gave you all those books? You've got a power, boy." Mrs. Jeremy fussed over him as he lay in the hospital bed, fluffing his pillows and patting his hands. Although well past visiting hours and deep into the night, maybe even early morning, she seemed totally unconcerned about being tossed out. How did she manage to get around rules that the rest of society found unbendable? Outside his room, the sterile, cold ceiling lights gave a dull illumination to the vacant hallways.

"I think it was the thing in the office that finally did it," Dane thought out loud, speaking softly so he wouldn't disrupt the wrapping around his ribs. One broken and two fractured, the doctors said, along with bad bruising. His entire body sported an odd mixture of green and blue hues along with an assortment of bumps, scratches and lacerations.

"Wasn't the office, boy," Mrs. Jeremy said, pulling a newspaper from her purse. "It was the accident a year ago. Shut up. Go to sleep." She opened the paper and began to read.

Jake hobbled out of the bathroom and wobbled uncertainly on a pair of metal crutches. He lumbered his way to the bed. The foot Christian had smashed was now sporting a thick cast. "Hey." He whispered, sitting on the edge of the bed gently, as if Dane were made of glass. "Where's Gilbert?"

"Jeannette took him home. It was his curfew." Dane said.

"Funny guy. I like him."

"Good," Dane responded, "I invited him to our next dinner party."

Jake chuckled. "What a day."

"You two do this young love shit, I'm going home." Mrs. Jeremy declared, rising from the chair and shoving her assortment of magazines, newspapers, and books into her gypsy bag. She crossed to kiss Dane on the forehead and squeezed Jake's shoulder before heading out the door.

The two men stared at each other a minute, listening to the night sounds of the hospital. Dane smiled as he studied the energy patterns that surrounded his partner—Jake's rugged, defined face shone with a pale yellow and a misty green. When he spoke, Dane watched as multi-colored hues emanated from his mouth.

"Kevin said Sean was like a wild man," Jake chuckled. "Before Kevin pulled the car over to the curb, Sean jumped out, ran to the lobby doors and kicked at them until the glass shattered."

"Get out!" Dane said, trying to smile without hurting his scarred face.

"That's what Kevin told me. Then, of course, Ace–"

"The wonder dog." Dane sighed. He screwed up his courage and said quickly, "I didn't know the flight was cancelled and I didn't know where to find you."

"Yeah," Jake said, nodding. He stared at the cast and adjusted his broken foot.

"I want to go home."

"Me, too." Dane sighed.

Jake nudged Dane over a few inches and crawled into the bed next to him, hanging his cast over the edge of the bed. They both lay staring out the window enjoying the lights of the city.

THE END

Made in the USA
Columbia, SC
31 December 2017